Abomination

Abomination

The Story of David and Jonathan

BY JEZA BELLE

RESOURCE *Publications* · Eugene, Oregon

ABOMINATION
The Story of David and Jonathan

Resource Publications
An Imprint of Wipf and Stock Publishers
199 W. 8th Ave., Suite 3
Eugene, OR 97401

www.wipfandstock.com

PAPERBACK ISBN: 979-8-3852-5960-1
HARDCOVER ISBN: 979-8-3852-5961-8
EBOOK ISBN: 979-8-3852-5962-5

VERSION NUMBER 09/05/25

To *Spyder* who is a warm smile, an encouraging hug, a shared cocktail, a loving family member, and a good friend.

"Your love for me was wonderful, more wonderful than that of woman."

—2 SAMUEL 1:26

Contents

CONTENTS

THE SACRIFICE

Acknowledgements

My partner in life—for years and years of love.

Dylan Garity—for being an amazing editor.

Thomas Evans Photography—for the fab press photo.

Wipf and Stock / Resource Publications—for relentlessly saying "yes."

Prologue

Alongside a small patch of acacia trees covered in golden-yellow spikes, a pale sun beat down on an open bedouin tent. The sides were lifted so as to allow air to flow through, lest its inhabitant be suffocated in this land of dusty mountains and wadis. Though the camel-hair hides it was constructed of were suited to these harsh conditions, an almost unnatural, hell-like heat lay across the land, stifling it like a fiery hot blanket. Even the riverbeds, which had recently bloomed—as they had every year since the days when the Nephilim walked these lands—had died off, and the pastel roadways in the desert, accustomed to clay-baking heat, had been replaced by deep, barren craters of fine grains of sand.

Inside the tent, which stood on top of a small hill on the edge of the nearby village of Ziklag, a ruddy man reclined, his body laid across a large cushion dyed the same golden yellow as his hair. He was deep in thought when a servant brought in a young man, who collapsed onto his knees.

"Are you David?" he asked tentatively from the ground.

"Yes," came the firm but simple response.

"Then please, have mercy on me," the young man cried out, throwing his arms in front of him and resting his chest against the carpet.

David stood up so that his muscled body towered over the prostrate figure on the floor of his nomadic dwelling. "What need would I have to show you mercy?" he asked curiously.

"They are dead," the young man answered into the ground.

"Stand up and tell me your tale," David commanded. "But first, I must know your name."

"Eliphaz, a descendant of Esau." The man pushed himself off of his knees and stood upright.

"An Amalekite . . . which makes your journey to my tent more confounding." David's brows furrowed, and his eyes, the same azure as his loose tunic, bore down onto this ally of the Canaanites.

"You must know, I only did what he begged of me."

"He?"

Eliphaz lifted his hands, which shook with tremors. "Saul, your Israelite king." His voice rose in fear.

"And this means?" David pressed.

"King Saul is . . ." The young man hesitated to finish his sentence.

David's eyes widened. "Saul is dead?"

Eliphaz nodded. "That's not all." His whole body was convulsing now.

"What could be worse?" Concern laced David's voice.

"Jonathan—" Eliphaz began, but David put his hand up to silence the Amalekite.

"Do not say it."

The tent was silent except for the scurrying sound from the short legs of a mottled sandgrouse that was wandering along the edge of the shelter. Something startled it so that its wings rustled in a beat, and it took off into the air with a high-pitched whistle. It screeched, then it was gone. In its absence, David released his own twisted groan before he fell to his knees and cried.

THE ANOINTMENT

Youthful Ignorance

The echo of fists beating against countless breastplates rattled across the hot desert air. It could easily have been mistaken for thunder, except that the morning sky was clear from Socoh in the east to Azekah in the west.

"I will make a chain out of your snipped Israelite cocks to wear around my neck if someone doesn't come down and fight me soon," a giant covered in bronze-scaled armor yelled out across the Valley of Elah.

Every day for weeks, Jonathan had watched from the edge of his father, King Saul's, encampment on the opposite knoll as the morning light tore at his eyes. Even the sun fled in terror as it reflected back against the polished helmet on top of the head of that Philistine they called Goliath, who stood as tall as two soldiers, one on top of the other.

Yet where celestial bodies had the safety of distance, the king's army had only the space between two hills. There stood this creature so fearsome who freely mocked an army of thousands and not one of them did more than tremble in response.

A palm pressed against Jonathan's shoulder and forcefully pushed him a few steps forward. "Why don't *you* go down and face Goliath," snickered a familiar voice, and another cackled at the prospect.

Jonathan turned around and glared at his annoying half-brothers, Armoni and Mephibosheth. With their large heads and bulging eyes, the twins looked like a pair of matching desert spadefoot toads, though where Mephibosheth was squat and thick, Armoni was long and thin. The incessant croaking from the real nocturnal amphibians each night was less irritating than these two, who plagued Jonathan constantly.

5

"I don't think his balls have dropped yet, and you want him to play the role of a warrior?" Mephibosheth said, his double chin shaking with laughter.

"And yet he thinks that he is better than us because his mother, Ahinoam, lay with our father first?" Armoni spit.

"Doesn't that just make him the son of a loose harlot?" the other twin teased.

"Piss off," Jonathan replied as the two of them marched away, arms across one another's shoulders, in fits of pubescent tittering.

Jonathan and his full-blooded brothers, Abinadab and Malchi-shua, had certain privileges that came with being born of a true wife, and his father's concubine, Rizpah, had raised her twin sons to be scornful of their place and to seek gain wherever they could. So, Armoni and Mephibosheth were ever the hair that lurked in the morning curds. Not a day went by when they did not bring some unpleasant sensation to his life, from the time of waking until he was once more wandering asleep through dreams, there was an incessant desire to cough them out. But they were family, and as such, Jonathan could not escape their presence, however loathsome he found them to be.

While his half-brothers were tiny gnats that constantly bit at his neck, Goliath's voice thundered in this moment as if he were a god, and the knees of the many men who were just behind Jonathan knocked together at the mere thought of being sent down by their king to face him.

Across the valley, on the hill of Ephes Dammim, another army stood, and they hooted and howled at each taunt their massive brother hurled up at the Israelites.

"I think they must have sent their women out to fight us," one of the Philistines called, and Goliath's chest heaved as his mouth released a guffaw of thick bass notes. Its sound vibrated up the nape of Jonathan's neck, and he ran into the tent where his father sat among a mountain of cushions, his head in his hands.

"Is there not anyone in this whole land who will fight on my behalf?" Saul moaned. "I've offered great wealth and would even seat them at my side if only someone would go out there and kill that cursed beast!" He stood up and began to pace. "What was the point of being anointed a blasted king anyway if I'm to sit here and be made a fool of day after day?" Spittle sprung from the corners of his mouth. "Am I forsaken altogether?"

He lifted his eyes to the ceiling. His servant stepped forward to appease him, but Saul pushed the man away. "And where in Shiloh is Samuel?" He stomped over to his brother, Abner, the general of the Israelite forces. "We are staring down an army of twice as many Philistines as you had told me to expect, and our so-called prophet isn't even here to pronounce something—anything—or do a damn thing for us!

"You are all useless," he shouted again, then turned on his heels and paced.

Saul was frantic now, as he'd been more frequently these past few months, so Jonathan tiptoed back out and into the camp, where he found a place on the edge of the hill to squat down, watch, and think.

He had just settled when, behind him, he heard the cracking voice of a young man going through a familiar hormonal awakening. "Aren't any of you brave enough to do something other than stand here and look like washerwomen?" The boy's pitch dropped low, then rose to a high note.

Jonathan didn't bother to turn around to see who was speaking. It was just another rambling dissenter wondering aloud why they'd been camped out here for weeks rather than rushing into battle.

What does anyone, let alone a boy, know about leading a nation? Jonathan shrugged. Only he knew how the decision weighed on his father, and this youth's criticism was nothing compared to the crushing pressure King Saul himself felt to act.

But the teen's voice grew louder, until with a shrill declaration, he squeaked, "I will do it myself!"

Suddenly, the lanky young man rushed past on Jonathan's left side, almost knocking him into the sand. Jonathan steadied himself, then stood all the way back up. His mouth fell open in disbelief as he watched the boy head straight down the hill. Scores of men came up behind Jonathan and began to yell out at the golden-headed adolescent as he carefully zigzagged down between rocks and dirt.

"Come back here, child," someone called.

"You will get yourself killed and make us all into slaves, you stupid boy!" cried another.

A great roar rose up from the Philistine camp on the other side as they gathered at the edge of their own hilltop.

"What is going on here?" Jonathan heard his father call out from nearby. "And why is there a young boy walking down this hill?"

"That's David. He's the son of Jesse, an Ephrathite, I've been told," Abner answered.

"I didn't ask who he was," King Saul barked. "I want to know why this babe who is barely off his mother's tit has taken it upon himself to head toward the lair of the lion. How can this be happening?"

Saul's screams rang out, and Jonathan felt his father's fear. After all, he knew of the Philistine offer. If someone killed Goliath, the battle would be over and the Philistines would pledge themselves as slaves to his father's crown. But if a man were to face the giant and lose, the Israelites would have to bow to the Philistines, and it was certain that this boy, descending the slope at his own urging, had now sentenced them all to a life of chains and shackles.

"Damnit," Saul grumbled.

"What the hell is this?" Goliath laughed from down below. "I know the great King Saul, who claims to be protected by his god, did not send a boy out to meet me—unless he's come to rub my feet and wipe my ass after I devour all of his people, then shit them out!" Goliath's broad shoulders shook with delight as the Philistines behind him laughed in glee at his words.

"I've killed bears fiercer than you," David replied with youthful arrogance as he neared the bottom of the hill and stepped out onto the valley floor.

"Is that so?" The giant sniggered. "I think I have a boil on my ass bigger than you . . . though less irksome."

But David continued his approach, and a look of satisfaction spread across Goliath's face. "Come closer, then, so that I can shove my javelin down your throat and roast you over an open fire like a venison steak," he said. Then he pulled a mammoth spear out from behind his back.

Jonathan looked on with a mix of fear and wonder as he watched the young man swoop his hand down across the ground and scoop up a few rocks without slowing his approach. David then pulled a slingshot out from the small bag he had strapped across his body and loaded it with one of the stones.

Goliath released another howl from his belly at the sight of the weapon. "This has to be some kind of jest." He threw his head back with laughter, which caused his helmet to slide off and land on the hot sandy ground near his enormous feet.

8

Just as he did so, David lifted his slingshot and let loose the small stone, which whistled as it flew through the air. It landed with a thud directly against the giant's forehead, by his left temple.

Goliath's laughter faded, and he straightened his head and glared down at David. Then he dropped his spear and lifted his right hand, pressing it to his face. Liquid began to drip out between his fingers until it flowed steadily, the color as red as the Nile when it was hit with the first of the ten plagues.

"You little sh—" he started to say, but his legs gave way midsentence, and he wobbled from side to side.

He swayed like a cypress tree in a storm before he teetered and tipped. The air shook with a crash of metal and flesh that ricocheted across the valley and onto the two hills of the opposing camps, until at last all went silent.

Jonathan could not hear the sound of his own breathing; his lungs had ceased to contract. For just a moment, it seemed as if all of earth waited breathlessly for the stirrings of the giant. But they did not come.

No one moved as they watched David walk forward and kneel down beside Goliath's body. The boy clumsily pulled out the large sword from the sheath that rested against the giant's right hip, straining greatly to lift the weapon up over his head. Suddenly, there was a loud swoosh, initiated more by the force of gravity than by the strength of the blade's wielder, and it fell downward. The squelch of flesh and bone ricocheted as it sliced through the neck of the giant, until at last, David stood and held up Goliath's head, which had been removed from his body.

Jonathan's ears were at once filled with shouts of jubilation, and he was all but trampled by the surge of men that ran past him and down the hill with their own swords extended. From across the way, he watched as the Philistines turned on their heels and ran frantically in retreat across the plains and back toward the entrance to the city of Gath, from where they had originally come. Then his eyes fell back down and searched for David, but the young hero was nowhere to be found. Only a mass of humanity now covered the broken figure of Goliath, which lay at the valley's center, though the memory of the boy Jonathan had watched sever its form in two was burned forever into his mind.

#

There was a wild rush of sound and vibration. Unsure of where he was, David turned around in confusion to see thousands of soldiers. The rushing crowd broke upon his body like he was a bulwark splitting the ocean waves in two. Their guttural cries released a wind as forceful as their movement, which carried on for several minutes, until at last they were gone. He looked up at the empty Israelite camp, and the realization of what had transpired roared back into his mind.

Turning back around, David looked down to see the split form of Goliath. The giant's head and sword both lay by his feet.

Tempestuous. That was how his family often described him, and he could hear them reprimand him with the word now. *You are prone to act first and think later,* his father might say, as he had so many times before. None of this would be wrong.

All David could recall was being infuriated. When he first arrived at the encampment only a few hours earlier, he'd been mad at his brothers. There they were, far from home, having been sent to save the land of milk and honey that their God had given to them. Instead, he'd found them full-bellied and idle. And they weren't the only ones. Tent after tent—so many temporary homes that they seemed to go on forever—had sat there filled with Israelite soldiers. David's fury had shifted to these lazy cowards, their feet up as they drank beer and waited, all too patiently, for someone else to save them.

"Your wives and daughters will be sold off," he remembered yelling at a group. They'd laughed and flung the bones of waterfowl, which they had picked clean with their teeth, at his feet.

One of the men chided at him, "Go home to your mother and come back when you have hair around your *shteikh.*" The others howled with laughter.

Another lifted up his robes and dropped his *ezor* to reveal his manhood. "Like this," he teased as he grabbed hold of his piece and twirled it around in the air.

It was this insult that made David's eyes go dark with rage and they had remained so until now.

He could find the traces of memories of his actions in between spots of pure redness, the color one saw when one stared into a fire.

There were the steps and stomps down the hillside, and the fury that had shot through him like an arrow through a lion's heart when the giant likened him to an ass-pimple.

"I guess I lanced it," he thought aloud, then chuckled into the air at this. That was followed by a guffaw that led to a burst of pure hilarity as he threw his head back. At last, all of the tension that had surged through his lanky limbs poured out through fingers and toes.

"I just killed a giant," he said with wonder when his laughter ceased. His hands shook with fear as he knelt down and took hold of the incredible sword that he had somehow managed to wield. "Good Gideon."

With effort, David heaved it into the air. Once he had control of it, he rested the sword so that its blade sat gently against his shoulder. The weight of the iron was a burden on his young body, and it caused him to bend at the knees. This shortened him just enough to sweep his fingers along the ground and find the coarse locks of the bodiless head, but not enough to render him immobile. As he passed, he gripped the hair tightly and then pushed up as hard as he could until he stood back up fully. Sword and head in hands, he clumsily wobbled away.

For a few moments, he limped on, his burden slowing his pace, until at last he reached a large tree beside a small stream. There he dropped the head and sword with a crash, sat down next to them at the water's edge, and exhaled.

David tried to catch his breath. Once he felt calm, he cupped his hands down into the coolness and lifted the refreshing water to his mouth.

"Ahhh," he moaned as it rejuvenated him. Rehydrated, he moved his body back, leaning against a tree and closing his eyes.

You are willful and not easily restrained, he imagined his father yelling at him as he disciplined him harshly. After all, he hadn't asked permission to leave his home in Bethlehem and run off to join his brothers in battle.

"Then again, there was no battle," he said.

Perhaps it was his brothers that his father would scold. *It did take their youngest sibling to show them what it meant to be a man of Israel*, he thought proudly.

"Meh," David answered himself with a shrug.

It didn't matter much what his father would say—he knew it was more than likely that they would all froth at the mouth and gnash their teeth at his actions. In fact, he would not be surprised if his father asked that smelly old man in rags to come back to their home and dump another clay jar of oil over his head.

"You are blessed," the frail creature had uttered. But David knew that his father was so worried about his temperament that he'd brought the kook out to give some kind of false sense of protection to his own mind, not David's.

"Maybe he believes that this kind of oil repels lions," David had said to his brothers, laughing.

"They wouldn't eat you before the oil," Eliab teased. "There's no meat on your bones!"

"I don't know," David answered in jest. "Some creatures find me incredibly edible."

Well, the giant did. That did not go to well for him, I suppose. Once again, he laughed heartily at his own humor.

David liked to laugh . . . a lot. It did not matter if it was with his brothers or alone. In fact, maybe it was better alone. When you spent as much time by yourself as he did, unless you called a herd of sheep company, you learned to be your own amusement and to allow yourself the right to be perfectly amused by your own musings.

"Not even my brothers realize just how hilarious I am," he assured himself.

In the far distance he heard the clanking of weapons, and he wondered how his brothers were faring in the battle.

I suppose I'll just go home now, he thought, but his body decided otherwise. Killing giants and saving nations was hard work, and so as his ears moved away from the battle and toward the gentle sounds of the stream rolling over the bed of rocks beyond his toes, his eyes became heavy, and he slept.

A Gnawing Ache

In the hours of melee that followed after David had killed Goliath, Jonathan joined the other Israelites in pursuit of the Philistines. Though young, he had cut down many on the Shaaraim road. While the Philistines possessed superior weaponry, and their military tactics were far more sophisticated, the loss of Goliath stripped all of his kinsmen of their morale and sent them fleeing in terror. Jonathan had loosed his bow into the backs of many as they fled, until at last, covered in blood and sweat, he returned to the camp where his father had remained.

Before he could head to the king's tent, he entered his own, which he shared with his younger brothers. As the oldest male heir, though a mere sixteen years of age, he had seniority over Abinadab and Malchishua, who were just behind him at fourteen and fifteen. As such, they'd remained in the camp at Jonathan's behest and had not participated in the killing that day.

"You are bloodier than an altar." Abinadab smiled as his elder brother came inside and began to undress, removing his garments of war.

"Eww," Malchi-shua said with a puckered face. "Is there anything dirtier than gentile blood?"

"Your breath, Shua," Abinadab shot back with a grin, and the two began to wrestle on the floor.

Jonathan smiled and walked over to pick up a laver of water, which he poured over his arms. With a soft cloth, he wiped away the bits of gore from the Philistine men he had flayed alive.

"How many *did* you kill today?" Shua grunted as Abinadab pulled him into a stranglehold and smashed his face into the dusty woolen carpet.

"Let's just say more Philistines died today than since all of the Canaanites who moved to this land from far away islands were killed by Rames III—and he nearly decimated those sea people more than a hundred years ago."

"Oh, now he thinks he's a pharaoh." Abinadab laughed as Shua freed himself and then pounced on his brother's shoulders.

"While you two play, I have to go see our father now, as I am sure he will want a full report," Jonathan informed his siblings, but they just muttered short acknowledgements from under locked limbs.

A servant came in and helped to dress Jonathan in more suitable clothing, and the bloodied, rugged young man who'd entered the tent minutes before soon looked nothing like the well-dressed prince who exited.

The walk to Saul's tent took less than two minutes, and Jonathan entered to find his father once again pacing to and fro.

"Where is the boy who slayed the giant?" he asked Jonathan forcefully, as if he had come in with some sort of news on the Philistine's killer at his father's request.

"I could not tell you." Jonathan bowed his head gently.

His father sucked at his teeth and walked over to his cushions, where he flopped down with a sigh. "Well, at least share with me how it went today?" he pressed, picking up a bowl of olives brought to him in a bushel from Carmel and examining a wild green one.

"We followed them to the gates of Ekron. Those that made it inside were few, and your territory is once again safe and whole, just like our God had told you that it would be."

"Hmm." Saul plopped the morsel into his mouth and chewed. "Yes," he said as he swallowed. "I did know it would all be put right. That's why I am the king and you, my son, will be king after me, and so on until the end of time."

Jonathan's chest swelled at his father's boast, but he could have sworn he then heard him mutter something under his breath about Samuel.

As Saul finished speaking, a servant came forward and whispered something into his ear. "What?" Saul's eyes widened. "Well, bring him in immediately!"

The servant left and quickly returned with the boy named David. He carried with him the head of Goliath, which hung down from the locks of blood-matted hair that were twisted around his fist.

"I bow to you, oh anointed one," David said as he placed the head on the ground.

Saul stood up and stepped forward, his hand extended for the boy to kiss.

It was at that moment that Jonathan at last got a good look at the young man who had turned the tides of war, and what he saw astounded him.

Where Jonathan was dark-featured and rugged, David was fair-haired and peach-skinned. His face was almost as fine as those of the most beautiful of women. Jonathan admired the exquisite positioning of the boy's deep-blue eyes, set on either side of a symmetrical nose that seemed to be carved out of the finest pale stone.

The view of David's profile caused the breath to leap out from Jonathan's lungs. His eyes moved up and down as he studied the Judean stripling from his perfectly proportioned head to his dusty sandaled toes, which were decorated with the lightest of blond hairs. An unfamiliar gnawing began to ache in the space where his heart lived, and he felt it pulsate. Jonathan could hardly even remember where he was when he heard the distant sound of a muffled voice call out to him.

"Jonathan . . . um . . . Jonathan," Saul repeated in his direction.

It was as if he had just swum up from the bottom of a lake and his ears were still filled with water. While he heard his father speak, it was garbled, and he found himself unable to respond.

Saul laughed. "This is my eldest son, Jonathan," he said to David. "It's been quite a day, for him as much as everyone."

"Hi," Jonathan managed to cough up at last as his father began to back away.

"Nice to meet you." David nodded his head. "I'd shake your hand, but . . ." He looked down at his side, where Jonathan saw the hand that had been stained with dried blood from the gnarled head of Goliath, which lay on the ground.

"Oh." Jonathan looked back up and grinned. He waved for the servant to bring their guest water and a towel.

"Well, I will leave you two to talk," Saul said to the young men. "Now that you have presented yourself before your king, David, I must excuse myself and go speak with the cook. I have decided that we will have a feast tonight in your honor."

"For me?"

"Oh yes, and one like no one has ever seen before throughout the land of Israel—certainly bigger than anything you have witnessed in

Bethlehem. After all, you will have many tales to tell your family when you return to your fields as a shepherd, but let one of them be how your king fed you from his finest of wares."

At that, Saul disappeared behind a large curtain. David looked around the tent and then over at Jonathan and smiled. "Well, this certainly is fancier than a field of sheep," he said breathlessly before he furrowed his brow, "though I thought I might get to stay a while longer. I do not relish a quick return to wool and sheep dung."

Jonathan laughed. "Don't be confused. My father is actually doing you a favor, even if it doesn't seem like it now. It is really far less peaceful here than sitting under open skies and listening to the sounds of newborn lambs. Instead, I just get the incessant bleating of my younger brothers!"

"I have a bunch of them too, though mostly older, so I understand," David commiserated. He stepped forward and put his newly cleaned hand on Jonathan's shoulder. "Anyway, it's nice to meet you, Jonathan."

The sound of his name on David's lips was like music, and the touch of David's palm on his robe seemed to burn right through the fine fabric and sear Jonathan's skin. He stared into the Judean's eyes and found himself completely enraptured.

"Wow, that is beautiful," David said as he admired Jonathan's clothing.

"It really is," Jonathan responded, in awe at the young man's presence.

"I've never seen a robe so nice!"

"Oh." He recovered himself. "Um . . . oh . . . you mean this?" He lifted a piece of the fabric into the air.

"Yes." David laughed. "What did you think I meant?"

"I—I really . . . I really don't know," Jonathan stuttered.

All of a sudden, without thought, he found himself pulling his linen robe up over his head.

"Wait, what are you doing?" David's blue eyes widened, but soon Jonathan had slid off not only the robe, but his sleeveless *ketonet* as well.

"Here," he said awkwardly, thrusting them into David's arms.

"Huh?" David took a step back and put his hands up in the air.

"No, really, you can have them," Jonathan whispered as he laid them both at David's feet.

"Oh I couldn't," the young man replied in shock.

"You must," Jonathan insisted.

"But why?"

The deed was already done, and Jonathan realized he needed to say something to make this gift seem less weird than it felt, because frankly, he did not know why he'd done it.

"Just consider it a small thank-you for your service to my father . . . and to the entirety of Israel, if that makes it easier," he said with feigned confidence, though in his mind he was furiously asking himself what had made him do something so ridiculous.

David looked up from the garments and studied Jonathan, who stood there practically naked in front of him. He wore only his ezor, which hung loosely around his hips, and even that barely covered his loins. Jonathan had never felt so vulnerable before another person, and a shiver moved across his abdomen as he noticed David's eyes stray briefly to his lightly furred stomach and down the darkened trail that disappeared beneath his thin garment below.

"Oh . . . um . . . this really is most generous," David mumbled, and now it was he who appeared to be embarrassed. A strange tension hung in the air. "I have to ask—you hardly even know me, and yet you make such a grand gesture? Not that I'm complaining." He laughed, and once more seemed to take a quick peek at Jonathan's body.

"I'm not sure that I can explain it myself, to be honest," Jonathan responded in embarrassment.

"Lucky me, then."

Jonathan cleared his throat. He contemplated leaving the conversation, but something pushed him to say more. "I seem to have this strange feeling," he began timidly. "Ordinarily, I would not be this forward, but . . . it is as if we have already met before, even though we are strangers."

"I do not know what to say," David said softly.

"Maybe not, but I just know that, somehow, it is as if we are bound together and always have been."

They were both quiet.

"Why else would I find myself standing before you bare in both body and soul?" Jonathan finally added, with a hiccup of embarrassed laughter. The blood rushed to his face, and he suddenly felt terrified that he had shared his feelings so willingly with this boy.

Stupid, he scolded himself furiously.

There was silence from David still, and the more seconds passed, the more Jonathan wanted to crawl under the many carpets that lay on the ground of his father's tent. There, he would hide his shame until David left him in humiliation.

But finally, David answered. "I also cannot explain this, but everything you have said to me, I too feel the exact same way," he confessed.

Jonathan beamed, and they stood there together, not knowing what to do or say next.

Jonathan broke the moment. "Well, since we are both bound, then, you will come with me to my tent?"

"That moved quickly." David giggled, and Jonathan felt a surge of self-consciousness.

"Oh," he gasped. "I meant that you would come with me to get cleaned up for tonight."

They both laughed awkwardly.

"Also, I wanted to give you my sword and sheath as well."

"Haven't you given me enough already?" David shook his head in surprise at the honor.

"I mean, clearly you have Goliath's. But I imagine that his blade will be far too heavy for you to carry around day after day.

"Yes, but—"

"Do you have another sword?"

"No, but—"

"Well, as a new military hero, you have to have a sword, don't you?"

"I suppose that is true, but—"

"So, you can carry mine, if you like."

They stared into each other's eyes.

"I was going to say that you need to have a sword too, don't you?"

"Oh, I have my bow," Jonathan explained. "There is hardly anyone, young or old, who can shoot a shot like me. Besides, my father is the king. I can get another sword made any old time."

"Well in that case, I gladly accept." David nodded and reached out his hand in thanks.

Jonathan looked up and smiled before he lifted his own hand and grasped David's firmly. But before he knew it, he found that David had pulled him into a hug.

"Thank you," he said softly into Jonathan's ear.

Jonathan tingled at the touch of David's body, which pressed up against his bare skin. It was like a cold wind that the pelts from a thousand badgers could not protect against. He put his arms around David and held him close, as if to share his heat. Then he felt his knees buckle, and he wondered what this feeling was that seemed to come on like the heavy rains of winter. It was as if he were soaked through and his body had gone limp from saturation.

When they pulled back from each other, he noticed the flush spreading on David's cheeks as well, and they both shuffled their feet awkwardly, until at last Jonathan regained his composure. "This way." He pointed. "At the very least, I need to get some clothes on."

They both giggled as they stepped out into what was now the early evening air, and together they headed to Jonathan's tent.

Inside, all four of his brothers were lounged about on carpets, limbs strewn in every direction.

"What in the land of milk and honey?" Armoni laughed, spitting out some water. He wiped the back of his hand across his mouth. "Did you lose a bet that you had to walk around the camp in that state?"

Mephibosheth's plump cheeks blew out a push of air. "That's the most hysterical thing ever," he cackled. Then uncharacteristically, even Abinadab and Malchi-shua joined in and laughed along.

"Okay, okay," Jonathan replied. "Unlike you lazy locusts, I was attending to the king."

"What, as *Qadištu*, the temple prostitute?" Armoni continued. Then he looked over and noticed Jonathan's clothes in David's hands. "Or were you sold as a bride by our father to his precious hero?"

Everyone guffawed, as Armoni was often the rudest, but Jonathan was embarrassed by the comment and reprimanded them all strongly. "How dare you speak like this with a guest in our presence?"

All four immediately stopped their laughter, as it was a severe sin to be unkind to a visitor.

"Our apologies," Abinadab said, and they all stood up to greet David with bows. "My name is Abinadab," he continued, "and that is my brother, Malchi-shua, who we all call Shua."

"And what about us?" Armoni growled.

"I wanted to spare our guest the unpleasantness of your association," Abinadab ribbed, but the twins both scowled. "Alas, here are our half-brothers, Armoni and Mephibosheth, sons to Rizpah, our father's concubine."

Jonathan elbowed David lightly in the ribs. "These two will be the reason the Lord probably sends another flood down to destroy the earth."

At that, Armoni and Mephibosheth stormed out of the tent, though they bowed their heads to David on the way out.

"Don't mind them," Jonathan said. "They rarely come in here, as they have their own tent that they live in a row back from ours. When they do though, they are more dung beetles than wolves."

A servant came in with clothing for Jonathan to choose from. He looked the garments over and chose a new *ketonet* and robe. As he lifted each over his head, the servant helped to pull them down over his arms.

David blurted out, "So what's it like, being the son of a king and all?"

"There's very little privacy," Jonathan confessed, shooing the servant away.

"Maybe, but it has to be quite something having servants dress you." David stared at the attendant, who walked out.

"I can remember back to when my father was a humble farmer, much like yours," Jonathan explained as he changed his sandals. "Don't let all of this confuse you, as we were as lowly as the rest until Samuel told us otherwise. And while I cannot say that there are not great benefits to being royal, there was something simpler about my youth."

"Oh?"

"There was a sense of abandon when I ran around free from the watchful eyes of guards or the endless glances from desperate women hoping to marry their way into my father's household."

Now dressed, Jonathan turned to his brothers. "Go and get changed. We will go to our father's for supper shortly." The two scurried from the tent.

"That doesn't sound all too bad, having girls throw themselves at you," David teased.

"It doesn't, until you realize that most of them will say or do anything—"

"Anything?" David interrupted.

"Yes, including feeding you a flood of lies, if it means any chance at being a princess." Jonathan paused. "It's very hard to know who is really your friend and who is simply interested in the proximity to power."

He sat down on a cushion and tapped the one nearest to him for David to do the same. "We will wait here for my brothers, as they won't be long."

"How do you know that I am not interested in gaining power from you as well?" David asked.

A smile spread across Jonathan's face. "Because after today, you already have it." He laughed. "What more could you possibly want from me now that you are the most well-known person in the land? Outside of my father, of course."

"I didn't do it for fame," David explained. "I did it because I had to."

Jonathan raised his brows toward his guest. "And that, my new friend, is why I am as comfortable with you as if we had nursed from the same breast. Your companionship is already anything but transactional."

But inside, he confessed to himself that his comfort with David was beyond any words he had learned in his sixteen years of life. *I already have love for you, though it perplexes me how it has rooted itself and flourished to the leaves so suddenly*, he said, but only in his mind.

Jonathan sat back, and for the next while, the two boys talked about many things, until it was time to feast at the king's table.

#

"I didn't realize how hungry I was until right now." David licked his lips as the smell of roasted lamb hit his nose.

He was led by his new friend into a large tent that was only a few steps away from where they had been waiting for Jonathan's brothers. Inside there were already dozens of men standing around in whispered conversations. An equal number sat on cushions and drank from vessels of silver and gold, which were topped up by servants who passed by with skins of wine.

"Welcome to the family," Jonathan announced, lifting two goblets filled with a dark red libation from a tray and handing one to David. "And a toast to your first successful evening in my father's household. May it be filled with much drinking and little backbiting, though I doubt the latter."

David noted Jonathan's eyes, which strayed toward the back of the tent as he said those last words. There sat King Saul on a simple throne carved from a single piece of cedarwood. He was surrounded by three men, two of which sat at his feet, while the third was positioned by his side.

"Who is that?" David asked as he eyed the man who stood with such authority and laughed so loudly with great confidence.

"That's our uncle, Abner," Jonathan explained. "He leads the army, and I am certain he will be anxious to meet you."

"Me?" The thought seemed ludicrous.

"Then again, maybe not." Jonathan grimaced. "After all, you did in one day what Abner himself could not do in many weeks, and he had an entire battalion of troops to work with."

David's eyes wandered the room and took in the opulence of the setting. The splendor was a far cry from anything he was used to. While his father, Jesse, was by no means poor, in comparison to Jonathan's family, he may as well have sat at the city gates begging for alms.

Mouth gaping and eyes staring, David followed behind Jonathan as they approached the throne. Abner was in the midst of explaining how the Israelites had rained down death between Gath and Ekron when King Saul suddenly put his hand up to silence him. There was a moment of awkwardness as David took note of Abner's jaw, which stiffened at Saul's action. The general recovered quickly enough to smile and pat the shoulder of their guest when Saul introduced David to the crowd.

"The boy who slew the giant!" the king declared as he lifted David's arm into the air. All around the many voices of the men cheered in reply, and David could feel the embarrassment flush his cheeks.

One of the men who had been at King Saul's feet stood up and approached him. He grabbed David's hand and shook it enthusiastically. "I am a shepherd too," he announced proudly as he pumped it up and down.

"This is Doeg," Jonathan explained with a frown. "He's an Edomite, and his job is to take care of all of my father's sheep." He stepped in between the two men. "But you are no longer a man of the ovine, David, and as such, you need not trouble yourself with the sons of Esau."

At that, Jonathan pulled David's hand away from Doeg's, and David noted that the shepherd grew red-faced at the rebuke. His palm began to sweat at Jonathan's touch as the king's son led him to a table at the far side of the tent. There was an unfamiliar intimacy in the act, and when Jonathan released him, David had a strange inclination to hold his own hand up to his face and nuzzle it against his cheek.

"Sit here," Jonathan said as he pulled out a chair and sat him down on the king's right-hand side.

"Are you sure I should be so close?" David's eyes widened again.

"Of course." Jonathan beamed. "You are our guest of honor!"

"I'm used to eating whatever scraps are left over from my brothers when I return from the fields." David laughed in wonder. "A choice spot at a king's table is very unfamiliar to me."

Jonathan's hand found the back of his neck, where it squeezed as a toothy grin exploded on his olive-toned face, which David now examined more closely than before. *Wow, his brows are thick,* he thought to himself.

Jonathan released his grip and took a seat in the chair next to him.

Once everyone else was settled, a lyre began to play from behind a curtain.

"I play this instrument too," David leaned over to tell Jonathan.

But there was no time for a reply, as suddenly two dozen women burst out into the open, each one rattling a tambourine in time to the rhythmic beat of an unseen drum. One woman wore a *simlah* of light green silk that ran from her neck to her ankles, and it shimmered brilliantly in the firelight.

David gasped at the sight. "How majestic."

"That is my mother, Ahinoam," Jonathan explained.

David could not help but stare at the striking woman with the bushel of dark hair as she danced her way around the table and eventually stood next to her husband. He eyed her up and down with admiration, fascinated by the many rings she wore on her fingers and toes.

Such wealth, he thought to himself. But to Jonathan, he said, "My mother doesn't look like that!" His eyes followed the golden chain that ran from Ahinoam's right ear down to the perfect circle of gold that clung to her narrow nose.

Lost in the moment, he was startled by a wild shout followed by a ripple from a new tambourine that came from behind the curtain. All heads turned in the direction of the sound as yet another beautiful woman emerged, her hips gyrating to the music.

"And who is that?" David's eyes grew even larger than before.

"You are safer not knowing," Jonathan replied through pursed lips.

This was a slightly younger woman than the first. She wore a far simpler white linen dress, but was equally beautiful, though perhaps in a more rugged way. The sound of her tambourine rattled David's mind as she moved closer and danced directly in front of him. Her eyes made contact with his, and he felt as though she would swallow him body and soul. The feeling was not unpleasant, and it made his heart race with excitement.

At last she moved on, and when she did, David caught a glance of distaste from Ahinoam. The younger woman brushed her shoulder up against Jonathan's mother in a challenge. Then she broke her stare and quickly moved on to take her place on the other side of the king.

Another wife, perhaps? A low growl emanated from Ahinoam's throat, which let David know that, whatever this woman's title, there was tension between the two of them.

Jonathan leaned over. "If you must know, she is my father's most wicked concubine, Rizpah. Also, she is mother to those treacherous creatures, Armoni and Mephibosheth, who you met in my tent earlier."

The music stopped before David could think of how to respond, and large trays of food were brought out. Servants worked their way around the table while the dancing women lifted up great big serving spoons and dipped them onto the trays so that they could place delicacies and delights onto the plates of the men.

David licked his lips at the sight of the mutton stewed in sour milk and the loaves of bread that had been dipped in honey and then covered in sliced almonds. He moaned with delight at the small pies of roasted beef cooked in onion, egg, and chopped fig that were brought out next. He had never before seen these delicacies, which had been baked for hours in earthen ovens before they were dotted with aromatic sesame seeds, which glistened across their golden tops.

At each passing of the food, the men around the table complained that their stomachs would burst, but soon, flat dough that had been heated on rocks and filled with carob and pistachio was dispersed. This silenced all mouths, which were willingly stuffed once again.

When every morsel had been devoured and every drop of wine had been tipped onto tongues, King Saul stood up to make an announcement. "Tomorrow we will return to Gibeah," he roared, and the applause was thunderous. "Now that the Philistines have been neutralized, I, for one, would like to bathe in the hot waters of the Hamat Gadar. Then I plan to put my feet up and enjoy the peace that I have won here for our people. This has proven once again that I alone was meant to be the man to save all of Israel, and that my bloodline"—he pointed to Jonathan—"shall rule this land for as long as the stars shine in the sky."

The crowd of men cheered again, until they all were spent from the excitement of war. At last, they lifted their inebriated bodies up with great effort and slowly broke away for their own tents and bedding.

"Oops." David giggled as he wavered upon standing. "My father doesn't allow me too much wine," he confessed. The effects of the alcohol had left him feeling giddy.

"We only have a short distance to my tent, and you will stay with me," Jonathan said as he put an arm over David's shoulders. "This way, we can ride out together tomorrow."

David found that the unexpected closeness of their bodies was as intoxicating as the fermented juice he had guzzled by the hin. *Delicious*, he thought as he looked over and admired the plumpness of Jonathan's bottom lip, which moved up and down in invitation.

"I said that you can accompany me side by side for as far as our parties travel together," Jonathan repeated.

"Oh, I'm sorry." David looked up at his eyes. "Yes, sure . . ."

"With my father's permission, of course, I would happily accompany you from here all the way back to the land of your father, in Bethlehem."

"That would be wonderful" was all that David could reply, as he was beginning to feel more woozy.

"Are you alright? Your face looks a little green."

"I think I need to lie down."

"Let's get going, then."

David leaned his weight onto Jonathan and let him guide his body toward the opening at the end of the tent that led them out into the night air.

As the two young men made their way into the moonlight, they heard the sounds of an argument. It was on just the other side of the goat-haired flap, in the section of the tent from where the dancing women had emerged.

Jonathan brought them to a halt. "Shhh," he commanded softly, and they stood there in silence and listened.

"I was supposed to wear that dress of silk," a voice hissed. "You knew this, and yet you took it from me, just like you took my position."

"How could I take your position from you when I was married to the king for five years before you ever met him?" another voice said, dripping with frustration.

"Either way, that dress would have been far prettier on me!"

"I would not have had to wear it if you had not torn my blue *simlah*."

"Well, next time do not speak to me like I am not an equal, Ahinoam, and I won't have to tear it to pieces!"

"Equal? You somehow forget that you are not the first wife, Rizpah. In fact, you are not even a wife at all," Ahinoam responded sternly. "I do not know how many more times, over how many more years, you will seek to defy and disrespect me or try some cheap trick for attention, but always know this: a concubine is what you are, and it is what you shall forever be. Nothing more."

The concubine all but screamed in frustration.

"Rizpah, nothing more, but certainly nothing less." Ahinoam's voice softened. "And that should be quite good enough."

"We will see," Rizpah snarled. "Even a queen cannot live forever."

"Is that a threat?"

"I only speak the truth," she hissed.

Ahinoam growled back, then the two shadows faded away in opposite directions.

"Ah," Jonathan said sadly. "You just witnessed what true combat is. It is not the Israelites and the Philistines on the field of battle, like you experienced today. No, it is the never-ending war between Saul's wife, Ahinoam, and his concubine, Rizpah."

"It sounds frightening," David responded with concern.

"It usually is." There was silence for a second before Jonathan continued. "If only that woman and her spawn would realize that there's only one first family. It may not be perfect, but they also get enormous status and live lives that are quite desirable compared to most. But somehow for them, it is just not good enough."

David wanted to say something witty or comforting, but the only thing that escaped from his mouth was a loud hiccup.

Jonathan laughed riotously. "I could not have said it better myself."

They carried on, though Jonathan continued to talk about his mother and the king's concubine the entire way, and David was hard pressed to follow what he was saying. "It does not surprise me that she tried to outshine Ahinoam tonight in your presence. She wants everyone's attention. But it equally does not surprise me that my mother neutralized her." He rambled on, but all David could think about was drinking some water and laying his head down on a cushion.

A few steps more and they tripped into the opening of Jonathan's tent, where they passed through a divide that had been established by thick curtains. David stumbled a little, so Jonathan held him tighter, then led him into a large space. This room was nearly dark, and the floor was covered in thick carpets and piles of silk pillows and woolen blankets.

"Ahhh," David moaned. "I think this tent is spinning . . ."

"Easy . . . here you go." Jonathan gently guided him down to the ground by placing both of his hands on David's back.

As David slid to the floor, his own arms somehow became wrapped around Jonathan's shoulders, which pulled the neck of the king's son forward so that they were both suddenly nose to nose. Jonathan let out a small gulp of what seemed to be fright, but he did not remove himself from this position. For a long moment, they each stared into the eyes of the other. David found himself infatuated by the reflection of soft light from the nearby oil lamp that danced across Jonathan's brown orbs.

He could feel Jonathan's hands on his back begin to shake, and he wondered if it was from fear or excitement. When David closed his eyes, he could smell the wine on Jonathan's breath, and he found it to be as sweet as the fruit of the vine that he had imbibed throughout the night.

When he opened them again, he found his head moving. It was as if someone had placed a hand on the backs of both his and Jonathan's necks and was pushing them closer and closer together.

Desire spread its way throughout David's body, and he freely gave himself over to it. He moaned ever so softly as their lips closed in, but just as they were about to touch, the sound of boys' laughter pierced the night air.

David watched as panic erupted across Jonathan's face and beads of sweat burst out on his forehead. He quickly pulled back from David and let him fall to the floor.

"Ow," David exclaimed as he landed on his side. He lay back and let the air that had gathered in his lungs in anticipation of the kiss rapidly escape, exhaling in disappointment.

"I told you . . . my brothers . . . they are incredibly annoying," Jonathan offered as a sloppy excuse, backing away. "I, um, well . . . I had better go check on them. You—you can sleep here and, well, I . . . I will sleep in my brother's tent," he stammered as he made his way out of the room.

Damn. David was not sure whether he should be angry at the loss of opportunity or embarrassed by Jonathan's reaction. *Was he afraid of being caught, or just afraid?*

But as he settled his head onto a nearby pillow, his mind became cloudy from the wine and the events of the day. He closed his eyes, and as he did so, he could hear the sound of the soldiers shouting. The shouts turned to taunts, and his mind filled with the image of Goliath glaring down at him from his towering height. At last, the sight of Jonathan smiling at him rose up in place of the giant, and David smiled back. This brought peace so deep that exhaustion at last carried him away and into slumber.

Under the Witness of Heaven

The piping notes of the *zamir* tittered in Jonathan's ears as the birds called the morning revelry across the Valley of Elah. Outside he could hear the sounds of men packing and loading their belongings onto the backs of creaking carts and braying asses.

Rubbing the sleep out of his eyes, he sat up and stifled a yawn. He remembered that he had run out of his tent when David and he almost kissed.

So dumb, he chastised himself. *Why am I so damn awkward?*

It had seemed like a good idea at first, to get away. But his brothers would not shut up; the excitement of the great beheading and battle had left them too excited, even though they'd only watched it from afar. Finally, he'd thrown a pillow in each of their faces and stormed back to his own tent, where he found the son of Jesse sound asleep, snoring and snorting like a bull.

"So much for peace," he had whispered to himself, but the truth was, once he lay down, he rather enjoyed the sound of David near him.

Why did I drop him? He slapped his head with one of his palms. *Real nice,* had been his final waking thought.

Now it was morning, and all he wanted to do was to make amends for running off. It had been foolish, and he wanted to explain to David that sometimes he did foolish things, especially when he felt as clumsy as he did right now. There was something about David that made him go weird, and he had to admit that this descriptor was a bit of an understatement for the way he had behaved ever since the young man first entered his father's tent.

Jonathan groaned to himself as more of his actions from yesterday returned to his mind. *I pulled all of my damn clothes off, for goodness' sake. He must think I am such an idiot!*

Embarrassed, he slowly turned his head to look over at where David slept. However, all he found was an empty space. *He must have gotten up early. That's okay. I'll smooth this over, and hopefully when I do so, it will be without further embarrassment.*

With a stretch, Jonathan stood up. A servant walked in with water and helped him freshen up before he changed his clothes in order to be better suited for riding the long distance to his father's fortress.

"Have you seen David this morning?" he asked his servant once he was dressed.

"He left only a few minutes before you awoke, but he took no breakfast and was gone quickly," the man replied as he left.

Jonathan shrugged and made his way to another section of the tent, where he sat down to a bowl of thick yogurt with honey and raisins. After he'd lapped a few spoonfuls into his mouth, he stretched his body once more and walked outside into the bright light, which was already punishing to the eyes, though it was still early.

Men and camels moved in every direction, so Jonathan navigated between them until he reached his father's tent, where King Saul was scolding some members of his household.

"I'm the king here," he barked at the young men dressed in nothing but loincloths. "It is not for you to decide when to pack my things away for me, but for me to direct you when and how to do it. That is why your families have sent you to me to serve—so that you can learn your place in this kingdom."

When his father lifted his fist to strike one of the men, Jonathan gasped and rushed forward. "That is all," he said to the group of servants. "You are dismissed and can carry on with your duties."

Relief spread across the faces of the young men, whose shoulders were bent near to the ground. They scurried away in various directions as quickly as they could.

"It is not easy being the one in charge." King Saul sighed as he lowered his fist and sat down on the throne.

"That may be, but I hardly think those men did anything to warrant such a reaction."

"Do not question my decisions, boy," Saul answered bitterly, but Jonathan ignored his father, as he usually tried to do whenever he started acting like this.

"What time do you plan for us to leave?" he asked instead.

"We will depart in one hour." The venom in King Saul's voice faded. "The rest can stay behind and finish the packing, but I have ordered David to ride up front with me, you, and Abner. We will head toward Gibeah. Once we reach the Judean wilderness, you and I shall go north, but Abner will turn eastward and escort David to his home."

"What happened to having whoever faced Goliath sit at your right-hand side?" Jonathan asked.

His father sucked his teeth. "I did . . . for dinner last night. He sat next to me, and he ate like a sacrificial bull, I might add. Now we each go back to our allotment."

"That does not seem like much of a heralding for one who did so much."

"That is why I am giving him the privilege of riding alongside me."

"In any case, I was hopeful that I could go with David to Bethlehem myself, instead of Abner, when you do send him away." Jonathan's voice was eager.

"I supposed that we can arrange that, then," King Saul said as he stood up again. "But for now, go and make sure that your brothers are ready to leave, and that includes Armoni and Mephibosheth. Their mother tells me that you are unjustly harsh on her sons—always, and in public, too—and I will not have it."

Jonathan rolled his eyes at this twisting of reality.

"I do not care how much they irritate you. You are the oldest," Saul pressed. "Whatever they do, you must not rise to the bait, lest you look weak and unfit. Brothers will be brothers behind closed doors, but the one thing you as the future king must never do is to humiliate them, especially in public."

Jonathan opened his mouth to respond, but his father had already stormed off, so he turned his body around and headed out to look for his brothers as commanded.

He found all four of them down on the valley floor. As he descended, he saw them each pivot their bodies until their weight was shifted to the left, as if they were participating in some kind of dance. "What in Egypt are they up to now?" he muttered under his breath.

As he got closer, he watched all four toss heavy stone discuses into the air at the same time. When the circular plates landed on the ground with many thuds, a few slave boys ran out to mark the distance of each with rocks.

"You cheat as always," Jonathan heard Armoni whine.

"How does one cheat at throwing a discus?" Abinadab chuckled. "It comes down to strength, of which clearly I have more."

"He's right," Mephibosheth barked, his toad-like eyes bulging in anger. "I saw you take a step forward while the rest of us stayed behind the line."

Spittle flew when Shua ran up and yelled in Mephibosheth's face. "Now that's just an outright lie!"

Shoulders and bodies started to buck up as all four boys began to push one another.

"Stop," Jonathan commanded as he stepped in between them, his hands in the air as a warning.

"They started it," all of them cried out at the same time.

"This is just for sport, brothers," Jonathan reminded them. "Not everything is a reason to fight."

Separated but not calmed, the four slowly circled around him, ready to pounce anew, and they glared across the distance at their half-siblings with fire and brimstone.

"Our father is ready for us to leave," Jonathan explained sternly. "We need to join him shortly, so there should be no further problems between us."

"Tell that to the testy twins," Abinadab said as he rounded Jonathan's back.

"At least we have testes," Armoni sneered, then pointed at Shua and Jonathan. "Not like you and your sisters."

Mephibosheth snorted as he batted his eyes and curtsied. "Yes, your highnesses. Right away, ladies."

"Oh, whatever." Abinadab stopped circling and threw his hands up in the air. "It doesn't matter what we say or do, the two of you are always such prickly pears."

Everyone followed suit and stopped pacing around Jonathan.

"It's true. You are like cheap and coarse fabric that blisters the skin, just like your mother," Shua added.

"Don't talk about our mother like that," Mephibosheth warned, and he stepped forward once more.

"Or what?" Abinadab raised his voice again.

"One of these days, something is going to happen to you—to all of you," Armoni spat with venom.

"Enough!" Jonathan screamed. "The four of you are like the bleating herds that Doeg tends to. Now get yourselves together without any more mule shit, and prepare to depart. I will meet you at our father's tent in ten minutes."

His command given and his brothers rebuked, Jonathan stormed back up the hill to look for David. "Now let me sort this out with him without making a further ass of myself," he ordered himself.

#

"I'm supposed to ride on the back of that beast?" David eyed the horse suspiciously.

"You are a hero now," Abner stated directly. "And heroes do not walk." He pointed to David's leg. He was a general, and generals expected to be obeyed.

David sighed and rolled his eyes, but neither act of rebellion prevented the inevitable. So, he moved up alongside the animal and grasped its mane.

"Now do it," Abner commanded.

David threw his right leg up into the air in an attempt to get it over the back of the horse. Abner rushed up and pushed at his backside.

"I have always traveled . . . by foot," David explained through huffs as he struggled to get up. "I would be just . . . as . . . happy . . . to do so today."

"I am afraid the king has insisted," Abner grunted from behind him.

The horse whinnied.

David cried out as the sound startled him, and he lost his grip and fell backward. He landed with a loud thud onto his left arm on the hard ground.

"Fuck." He looked up from the dirt with a pout while he held his elbow with his other hand. "My falling has become a habit here."

"You think this is bad, I imagine you would feel much worse if you had to travel by foot along with the washerwomen instead of up front with the king."

"Ugh," David moaned, struggling to get back up.

"Again," Abner directed him sternly. "We will keep at it until your bony butt is on top of that thing."

"Here," he heard another voice say from behind him.

Just what I need. David sighed to himself as Jonathan stepped forward and approached them.

"Put your left hand over by his neck like this." He demonstrated.

Is he strange or what?

"Then do a small bounce from your knees before you swing your right leg up."

He allowed me to make a fool of myself last night and now comes over here acting like nothing even happened?

"Got it?" Jonathan asked.

"It's alright," David said coolly. "Your uncle has given me adequate instruction already."

"Oh," Jonathan said with surprise in his tone. He turned back to Abner. "Continue," he said with a nod.

"Well, um . . . actually, that was good advice that my nephew gave you," Abner admitted.

"Hmm." David pursed his lips.

"In fact, let's go ahead and try exactly that," Abner encouraged him.

David looked at Abner, then at Jonathan. He sighed and rolled his eyes. "Fine," he relented.

He placed his hand on the horse's neck and lifted his leg just like Jonathan had shown him. Then with a bounce, he swung it up into the air. The momentum was satisfying, and a small, quick push from Abner helped carry him over the side of the animal until he was at last seated right on the back of the beast.

"See?" Jonathan exclaimed through a bright smile.

I see, alright. I see you dropped me to the floor like a leper.

Out loud, David answered blandly, "Thank you."

While he might have appeared calm, frankly, between the humiliation of last night and his terror at sitting on the back of this beast, his hands were shaking so badly he buried them in the horse's mane so that they would be hidden from sight.

He turned back to Abner and smoothly asked, "And now, how do I make this creature move forward?"

"If you tap it lightly with your heels"—Abner grabbed the reins—"you will find that the beast will . . ."

As Abner led him away, David did not hear another word that the man said to him.

Maybe I misunderstood? But what does "bound" mean if not soul and body? I guess he just wasn't into me like that after all.

"Damn, I am really stupid," he said aloud at last, fuming.

"You won't be stupid if you never forget that the horse is at your command, not you at its," Abner replied.

"Huh?" David looked down at Abner and remembered what they were doing. "Oh . . . right. I got it." He grabbed the reins out of the general's hands. "I think I can handle it from here," he informed him with confidence.

"You do?" Abner said in surprise. "You seemed so hesitant."

"No point dancing around it all day. If I have to ride it, then I will ride it," David declared. Then he kicked the horse in its side and trotted off around the camp as if he had been riding all of his life.

"I got the hint," he blurted into the air as he bounded around. "And I won't be making that same mistake again."

#

Well that was awkward, Jonathan thought. *David was the one who pulled my face down for a kiss, not the other way around, but now he is mad at me?*

"I've made a complete mess of this." He sighed. "Maybe we can just pretend it never happened."

With no time to dwell on it, he shook it off and went to secure his brothers for travel so that he could find his own horse instead of worrying about everyone else's.

Abinadab and Shua were easy to corral, but the other two had not followed the command he had given them in the valley and were now nowhere to be found. After a few minutes of poking his head in and out of various tents, at last Jonathan saw their feet huddled with Rizpah's just behind the flap that led to the women's quarters.

"It's alright, my children," their mother soothed. "Just as I am more beautiful than Ahinoam, you, my special twins, are more wise and accomplished than her children will ever be."

"But they insulted you too," one of them whispered bitterly.

"That matters little," she said, "because I have seen the old soothsayer at Endor."

Jonathan could hear the boys gasp.

"What?" one asked.

"You did?" said the other.

"Yes." There was excitement in her voice. "And she told me that one day it is you who will be the princes, my sons. None of Ahinoam's children will see the crown on their heads," she exclaimed.

Jonathan had never heard Rizpah actually happy before.

"What will happen?" one of the twins asked in glee.

"She did not give any details, but she did tell me that all you have to do is bide your time, and that all of this will happen without either of you lifting so much as a finger."

"One of us will be king?"

"Mediums are rarely wrong. Why else would they have been forbidden?" Rizpah told her sons with confidence. "I promise you, my children, it will come to pass. But for now, you must obey your brother Jonathan in all that he says. For one day, he will be dead, and you will give the orders that the rest will follow."

Jonathan rolled his eyes. He knew mediums and spirits were strictly forbidden, but he also thought that their pronouncements were a load of hot manure. Unlike the prophet Samuel, or the priests that used the Urim and Thummim, these spiritualists had only empty words. These were great for fertilizing foolish minds, but piss-poor for predicting anything that would ever come to fruition.

He wondered what to do for a quick moment before he turned and tiptoed away. While he could easily have rushed forward and condemned them all for discussing a witch's proclamation, or run to his father to report Rizpah's wickedness, he decided to retreat and simply ignore what he had heard.

If believing some old hag's shit will keep these three in line for the time being, then so be it, he told himself.

He hurried quietly from the tent and went to find his place in the entourage that was lined up for travel. "They will find their way, I have no doubt about that," he mumbled about his half-brothers as he climbed onto the back of a gray mule.

Jonathan rode along, twisting his neck left and right to search the crowd. *I wonder where David is,* he thought. Whatever had taken place earlier, he couldn't stop himself from looking for him.

When he reached his father's side, he realized that perhaps David had decided to ride elsewhere after all. So much for acting like nothing happened. *He obviously just doesn't want to be near me at all after what I did.*

But just then, David emerged from the crowd atop the horse that Jonathan had helped him mount earlier. Jonathan noted how his head was raised particularly high as he trotted up alongside him. In their few moments apart, David seemed to have found his footing and now appeared quite confident on horseback.

His eyes lingered on the light freckles that dotted David's fair cheeks. *Wow, he is handsome,* he couldn't help but think.

Jonathan tentatively tried to break the ice between them. "Um, my father said that I will be able to escort you on your way back to Bethlehem after all."

"That won't be necessary," David replied, his eyes fixed forward. "I can travel alone." He urged his horse to continue ahead, where he joined another group of horsemen.

He hates me. Jonathan's heart fell.

"We will ride out as one until we exit the rolling hills and reach the rocky cliffs," King Saul suddenly announced with great vibration from atop his white horse. "From there, we will break into two formations."

Twelve men in armor marched out of the crowd, all on foot, and closely lined up on either side of the king. A trumpet blew, and a herald yelled out, "And now, let all the land see their King Saul, the mighty, who by God's grace has freed us all from the great threat of the Philistines."

A gigantic roar sounded from the crowd, and they fanned out and forward across the plains and toward the hill country.

As they passed through towns both small and large, people came out to wave and cheer. Women by the duos, dozens, and hundreds would ululate loudly, their tongues pressed rapidly against the roofs of their mouths as they released their high-pitched wails.

Everyone seemed happy except for Jonathan. His heart both lamented and leapt each time he caught a glimpse of David.

Then a song that had first been whispered in one of the small ravines along the road began to twist and turn its way across the desert plains until at last it became as powerful as a sandstorm.

"Saul has killed thousands and David his tens of thousands." The lyrics rang out until everyone and everything throughout the land had been swept up by their gale force. Finally, they sped on a gust of wind until at last they landed in the ears of the king, who raged at their meaning.

\#

Jonathan entered his father's tent once their caravan had stopped for the evening. There he found King Saul walking back and forth and cursing in a fit of anger.

"*Yimach shemo!*" he roared at Jonathan.

"Whose name should be blotted out?" Jonathan asked with great concern.

"That boy! That stupid shepherd from Bethlehem." His father fumed.

"David?" Jonathan was confused. "Only yesterday you were willing to have him sit at your side in front of everyone."

"I should have known it was all a plot." Saul was frantic now. His head shook back and forth, and his eyes looked across the space between him and his son as if they would pop out of his head and roll onto the ground by Jonathan's feet.

"Did not that damned Samuel tell me that I had fallen out of favor? That someone else would be anointed?"

"Slow down and breathe." Jonathan lifted his hand up to urge his father to be settled. "Then slowly tell me what you are talking about." He could feel the squeezing at his temples that always gripped him when his father got like this. "You said Samuel, but the prophet is not here. Did he come to you in a dream or are you having some kind of an episode?"

At these words, Saul threw his palms in the air and bellowed, "What that prophet did to me at Carmel was no episode. It was a curse!"

"You're not making any sense. How did Samuel curse you?" Jonathan took his father's hands and tried to steady them at his side.

"He said the Lord had rejected me." King Saul's eyes went wide with terror.

"I am worried. I should find an herbalist to give you some tea to rest your spirit."

"A potion cannot undo what has happened on account of the Amalekites." Saul's voice now softened, and tears began to spill from the bags that had formed under his eyes from too many sleepless nights.

"Here." Jonathan guided his father to his throne. "Sit down and tell me slowly what has you so troubled."

"I should have killed them all," Saul's shaky voice whispered.

"But you did," Jonathan insisted. "It has been almost a year since you rode out and put King Agag and all of his people to their death, just as you had been commanded. So there is nothing to worry about. You just need to rest."

He reached for a nearby empty cup and filled it with wine from a skin. Then he lifted it to his father's lips. "Now drink," he insisted, and his father obeyed. "You did what was asked of you, and that is all there is to it. You're just tired."

The king stopped his drinking and shook his head. "I let the men keep the best of their animals." He sobbed, unconsolable, then stood back up. "And I myself waited too long to slay Agag, their king."

"But you did kill him," Jonathan tried to reassure his father.

"Yet only after Samuel had already told me what God had declared," he said so softly that Jonathan could barely hear him.

Jonathan rubbed his father's arm. "Then whatever Samuel shared was just. Whatever he pronounces is the word of the Lord. Remember, it was at his behest that you became king at all, so you must accept his prophecy, no matter what. We all must."

"Oh my son," King Saul cried out again. "I am sorry that I have forfeited your inheritance, as that was what was pronounced to me at Carmel. That someone else will come after me, and that it will not be you but another unnamed. One who is not from our family."

They stood in silence for a minute.

"The cries of the people today make me afraid that it will be David," Saul said at last. "He's young, he's beautiful, and he's already achieved much in a matter of mere days."

"I think you single him out too readily just because of one song. I hardly think that has earned him the right to be feared by you. But what if God did proclaim that he will be the next king? If he is, I will serve him, or whomever it will be, just as I serve you," Jonathan replied quietly. "What's most important is to stay loyal to our God and to our nation."

"No!" Saul yelled. "I will not give up so easily."

"You cannot give up that which you do not own. We are only in this position by the Lord's will."

"No." Saul shook his head. "I have thought it over, and if I send that boy away now to his homeland, he could come back with an army twice the size of our own and have us all killed."

Jonathan laughed. "I don't think that David seems likely to murder us."

"No, my son. I will not do it. Instead I will have to keep him close to my side." Saul began to pace again. "I will pretend that he is a trusted and valued member of my household. But in reality, he will be my prisoner, and if necessary, I will kill him before he can kill me and take this crown off my head." He was frantic again.

"Sit," Jonathan commanded, and guided his father back to his throne. When he was seated, he soothed him with reason. "If the Lord has decided, then he has decided. We cannot change that, even if it means the kingdom is not to be mine."

"You are not angry?" Saul's eyes widened, and he reached up to touch Jonathan's face.

"What good will that do?" he replied softly. "I have to trust that it is the right decision, just as I trust that, for now, you are still the king and must act like it." He took his father's hand from his cheek and held it.

"Let David return to his home," Jonathan said at last. "For one, it is more than likely that it is not he who will succeed you. It's not like this young man has already been anointed by Samuel, or we would have known about it by now."

"I suppose that is true," Saul relented.

"Whether you keep this one boy close or not, what is to be will be, and you and I both must accept that. But none of this is any fault of David's, and he should not be kept from his family due to our disappointment or your paranoia. Instead, you will do what is in the best interest of our country and all of our kinsmen, as that is what is most important."

His father settled, and Jonathan called in a servant and instructed him that the king be given a calming brew and taken to his bed at once. Afterward, he stepped out into the night air alone and stared up at the stars.

He was in solitude for just a few moments before he heard the soft patter of a pair of feet that approached from behind. He turned his head and found David standing there.

"I must apologize for the way I acted today," the teenager said nervously. "I was rude to you because I was embarrassed by my ridiculous behavior last night."

"*You* were embarrassed?"

"Not only was I drunk and needed to be practically carried to bed, but I, perhaps, was a little too forward. You had every right to turn me down—"

"I didn't turn you down," Jonathan interjected. "I panicked and ran out of my tent like a frightened child."

"Oh, you mean . . . ?" David looked at his feet before he continued. "Look, I seem to get all strange and twisted when you are around, so I don't want to say the wrong thing here."

39

Jonathan sighed. "It's alright. I cannot say that I know how to act. I would call myself something of a bumbling *kesil*. Usually I'm the one with good steady judgement in my family, but . . ." He paused.

David nodded and then stepped up so that they were standing right alongside each other. He pointed up into the night sky. "My father tells me that the stars are each part of a great host that stand ready to protect the Lord from the serpent and to enforce his commandments."

"I have heard the same," Jonathan responded as their arms gently brushed up against one another and rested there. He could feel the static electricity where the hairs on their forearms touched.

"And what do you think?" David asked in a whisper.

"Whatever they may be, they excite me as much as they terrify me." Jonathan shivered.

"Mm-hmm," David agreed.

They languidly leaned against one another in silence for a moment, then David turned his head to face Jonathan. His voice grew soft. "Isn't it amazing how something can make you feel both out of breath and ready to run across the desert at the same time?"

Nervously, Jonathan pulled his gaze down from the stars and over to David's eyes. The giant-slayer tilted his head and began to move in slowly toward Jonathan's face, his blue eyes filled with great longing.

Jonathan giggled uncomfortably. "What are you doing?"

"What I should have done last night, only this time without the help of wine," David answered in a huffed breath.

There was panic in the pulse that began to thump along the side of Jonathan's neck. While something urged him to flee like he had done the previous night, his feet felt stuck in place, as if large boulders sat on top of each of his sandals. Unable to break free, he surrendered and shut his eyes, and at last, he felt the soft padding of David's lips gently press against his own.

His body tingled, and he felt the stirrings of movement below his waist. *What is happening?* he thought in fear, but the salty taste of David's mouth lured him back into the moment.

This was the answer to that ache in his soul, that deep yearning he'd felt from the moment he met David face-to-face.

Two quick whoops from a hyena off in the distance rang out, and they nipped at Jonathan's conscience, so he pulled back. As he did so, he gasped loudly, as if his head had just emerged from being dunked into the deepest of cisterns.

What am I doing? It felt as if he were riding across the land in one of the two-wheeled chariots that the Philistines had used so effectively against them in battle. Only the chariot would not stop, and now it ran straight off a cliff's edge.

"Is this wrong?" he suddenly blurted out in frightful confusion.

"Hey, hey, hey." David put his hands on Jonathan's shoulders. "If this was wrong, we wouldn't have been led to each other."

"I know that is true, but—" Jonathan started to say, but his words became lost somewhere between the arms that pulled him in close and the gentle kiss that landed on the nape of his neck.

"Wasn't there something about an abomination?" He let out a gasp of sexual freedom as David made his way up to his jaw. "Or was it l-la . . . lamentations . . ." he stuttered as David's mouth found him again.

They connected in fiery fervor.

When they unhooked, David growled, "The only abomination here would be to deny what we feel for one another."

"Yes." Jonathan exhaled shakily. "Maybe I just needed to hear you say it."

They embraced, and the youthful ignorance of lanky limbs and clumsy hands turned to passion and everything else in the world stood still.

"Whatever this feeling is," Jonathan finally shouted into the air, "I want more!"

Then, under the witness of the heavenly host, they kissed again, and even the stars did not burn with the same intensity as the touch of their lips.

An irksome sound began to emerge in the distance. "Jonathan?" it yelled repeatedly, and ever more loudly, until both boys were pulled back from the stars. As they moved their heads away from each other, David grabbed Jonathan's hands and squeezed them.

"Jonathan!" the voice called again.

"Ugh!" He threw his head back and moaned. "I told you, it is times like these that I feel the urge to leave the royal entourage and become a lonely hermit who lives among the rocky crags with lizards and mice."

"I need to be going now anyway," David replied, laughing as he swung Jonathan's hands to and fro. "Your father has sent word that I am to move on this evening without waiting for the sunrise. That is why I came to find you."

"I'm glad that you did."

David backed away, slowly extricating his hands from Jonathan's with each step, until they fell at his side. "As much as I was starting to like all of this attention, it appears that my fate is not to be among kings and princes after all."

"I had planned to ride to Bethlehem with you, but I believe that is no longer an option," Jonathan confessed sadly.

"Hey,"—David shrugged—"I walked on foot along the valley road to the battle all by myself. I think I can manage half a day's ride on the back of a horse."

"Then this is farewell?" Jonathan asked as a mild tightness began to squeeze his chest.

"I hope not forever . . . but I don't know when we will meet again," David said with sadness in his eyes.

"Perhaps when the Philistines send more giants." Jonathan awkwardly giggled, an ill-timed adolescent jest.

What did I do that for? he admonished himself sternly once the silly words were already loosed.

He tried again. "What I really mean to say is that I do not know if I will ever find a person I'm more connected to than I have found in you during these past two days."

The words spoken, Jonathan felt the muscles in his body tighten. Without thought, he lunged forward in a rush right into David's arms. The move practically knocked David over, and they hugged each other tightly.

"I feel the same," David admitted. After a few seconds, he gently pushed Jonathan away again. "Goodbye," he said simply, then turned and walked toward the tents.

Jonathan watched until his body disappeared among the temporary dwellings. He looked back at the stars and dabbed at the water that had unexpectedly formed at the corners of his eyes.

#

The road back seemed more difficult than it had when David traveled it only a few days ago to find his brothers. True, the landscape was the same, and this time he had the aid of a horse to make the steps lighter and quicker, but he was a different person than when he'd made his way to the Valley of Elah.

All he had planned to do was to bring food to his brothers—or at least that was what he'd told himself when he grabbed some loaves of bread and charred meat and ran out the door. The food wasn't very fancy, but it made for a great excuse. Not that he'd offered it to anyone.

He had not asked permission to leave his father's household. Instead, he yelled to a pair of his sisters who stood bent over a stone quern milling wheat that he was going to find their brothers. The girls looked up in fury, and David knew he was leaving them to explain to their father where he had run off to. But he hadn't considered the repercussions then, and now he was headed back home to face whatever awaited him.

Things had been lighter before he ran off in boyish curiosity to see the battle his older brothers were engaged in. Thoughts of war seemed exciting and even romantic. He'd left home with a certain amount of in-nocence, he told himself as he began to recognize the familiar terrain of his father's land. Of course then he had not known the way blood oozed out of a man's neck when it was severed from its body. He had not known a thing about fine food or thrones, or even women in silk and jewels. And he certainly had not known the itch of emotion and physical attraction to a boy named Jonathan, the thought of whose brown hair even now brought a smile and a sigh.

David's horse made its last steps up a Judean hill, and his father was there and waiting. David braced himself for the lashing of a rod as he sheep-ishly slid off and the man let out a great big yell.

"David!" Jesse roared.

Wait. David's brow furrowed. *Is he laughing?*

"My son," his father bellowed as he rushed forward and embraced him in a strong and loving hug.

From the dwelling behind him, out poured David's mother and sisters, who all ran to him and stroked and patted his back and arms, which were still entwined in his father's embrace.

"And where are your brothers?" His mother beamed. "We have been preparing food since yesterday, awaiting your return."

"My brothers?" David giggled. The question dumbfounded him. He had not given them a single thought since he'd stormed off and away from them and right over the hill that led down into the valley.

"They did not ride with you?" his father asked in surprise. "How could they not protect their younger brother, or smother him with pride for his deeds?"

"They will have to eat the scraps of our food then." David's mother laughed and grabbed him by the hand. She led him inside, followed by his sisters and father.

In all of his years, David had never seen his family so excited to see him, nor had they ever feted him a hero. He could get used to this. Maybe life back in Bethlehem wouldn't be so bad.

"Sit and eat," his mother commanded.

"Yes," Jesse agreed, and took a seat next to David. "And then you will tell me all about how you, my child that was anointed by the Lord himself, slew the giant and saved the nation!"

Am I asleep? Did I climb Jacob's ladder to find myself in some kind of a strange dream?

"Did the king marry you to his daughter, and what kind of positions have you secured for your brothers?" David's father asked excitedly.

"No," David said between bites. "He sent me back to our home forever, and I know nothing of my brothers, as I have not seen them since before we slew the Philistines."

Mid slurp, he watched his father's face fall.

"You mean to tell me that you killed this Goliath and got nothing from it but a silly song about ten thousands?"

"I'm afraid that seems to be about it." David sighed. "The king wanted me to leave, as that song made him jealous, so he sent me back to Bethlehem with no further instructions."

"Did he at least give you some type of reward? A few animals, perhaps? Maybe some shekels as payment?"

David pushed the food away and stared down at the tabletop.

"Oh." Jesse's voice quieted. He stood up, which caused David's sisters, who had been standing over him, to back away. "In that case," he said sternly, "you can tend to the flock in the lower fields this evening."

"Huh?" David asked. "I just got home after a long journey."

"You may not be anything to King Saul, but here you are a good shepherd boy, and your father needs one to keep our sheep safe tonight."

With that, Jesse removed himself from the tent with slumped shoulders, and David watched as his mother and sisters slowly walked out to return to their chores.

Alone, he felt heavier than he had on the journey.

"Well, this sucks," he groaned to the empty room.

THE COVENANT

Bitter Vetch and
Goat's Milk

T he high sandstone walls of the fortress at Gibeah were still warm to the touch despite it being after dark. Jonathan leaned up against a pile of stacked rocks that sat atop the fortification and made up the lone tower as he looked out on the central highlands. Around him, archers stood at his command, ready to rain down hell on any raiding enemy parties that made their way this far into the land of Benjamin.

It had been three years since their victory in the Valley of Elah. In that time, the Philistines had nursed their wounds and regrouped, and were now a more formidable force than before. They had become extremely bold in their jaunts into King Saul's lands, as they openly dared the Israelites to face them head-on once more.

In addition to them, there were Moabites, Edomites, Ammonites, and a number of other assorted small Semitic kingdoms and nomadic tribes, each of which clawed for a piece of the land that the Hebrew god had promised the Jews was now theirs for all of eternity.

Content that the night was filled only with animals that roamed on four legs, Jonathan took the slender staircase down from the wall and walked through the small enclosure that circled the city. Within these walls stood about two dozen buildings. Many of them housed the staff that tended to the royal family, as well as groups of soldiers who were on constant call to protect their king at all costs. The rest of the buildings were for King Saul's family and the various arms of government. Outside, the low land was encircled by small clusters of homes made of stone and wood that pressed up against the fortress walls, as well as hundreds of tents. Within them, tradesmen and families clung to the lifeline of protection that the king's presence provided. Beyond these lay a vast expanse that allowed those on the fortress walls to see a great distance in every direction.

In a large building at the center of the city, Jonathan's father sat on his cedar throne and made daily decisions in the interest of the nation. The location at Gibeah allowed him central rule of his lands and also easy access to the priests who resided in the town of Nob, less than half a day's ride away.

"Your father is in a state," Abner said, sucking his teeth as he passed Jonathan on his way up to stand guard for the night.

"What now?" Jonathan asked with a sigh.

"Damned if he tells me. What I do know is that I stand ready to ride out tomorrow to confront the Philistines once more, if he would only give the word to gather the rest of our forces."

"Let me see if I can talk to him," Jonathan told his uncle, then he made his way into one of the short buildings near the tower.

Inside, Judith, daughter of Elim—another of King Saul's generals— smiled at him and brought a bowl of steaming venison stew and a spoon over to the table.

"Thank you." Jonathan smiled back, and sat down to enjoy the food his new wife had prepared for him. They had been married in the spring, at his father's insistence.

"You have gone too long alone," King Saul had scolded. "Since you have been unable to select an appropriate bride for yourself, I have negotiated an adequate bridal fee myself with Elim. This has brought you the comfort of a woman and brought us both assurances that Elim's large family will protect your claim to the throne whenever my time comes to rest with my fathers."

While Jonathan did not feel much more than a passing physical interest in Judith, he did what was expected of him, as at the very least, he was honor bound to provide an heir. While he admitted to himself that ultimately he longed for a partner with whom he had a stronger bond, Judith was what he had. So at every chance, he took advantage of her willingness to bed him, as he decided that even if there was a lack of connection, he could try to enjoy having sex, and Judith was ever the ready and willing participant.

Long gone from memory were his father's words regarding the prophet Samuel and their bloodline. Though Saul traveled back and forth between two distinct personalities, the reasons for his frequent visits to madness never resurfaced. Thus, they were forgotten, along with any mention of the boy from Bethlehem. These thoughts had spilled out along the same trail between the rugged wilderness and the dusty road to Gibeah where the whisperings of the witch at Endor and the kisses of a certain Judean shepherd had fallen. There they'd been swallowed up by both time and pressing matters of state, though in the quietest hours of the night, an unnamed itch would claw at Jonathan's spirit.

As he spooned a large helping of the food into his mouth and savored the pungent taste of cumin on his tongue, Judith came up behind him and began to rub his shoulders.

"Ah," Jonathan moaned.

"Now just relax," she purred.

But his muscles tensed. "As much as I would like to indulge in your attention, I must go see my father."

Judith stopped rubbing and leaned her face in front of his with a pout. "I won't get pregnant without us spending at least some time alone together each day." She sighed.

"You are a prince's wife now, and this means that duty always comes first," Jonathan explained.

"Oh, pooh," she whined. "It seems like every other minute, your father needs this, the army needs that, the priests need you to do one thing, and your brothers argue for you to do another. How boring! When do I get what I need?"

"And what exactly do you need that is so urgent?" he teased.

Judith's lashes lowered. "I can only show you."

Jonathan stood up and smiled. "As soon as I speak to the king, I will come back here for you," he playfully replied.

"Do you promise?" she begged.

"Just make sure you have the bed prepared. It is too warm for furs, so I expect you to be naked and in heat at the sound of my sandals at the door." He leaned over and kissed his wife.

They both laughed, and Judith tossed her hair about and cooed, "Don't you worry, my husband. I will be more than ready."

Jonathan slapped her on the buttocks and made his way to the door.

On his way to find his father, he passed through a long hall where his mother, Ahinoam, was addressing the cook and a group of servants.

"Tomorrow evening we will host the generals. I want a hearty meal prepared and each of the men to feel somewhat indulged," she instructed.

"So I believe perhaps something of a sweet pudding should round out the night?"

The baker nodded.

Jonathan noted the way his mother's chin was elegantly raised. She did not speak rudely to anyone but rather addressed them with the grace and dignity of someone assured of her station. Each member of her audience grinned and bowed before they left her, and Jonathan knew in his heart that there could never be another queen as self-assured and born to the position as Ahinoam.

"Oh," she said as she turned her body around in one smooth motion. "I did not hear you come up behind me, my eldest son." Then she smiled and leaned forward so that Jonathan could kiss her on the forehead.

"If only one day Judith will be as poised as you are." He winked at her.

His mother laughed. "I do not plan on dying for a long time, but when the time does come, I have every confidence that Judith will do splendidly. For now, though, you need to worry about having sons."

Jonathan chuckled. "So Judith keeps reminding me every chance she gets."

"Women have but a few purposes, my son. And until they run their own households, they really only have one, and that is to bear as many children as possible. Now make both your father and me happy by ensuring that Judith holds a baby on her hip come the spring. Otherwise, perhaps it will be time to look for a second wife?" Ahinoam raised her eyebrow.

"Oh no." Jonathan laughed. "I've already seen what having more than one wife can do to a family."

"I cannot fault you for saying this." His mother sighed loudly. "Only this morning, Rizpah tried to trip me. Can you imagine a grown woman trying to trip another grown woman?"

"My point exactly. No, one wife is quite enough. If I had a concubine, she would have to be a mute one." Jonathan said. "Anyway, I must go and find Father. Abner tells me he is unsettled."

Ahinoam lowered her eyes. "It seems as if the littlest thing sets him to yelling," she said with sadness in her voice.

"Perhaps if he had a less irritating first wife, he wouldn't be so agitated," Rizpah hissed from behind them as she entered the hall. Her two sons were alongside her, and Jonathan sucked his teeth at hearing such forwardness from his father's concubine in his presence.

"I would hold my tongue if I were you," he warned her. "You are speaking to the true wife of the king, and thus a queen. Not another mere milkmaid like yourself."

"Watch it," Armoni snarled as he stepped forward. "Our mother is only a quick accident away from being a queen herself."

"Is that a threat?" Jonathan responded with one eyebrow raised.

Mephibosheth stepped in between them. "My brother only seeks to return your own slight."

"It absolutely amazes me that after all of these years, the three of you still carry on with such fantasies about things over which you have no control," Jonathan said with a smirk.

"What I do have control over is what I shall wear tonight . . . Or maybe I'll wear nothing at all," Rizpah purred.

"Oh?" Ahinoam raised her voice in curiosity.

"It appears your husband has grown as weary of you as I have, as he has asked for me to sleep with him this evening," Rizpah boasted. She stuck her neck out as she brushed past Ahinoam. "In fact, my sons are escorting me to his chamber now. It seems the king prefers the sweetness of my melons over your dried, crusty cobs."

The twins snickered.

"Perhaps," Ahinoam replied coolly. "But it was I who suggested that he call for you."

A look of confusion grew across Rizpah's face as she stopped walking and turned back to face Ahinoam. "You did?"

"The king needs attending to this evening, and let's face it—he is getting far too old for his other, much younger, concubines." She laughed. "He simply cannot keep up with them."

Rizpah's shoulders tightened. "I should have pushed you with my hands this morning instead of just sticking out my foot," she snarled. "Then I wouldn't have missed."

"Hmm . . ." Ahinoam looked her over. "Yes, this was the right decision, as he really needs someone past their prime."

"That would be you!"

"Me?" Ahinoam chuckled. "Well, I am far too busy with something important. You see, I will be helping the jeweler tonight as we select precious stones for the new crown my husband has decided to have made for me."

Rizpah's eyes narrowed with envy.

"I thought my husband would benefit from having one of his lesser servants come and rub warm oil into his callused feet while I am occupied with rubies and emeralds."

"*Ata klava*," Rizpah growled under her breath.

"Yes," Ahinoam replied. "I am a bitch, but the *first* bitch around here. So scurry along—the king's corns await." She turned her back to the concubine.

"This plan will backfire, you know," Rizpah confided loudly to her sons.

"How so?" Mephibosheth asked.

"I happen to be ripe, so I may give your father another son tonight. Then we will see exactly which of us is past their prime."

"Oh." Ahinoam turned back to face her. "I highly doubt that will happen tonight. In fact, you may want to gather some dried flowers and herbs to scatter around the room. I fed my husband bitter vetch and goat's milk for supper, and you know how they both disagree with his stomach. He's likely to be quite gassy and uncomfortable."

Rizpah released a furious shriek before she turned and stormed out the door with her glaring sons following behind her.

"It's a shame." Ahinoam sighed. "If she were not always scheming or seeking to lessen me, I believe we could be quite good friends. But in the end, the only person she ever really trips is herself."

"Well, now that the demonstration of the love in our household is over"—Jonathan laughed—"let me go and find Father and see if I can calm his nerves. I confess though that my own are more on edge now than they were when I first walked in here."

He kissed his mother goodbye before he left and entered the small square room next door. Inside, there was emptiness.

Jonathan stood there for a minute and wondered where his father might have gone. A slight movement of the sheer gold curtains that were draped along the wall behind the throne caught his eyes. He looked down and saw ten sandaled toes sticking out from beneath the drapes. Turning his head, he scanned the room to see if anyone else was nearby.

Once he was sure that no one else was present, he rushed to the costly curtains and pulled them aside. Behind them stood his father, his back pressed against the stone.

"What are you doing behind here?" Jonathan asked cautiously.

"They have thousands . . . thousands," Saul muttered, with no affect to his voice.

Jonathan accepted that his father had become two people. One was the self-assured man who had been handpicked by a prophet to rule. He was confident, strategic, and intellectual. This man was a leader through and through. When King Saul ordered, all obeyed.

The other, less predictable, stood before him now. Though he was half a foot taller than almost everyone Jonathan knew, he was but a small child. This Saul often raged from paranoia, but at this moment, he seemed positively broken and feckless, more fool than king. Yet Jonathan understood that his duty as both a subject and a son was to protect both Sauls at all costs.

"What troubles you, Father?" he soothed. "Let's come out from behind these curtains, lest the servants see you."

"I am told that the Philistines are gathering a force of thousands of men at Mikmash," Saul responded softly.

"We have defeated large armies before, have we not?" Jonathan insisted with a smile.

"But not ones with so many chariots," Saul whispered.

Jonathan took his arm and led him forward. "Come now." His voice hardened. "You have ridden out with nothing but a small smattering of soldiers over and over again only to see our God show his strength repeatedly. Surely some chariots cannot scare you."

"No. I-I . . ." his father stammered in confusion. "I suppose not."

"Good. Good."

There was a change in Saul's eyes as he appeared to be approaching the line that separated him into his two selves.

"Now we just need a plan." Jonathan said.

His father shook his head from side to side, and Jonathan wondered which version would prevail.

The leader finally emerged. "Yes, a plan."

"Should we inquire of Samuel, or perhaps summon the priests so that they can consult the Urim and Thummim?"

"No," Saul said curtly. "Samuel is not an option."

"Any reason why not?" Jonathan asked.

"He is not speaking to me—again." Saul looked away from his son.

Afraid that his father would become lost in his head once more, Jonathan quickly searched within his own for an idea. "You have four thousand troops here in Gibeah?"

"More or less," Saul replied. "But that's hardly enough to—"

Jonathan cut him off. "Take three thousand of those and head to Gilgal tomorrow."

"Why on earth would I go to Gilgal and leave the safety of this fortress?" Saul's voice grew stronger.

"Gilgal is far enough away from the Philistine encampment that if they moved out to find you, they could not reach you in one day. It is also close enough to catch their attention, as why would the king of Israel go the opposite direction from their amassed forces if not to flee?"

"And if they do break camp and rush to Gilgal?" Saul pressed.

"Leave that to me. Meanwhile, have Abner ride throughout the land and gather as many men from the countryside as he can. He will lead them to where you are in order to form a more sizable army."

"Our men will have no weapons, though," Saul challenged. "There's not a blacksmith for *tsemeds*."

"Let the men of Israel bring whatever they can find to defend their land. Axes, rakes, shovels . . . They'll use their own bare hands to hurl rocks and choke at the necks of our enemies if they must. Either fight for their lives or watch their wives and children be led off in chains," Jonathan argued.

"Hmm." His father rubbed his chin and began to pace. "It would be better to have many men than a mere few thousand."

"In the meantime," Jonathan said, "while the gathering force at Gilgal draws the eyes of Mikmash, I will take the remaining one thousand soldiers and attack the Philistine outpost at Geba."

"Once you do, the full force of the Philistine army will turn to destroy you," Saul protested.

"Exactly. In seven days, we will fall on Geba like hail from the sky. When the Philistine army hears of our attack, as you say, they will move with all of their might to repel us. With their attention toward the west, you and Abner will come up from the south swiftly. It is close enough that there will be no time for any lookouts to report back to the Philistine commanders about your movements. Once you reach Beth Aven, you will turn and attack the Philistine forces from behind."

The worry lines on King Saul's face calmed and a smile spread across his lips. He stomped his right foot. "Yes," he roared at last, his eyes as bright as his teeth.

Jonathan's shoulders relaxed at the change in his father's tone. King Saul had at last defeated his other half.

"This is a brilliant plan," Saul announced. "Go now and instruct Abner of my scheme, and may the Lord be with you at Geba."

"Yes, Father," Jonathan answered firmly.

"We ride out tomorrow," Saul emphasized to his son.

"Rest now then, my king, and when I see you next, we will be standing on the broken backs of our enemies."

"Bring me the maps of Gilgal and Geba," Saul yelled out, and several servants scurried in from another room.

With his father sorted, Jonathan knew that he now needed to go and speak to Abner. As he headed out the door with plans to make his way to the tower, thoughts of Judith's naked body floated into his mind.

Abner can wait until I've had a quick tumble, he thought to himself with a grin and a shrug.

#

One lone oil lamp glimmered in a small stone alcove along the wall. It cast a long shadow over Judith's smooth, curved thigh, which lay across Jonathan's naked frame.

Judith's breasts pressed against Jonathan's chest as he lifted his head and leaned over to gently grab her bottom lip with his teeth. She returned this move with a forward burst of tongue that entwined with his, then pulled her body fully on top of him.

Jonathan moaned, and he reached his hands behind her to cup her buttocks as she threw her head back and gasped.

"*Ahhh . . . lazazel!*" he screamed out at last in a raspy voice.

Judith then released one last cry herself before she fell onto his chest with a satisfied sigh. Their two bodies were slick with sweat that glued them together.

Jonathan lay there for a moment in silence. At last he lifted his arms and gently took hold of Judith's frame, slowly moving her off of him. As she lay there next to him in contented peace, he swung his feet onto the floor.

"Why are you getting up?" she asked sleepily.

"I have one last task to do before I can rest, but I'll be quick," he announced, standing up and reaching for a cloth, which he used to wipe his body down. As he rubbed it across his chest and down over his softening root, he whispered to Judith, "Sleep softly."

He studied her as she began to gently snore. *You are a good time, if nothing else,* he thought to himself, *though I fear there is nothing between us beyond this bed and an arrangement between our fathers.*

With a sigh, Jonathan tossed the rag onto the floor and threw on a robe and sandals.

One day I suppose I will make the same sort of arrangement for our own son. When I do, I just hope that I match him with someone he loves.

With a shrug of his shoulders, accepting his fate, he left to find Abner.

The Waters at Mikmash

"Avraham's daughter wants to mount you like a mule," Eliab yelled at David, running away from him and jumping naked into the pool of water.

"I'd tell you to go dive in a lake"—David laughed as he ran after him, just as bare bottomed as his brother—"but you already did!" His voice echoed against a cliffside before it was lost in a splash of joy.

David had grown up. Gone were the cherubic leftovers of youth. His soft teenage face was now chiseled, but not as much as his lean and muscled body. It had arms that were plump with biceps and legs like those found on a prized stallion. He was smooth all over, except for the blondish fuzz that had cropped up in all the right places. But while his appearance was that of a man, the carefree attitude of youth still flowed through his mind, and a vitality of spirit rippled through his veins.

"We need to be back in less than an hour. I told Father that we would help sort the newborns," Eliab said. His hands rose from the deep and splashed a stream toward David.

"Dirty *chadal ishim*." David threw some water back at his brother.

"Besides," Eliab said, smiling again, "there isn't enough water in this lake to wash off the love of Tzitta."

"You son of a whore." David jumped up with a laugh and dunked his brother into the abyss.

They splashed and wrestled until their time was up. Exhausted from the fun, they rushed onto the bank, threw their robes over their bodies, and marched toward home.

"Last one back has to clean the goat pens," David challenged his brother to a race before he ran with all of his might through the trees.

He could hear Eliab's big feet coming up behind him just as the house came into view.

"Avraham sent a note that he wanted to speak to me," their father yelled out across the yard to David as they approached. "But I told him that he would have to wait for any discussions about anything involving his daughter, Tzitta, until after the lambing season."

"Thank goodness." David rolled his eyes. "Maybe by then she will have forgotten about me." He looked up to the heavens and prayed it would be so.

"You don't fancy the size of her *shetha*?" Eliab joked, tossing a small knife at David's feet.

"I imagine it would be like having an entire bear sow come crashing down on you." David laughed. "But it's not specifically that which I mind, as a sow can be nice, I suppose. It's the fact that she cackles that annoying laugh of hers, minute after minute after minute. I would rather be mauled by a lion than have to listen to that sound for the rest of my life."

Eliab's whole body was shaking. "Ahahaha," he howled, until his father leaned over with a walking stick and thwacked him in the stomach.

"Oww." His cry changed quickly.

"Stop wasting time and get to notching, or it will be winter by the time we are finished," Jesse commanded.

Both boys sobered up from their fun and walked to the pen, where they divided the lambs into two groups. They marked the animals' ears with a knife. On one set, they cut two parallel slashes at the tip, and on the other set, they branded them with a semicircle.

"These will be used for sacrifices." Jesse pointed to the ones with the half-moon.

David worked with his brother to herd that group to a different pen one by one, until finally their work was done. "I'm off to sit with the flock until dinner," he announced.

"But—" Eliab began.

David started to run away.

"Get back here," his brother demanded, which brought on a burst of laughter.

"Have fun feeding all of those lambs by yourself," David called back, speeding into a full-on sprint. Oh, how he howled until the tears rolled out of his eyes.

Poor Eliab, he thought to himself. He knew his brother was more than likely cursing him furiously for abandoning him to do work that ordinarily took three people. *That will teach him to mention Tzitta again.* He guffawed one last time.

As he slowed his pace, his shoulders shook from the joy of taunting his brother. The path he was walking was well-worn and familiar. There was no need to pay any special attention, as when one traveled back and forth over the same few hills and fields the way he had over these, one's body just led itself without thought. He was free instead to think on other things, like how Eliab would try to one-up him when he came back home late in the night after he'd checked on the sheep.

There was glee in his heart at the dawning of an idea that, whatever his brother did, he would respond by filling his bedding with grasshoppers. David's mind was deep into the plan of attack when he rounded the date palm that sat on the edge of the field where his family's herd grazed. As he passed its rough gray trunk, he found himself staring at the backside of a large male lion. The beast was eyeing the herd from the shade of the tree. His tongue had been wagging as he scanned the flock to select his afternoon meal until he and David were startled by each other's presence.

David sucked in the air around him so loudly that the lion quickly turned his head. It glared menacingly, then shifted its body around until only a handful of cubits of empty ground separated them from each other.

It was then that David realized that, in all of the fun he'd been having with his brother, he had run off without his slingshot or even a stick to defend himself. The lion seemed to realize it too, as it roared in a thunderous fury before it leapt into the air. Its neck was thick with muscle, and its paws reached out toward David's face with extended claws.

David roared back, and without any time for thought, he reached up with his right hand and grabbed the devil by its short brown beard and yanked it downward with all of his might until it smashed onto the ground. At the same time, the small notching knife that Eliab had tossed him to use on the newborn lambs appeared from within his tunic. With his left hand, he swung it into the air in an arc so that his arm avoided the lion's mouth. The needlelike blade pierced its thick fur and directly struck its carotid artery.

The great beast menacingly gurgled as blood filled its mouth. Red liquid pumped out of the wound on its neck until, with one last roar, it fell over. As the animal landed on the ground, its eyes glossed over, and its tongue, which had savored the thought of lamb, hung lifeless out of the side of its mouth.

#

"Was this the *whole* plan?" Abinadab asked as he rode up alongside Jonathan.

Jonathan scowled at his brother, whose blood-smeared face was twisted in confusion.

"We go to Geba to get massacred, then ride back to Gibeah?" he pressed. "I fail to see the point."

"We are not going back to Gibeah," Jonathan spat, his eyes set on the path ahead. His jaw was clenched, and his mind raced through the many different scenarios that might have kept King Saul from attacking the Philistine camp at Mikmash as planned.

"We are going to Gilgal to find Father."

Jonathan had sacrificed close to half of the men he had ridden out with for this distraction. Too many lives had been lost so that his father could deliver a shocking blow to their enemies from behind, but the ambush never materialized, and it wasn't just Abinadab who wanted answers. Jonathan wanted them too.

He stewed over his father's absence for the entire two hours it took to ride to Gilgal. At last, the six hundred men still with him of the thousand he had left the fortress with marched across the flat and barren plains to the lone hillock that rose up from the vast landscape. There they stopped. At the bottom, they strained their necks in confusion at the hill. Instead of being greeted by lookouts and guards, they saw only a large number of empty tents that flapped in the breeze.

"Where are all the soldiers?" Jonathan's youngest brother, Shua, asked with great surprise.

Abinadab replied in wonder, "There's not even a single man to herald our arrival."

The only voices that carried on the wind were those of a pair of brown-necked ravens, whose *karr-karr-karr* called down to the weary troops.

Jonathan slid down off his horse and took a few steps toward the hill. When Abinadab and Shua did the same, he turned around. "No," he commanded with a raised hand. "I will go alone."

"But what if something has happened to our father?" Abinadab asked.

"You must stay behind . . . for these men." Jonathan sighed as he pointed to the remaining troops.

Thoughts of how they had rushed to Geba flooded his mind. His plan had been solid, but the tiny outpost had been better prepared than Jonathan expected. While the battle was fierce and spectacular enough to distract the attention of the Philistines in the larger camp as intended, after two days, his father and uncle remained absent. Four hundred of his fellow Hebrews had fallen before Jonathan finally accepted that they would not be coming as planned. Now he and his men had barely managed to limp their way across the plains here to Gilgal for protection, only to find the encampment abandoned. Jonathan could not leave his men, bedraggled from fighting and their exhaustive journey, unprotected.

"I still want to go—" Shua started to say, but Jonathan interrupted him.

"In my absence, both of you will need to be in charge."

His brothers shuffled their feet at his insistence. Jonathan had never left them alone like this before. While they had always been around war against the Philistines, either they'd remained behind in the camp, or engaged, but only at Jonathan's instruction and in the most controlled of environments. Geba had been the first time he had taken them directly out into the field and put no restrictions on them. On the march there, he'd realized that he could never expect his brothers to become fierce warriors in their own right if they were always kept under the skirt of their mother back at Gibeah or left to sit in the tents at camp to wait for Jonathan and their father to return from bloodshed. Now he was leaving them alone. Although they would only be separated by a short distance, he could not defend them if they had been followed from Geba. Their training would have to suffice, because he would be up that small mountain, where he would find only God knew what.

"There is a possibility that we were tracked," Jonathan explained to his brothers. "It will be up to you to stand your ground until I return." He turned his head back to the hilltop and sighed. "Especially since it doesn't look as if we will get much help here."

He watched his brothers swell their breasts and ready themselves to take the lead.

"We will do as you say, brother," Abinadab assured him.

"Break into two groups and have each form a phalanx facing the opposite direction," Jonathan ordered. "Then you will push together with your backs to one another."

"Why this position?" Shua asked.

"Whatever comes, be it from the front or from behind, you will be ready." Jonathan grabbed them each and gripped them tightly. "And whatever does come, you will stand your ground until I can return."

"Yes, brother," Abinadab responded forcefully, and Shua nodded his head in agreement.

Jonathan watched as his two brothers divided the six hundred men into two groups with authority. As they began to take their positions, he accepted that they were both now fully in charge of his men.

This is how leaders are made, he told himself with a proud smile, then turned and began to huff his way up the rising ground.

When he reached the top, he looked around in astonishment. Pots of food sat over extinguished fires, and the wind whistled through empty shelters, where weapons and armor lay scattered on the ground. The ravens that had called down from on high were here now, hopping among the tents and plucking at whatever food remained.

Jonathan walked through the camp in an attempt to make no sound, until at last he found his father's large tent way in the back. He could see a small band of soldiers standing guard at the entrance. Certainly his father had not remained behind with all of his army absent?

The scene he looked upon was getting stranger and stranger, so he stepped out into view and sped his way toward the tent. The soldiers who stood guard grasped their spears tightly and prepared to engage.

"Jonathan?" one of them called out in surprise.

"Is the king here?" Jonathan inquired.

One of the two men at the entrance nodded weakly, and Jonathan patted him on the arm with a thank-you as he passed by and entered his father's dwelling.

Inside, it looked as if a bear had torn the place apart, splintering dry wood with its sharp claws in a search for grub worms. The dividing curtains had been shredded into pieces and now hung solely by wispy threads. Stacks of colorful rugs woven from brown, red, and yellow threads and laid out to cushion the king's feet were now tossed in every direction. Many of them were upside down, their knots and uneven structures exposed to the eye. Yet in the midst of all this chaos, in the center of this mess, sat an untouched throne, perfectly grand and undisturbed.

Jonathan put his hands on his hips and gasped. "What in Sheol?"

A slight moan broke the air.

"Father?" Jonathan craned his neck to look for the source of the noise.

When he heard it again, he rushed to the back of the room, where an overturned table lay on its side. With narrowed eyes, he tentatively peered over it. There on the ground lay his father, the great king of Israel. Only instead of pomp or grandeur, Jonathan found an old man, his golden cloak torn in two, with one wrinkled arm draped over his eyes.

"Are you alright?" he asked with grave concern as he climbed over and dropped to his knees beside his father. "Who did this to you?"

"Fine." Saul exhaled weakly. "I'm fine. Just leave me be."

"Where is everyone?" Jonathan begged.

"Gone," Saul groaned.

"I can see that, but where?"

He responded with only a slight whimper.

"Were you attacked?" Jonathan urged.

"I waited for as long as I could," Saul whispered, his arm still covering his eyes.

"Waited for what?" Frustration began to pepper Jonathan's voice.

There was no reply.

"Father." His tone became more forceful. "I must know what happened. Now, I don't see any signs of a fight here at Gilgal. The only thing destroyed is this tent. Who did this to you?"

"I did."

Jonathan moaned, realizing what he was looking at were the effects of a temper tantrum. "You didn't," he said in disbelief, but inside, he knew it was true.

They sat for a moment, then he sighed. "This tent can be cleaned, but I cannot help you if you don't tell me everything that I need to know. Now, why are you here, and why didn't you and Abner attack the Philistine camp at Mikmash as planned?"

"The men started leaving." Saul lifted his arm away from his face at last and stared off gloomily toward the top of the tent.

"For what reason?" Jonathan snapped.

"Three thousand chariots . . . they had six thousand charioteers to ride them," he muttered, shaking his head while looking back and forth along the floor.

"We knew that they had a large force, and yet still we had a plan," Jonathan insisted.

"The men just ran off . . . and left me . . . alone," Saul said, sounding defeated.

"So you threw a fit, then lay down here on the ground?" Jonathan's voice strained. "Why didn't you stop them? You are their king!"

"Yes, I am the king, not you!" Saul lifted his head at last and bit back with venom. "And I had no choice but to watch them desert me."

"There has to have been a reason."

"Samuel had not yet come," Saul hissed. "He told me that he would be here, but he wasn't. With the men getting anxious about attacking the Philistine camp, I made the burnt offerings *myself*!" He shouted the last word, then exhaled loudly. Throwing his head back onto the ground, he whispered, "And that . . . was the end . . . of everything."

Unable to control his fury anymore, Jonathan stood up and shouted, "I cannot take this any longer. What do burnt offerings have to do with all the soldiers leaving, and you being here in torn garments?"

"Because Samuel did show up . . ." Saul said softly.

"And?"

"And . . . now it is over. It is all over!" Saul rolled onto his belly and sobbed like a child who had been disciplined harshly, his shoulders shaking with each hysterical breath.

Jonathan had seen his father's highs and lows, but never had he seen him like this before. He squatted on the floor next to him and put a gentle hand on his father's back, lowered his voice to a whisper, and softly consoled him. "It will all be alright, Father. Everything will be alright."

Saul cried into the backs of his arms, and Jonathan had to strain to hear his response. "No, it won't be."

I'm used to rage, not tears, he thought.

With a final heave, King Saul lifted his head up and turned to face his son. His eyes were damp and deep with sadness. "I was only looking for favor from the Lord for a good battle." His lower lip trembled, as if he were a child.

"Shhh," Jonathan said, but suddenly Saul grew angry and shrieked into the air, causing Jonathan to jump back in alarm.

"Why couldn't Samuel have come in time?" his father screamed. "He could have done the damn sacrifice himself. Then we would have ridden to Beth Aven, and all would be well!" He threw his head back down and slumped into the ground so far that his body almost disappeared into the dusty carpets.

Silence fell.

After a few minutes, Saul calmly turned his body over and sat up. With a piece of his tattered golden robe, he patted his eyes dry and looked at Jonathan.

"The kingdom has been torn from us," he said plainly. "I know I have shared this with you once before, but I thought that maybe God had changed his mind in all these years, so I never mentioned it again. Only now, it is complete." He slumped his shoulders.

The distant memory of their conversation back at the Valley of Elah more than three years earlier resurfaced in Jonathan's mind. "Oh, that," he said.

"Before Samuel left this time, he told me that I would never see him again. You see, I made the burnt offerings that only a priest is permitted to make," Saul explained. "So he rebuked me strongly and told me that my kingdom would not endure." He let out a great big sigh. "You know the worst part? He told me that one day, another man, someone much better, who was *a man after God's own heart*"—he emphasized those words—"would lead all of Israel."

Jonathan understood now why his father had fallen to the floor in a state of depression, so he put his hand on his shoulder and squeezed. The loss of the crown meant everything to Saul, and especially to his pride. So, Jonathan allowed him this quiet moment and simply sat there and shared in his father's grief.

After a little while, Jonathan remembered his brothers, who were standing in formation on the plains below. Then he thought of his mother and his wife, who were in the fortress at Gibeah unprotected, and he knew that the time for sorrow was over.

"I understand your sadness," he said to his father. "But that does not solve the immediate problem of the twenty thousand or so Philistines who stand ready to squash us like crickets under their heels."

"What does it matter?" Saul shrugged.

"You are still the king, and it's your sole task to protect your people," Jonathan reminded him.

"But am I really, then? Isn't there another?"

"Not in this tent there isn't."

"Is not *my* heart after God's?" Saul spat. "I mean, after all, he chose me first."

"We can't worry about that right now," Jonathan said.

"It's important," Saul insisted, anger replacing the calm that had in its turn replaced the tears. "How can Samuel simply march in here and say that there is to be another king when I am not ready to give up the throne? I mean, who does he think he—"

"There's nothing we can do about that," Jonathan interjected. "Our only task right now is to fulfill the roles that we have each been assigned until they are no longer ours."

"But—"

"It's still our duty to defend Israel's people until our last breath, whatever position God sees fit to put each of us in."

"How can you just accept this?" his father roared, lifting himself up off the ground.

Just then, Armoni and Mephibosheth entered the tent covered in armor, and a feeling of disgust spread throughout Jonathan's body. "Where have you been?" he asked harshly as they approached. "Our father is alone here in his tent, and you two are not at his side."

"We went with our men to the hills, where they hid in wells and cisterns," Armoni responded, annoyed.

"You mean you left the camp together with the others?" Jonathan's voice rose with incredulity.

Armoni turned his head from his half-brother and looked to King Saul. "They asked me to come and tell you that they will not return until they know for certain that God is on our side."

Saul ignored him. Madness now swirled in his eyes, and they bore down only on Jonathan. "I will not allow it," he shouted. "I. Will. Not. Allow. It!"

Jonathan moved his furious glare from Armoni to his father. "Who are you or I to allow or to not allow? Are we God?"

Rage flew from Saul's lips. "I am the king, that is who I am! And I will remain the king until I say otherwise." His rant over, he transformed again and started to pace back and forth, all the while muttering unintelligible gibberish under his breath.

Jonathan realized that they would get nowhere until this new spell had passed, so he turned back to his half-brothers with disgust. "Go back to the hills and tell your armies that you were in charge of and who you were unable to stop from melting away, that King Saul and Prince Jonathan demand that they return to their posts. Anyone who does not return will be labeled a deserter and will forfeit their land and their wives to those who fight for their king."

"What makes you think they will come back here just because you demand it?" Armoni laughed.

"Not here," Jonathan said. "They should not come back to Gilgal, but they are to meet their king at Gibeah, where we will muster anew."

"We do not answer to you," Mephibosheth croaked, eyes bulging.

"I am the king's firstborn son." Jonathan flew furiously at them both. "You will answer to me in General Abner's absence, or I will have you both beheaded for desertion." Spittle flew from his lips as his brothers cowered from his rage. "You were to be leaders, and instead you served yourselves and ran off like young girls."

Jonathan stomped his way to the tent entrance and stuck his head out to motion for Saul's guards. "These two are leaving," he instructed them as they entered the tent, and his half-brothers scowled at their dismissal.

"We are royal sons too." Armoni scoffed.

"*Ko ya' aseh YHWH ve-kho yosif.*" Jonathan pointed to the exit as he threatened them. "And may the Lord strike you down, or worse, if you do not do as I have commanded."

A curse like that was a threat that not even his half-brothers wanted to chance, so Armoni and Mephibosheth reluctantly followed the soldiers out. Just before he exited, Armoni turned his head back and growled over his shoulder, "We will pay your actions back in time . . . dearest brother."

With the twins gone, Jonathan turned to his father, who was still talking to himself. Resigned to defeat, he angrily left Saul alone and headed back to his men to prepare for their march to Gibeah.

\#

By the next morning, Jonathan had convinced his father to head back to Gibeah with what remained of the army that had attacked the fort at Geba. When they had reached Migron, just outside the fortress, they stopped under a pomegranate tree for shade.

67

"Let us wait here for Abner to bring me the rest of the army," King Saul commanded. "He said he could gather a few thousand or so along the way, and even bring some of the deserters back into the fold. I expect him to be here sometime later this afternoon with a brand-new force, and then our enemies will see a sight that they have not seen in years: the Israelites raining down on them like giant balls of frozen hail!"

But the hours turned to days, and all that Abner was eventually able to muster was a mass of shepherds and farmers, some as young as thirteen and others as old as seventy. Yet none of these males had swords. Instead, they came only with plows, axes, and sickles.

"This is meant to fight off the Philistines?" Saul screamed at Abner on the fourth evening as Jonathan looked on.

"There is not a blacksmith to be found, as you know," Abner explained. "Every capable man left in the land I have brought with me here, and still the thousands of trained soldiers remain hidden in those caves in the hills with your sons, Armoni and Mephibosheth. And neither of those two have yet to respond to your calls."

"I will ride out and kill them with my own hands if they do not show their faces by tomorrow morning." Jonathan was fuming when a familiar voice suddenly grated his nerves from behind him.

"Kill who?" Armoni asked with ice in his tone.

Jonathan turned around and scowled at his half-brothers. "What took you so long? May the Lord help you if you failed to bring the men from our army back with you."

"Since our soldiers with actual fighting weapons number in the thousands compared to your lot of misfits and children, I really don't think you should be making threats to anyone," Mephibosheth responded with a laugh.

"The men are here." Armoni turned to the king. "Or at least as many as we could convince to come back with us after what happened at Gilgal."

"Fine." Saul huffed. "Abner will take over from here, as the two of you are no longer in charge but are to answer to your uncle as if he spoke with my own voice."

"But Father—" Armoni began to protest, but the king's voice grew louder.

"Your weakness shows that neither of you are fit to lead," he thundered. "You will each be counted as mere foot soldiers from today forward, and you are to be stripped of any titles that I have given to you."

"You can't!" Mephibosheth cried out.

"I think they should be made to go back to Gibeah and wait with their mother till this battle is over," Jonathan suggested with a smug tone. "They talk of children, but how could we trust the whims of these two toddlers?"

"Hmm . . ." Saul rubbed his chin and sat down.

The twins were incensed. "But we are the leaders of all of those thousands of men out there," Armoni responded angrily.

"Leaders who were completely ignored by their men, who ran away? Or was it leaders who perhaps chose to disobey their commander as well as hide in the caves rather than face battle? Either way, you showed yourselves to be weak and completely unworthy of your position." Jonathan waved his hand in dismissal.

"You cannot listen to our brother," Mephibosheth begged his father. "To send us back to our mother as if we were still nursing children would be a horrible slight."

"Maybe while there among the women, you might find yourselves to be more comfortable . . . Or if not, you might use the time to consider what it takes to be men," Jonathan cut in.

"You know," Armoni replied coldly, "I am getting tired of your dismissals and insults."

"Well, you would not suffer either a minute longer if it were my decision." Jonathan laughed. "I would have you both killed for desertion."

"Enough," his father yelled. "I have decided."

His three children eyed each other with great suspicion.

"Armoni and Mephibosheth will never learn to be true warriors if they are not in any wars," Saul said sternly. "They will remain here, but only among the shepherds. Their swords shall be given away, and they will fight with the sickles and the shovels of the other men, common men. Neither will possess any weapon of substance until they either pry them from the dead fingers of our enemies or prove to me that they are worthy once more of my household."

Mephibosheth mocked Jonathan with a smile, but Armoni's face reddened at Saul's proclamation. "This is madness," he grumbled under his breath.

It is better than nothing, Jonathan thought.

Content that at least there had been some punishment meted out for his half-brothers' actions, he sighed and left the tent. He found his way to his own, where he lay down and closed his eyes. There, behind those closed lids, he contemplated how to defend his father's land against a horde of Philistines now that they had a much smaller—and far more unprepared—army than before they had set out to attack Geba.

#

"Give us a song!" someone had yelled at David when he came home that evening. Then pandemonium broke out as familiar faces poured out from every window and door of their dwelling.

"I am sure he already has one in his mind about how he defeated the ferocious lion with his bare hands." Eliab slapped his brother on the back.

"Once again, my son has defeated what no common man could, or would." His father's breast swelled with the same pride he had shown when David had returned from defeating the Philistine giant.

An impromptu call for celebration was sent throughout the land, bringing siblings, uncles, aunts, and cousins, who traveled to Bethlehem from throughout Judea. After two days and nights of choice food and flowing wine, David's entire extended family had decided to take a small journey together to the nearby city of Carmel to offer a sacrifice of thanksgiving. They insisted that David come along, but he excused himself. While he admitted to himself that he loved the attention, something in his soul told him he should take some time alone. Once they had departed, he decided that he would go out into the wilderness and offer a sacrifice of praise on his own.

"It is wise for a man who has benefitted so much to worship in solitude," his father had said, agreeing to leave David behind.

So David took a bull and led it to the place where he had cleared the ground of all its debris and built a stone altar. There he spilled the animal's blood and burnt the entire beast up, saving only its hide, which he planned to have sent to the Levites to sell for profit.

As David returned on foot, he found one of his youngest cousins, who was around eight years old, sitting all alone and sobbing at the door to his family's dwelling.

"Why are you crying, little Schacna?" he asked the boy. "And where is the rest of the family? Surely they did not send you back to me all alone."

"We were in the city worshipping . . ." Schacna said, crying and running the back of his hand along his runny nose. "That's when the Amalekites invaded . . ." He was blubbering now.

"You were attacked?" David raised his voice. "What of our family? And how did you find your way back to Bethlehem?"

"My father sent me through a hole under the city walls and told me to run as fast as I could back to your dwelling in hopes that you could raise a party of men from the area to save them."

David put his hand on the boy's shoulder. "So you don't know if they are alive or dead?"

Schacna shook his head, flinging large tears to the earth.

"When did you run away?" David pressed.

"It was this morning," the child answered.

"You did good, Schacna." David squeezed his cousin's back. "And now, I will need you to go inside and rest. There is food in the pantry for two days or more. With any luck, I will be back with your father and mother long before then."

The boy nodded and stopped his crying. David did not look back to see what he did next, as a wave of intense anger took over his body.

He ran into the manger where they kept the horse King Saul had given to him and leapt up onto its back. Once mounted, he led the animal so that it tore through the doorway and out onto the hillside. There David dug his heels into the horse's hinds. It picked up speed, and they galloped at an intense pace toward his family.

He rode like that until the horse was covered in a thick sweat. It neighed and whinnied with exhaustion, so David led it to a small stream by some trees and turned it loose to find its own way home. "If it be the Lord's will, I will see that horse again someday, but first, I must find my family."

He skulked on in the weeds and among the trees until he saw the small city of Carmel in the distance and the smoke that rose up from its center. Once he got close, he picked up a trail of many footprints in the dust, which ran south toward Hebron. Without any thought, he continued on with great rapidity.

It was nighttime by the time David spotted a half dozen campfires clustered around in a circle. Even in the dim light he could recognize his father tied up among the group's captives. To avoid being spotted, he crouched down and whispered to himself, "Now what do I do?"

That he had not stopped to think about the fact that he would be greatly outnumbered if he tried to attack the camp on his own led him to chastise himself harshly. "Feebleminded." He gritted his teeth, as he now regretted his decision to ride off so quickly instead of raising a group of men to fight the Amalekites alongside him in order to win back his mother and father.

But he decided that it was too late to wallow in regret for long, as he was here and he was alone. "I'll be damned if I just crouch here and watch my whole family be led away forever in chains," he growled. His decision made, he stood up and marched directly toward the camp.

Unlike with his one-on-one match with the lion, this time David had his slingshot with him. He also had the short sword that he'd carried across his back when he went off alone to sacrifice the bull to the Lord.

Whoosh. Under the cover of darkness, he let loose a volley of stones that sailed through the air in the direction of the half dozen Amalekites who stood around one of the fires. Most of them fell over dead before they had time to run for cover from the mysterious assault. Those who lived were pelted nearly instantly by a second volley.

David let out a battle cry that sounded as if he were a force of a thousand, and like a wild man he ran into the camp, where he slashed and sliced every man he could find who had a weapon.

The entire assault took less than fifteen minutes. When it was over, close to thirty bodies lay on the ground. While they'd each suffered various cuts and stab wounds to different parts of their bodies, all were dead.

Within minutes, David had cut off the chains of the captured men, and they too began to free the others, including the women and children. There they fell on their faces and prayed to their God in heaven for his deliverance. Afterward, they kissed and stroked David's hands, which were blessed. A few of the men gathered stones and made a makeshift altar before they rushed to slay and sacrifice several of the lambs the Amalekites had looted from Carmel for their journey home.

The next morning, David and his family marched back to Bethlehem, having lost not even one of their kin to the Amalekites. Schacna ran out from the house and into his mother's skirts. David's own mother led all of the other women in preparations for a feast. Despite the endless yawns of exhaustion, there was not one person—of any age—who was not sated on the abundance of food and wine.

As the evening sun set, David looked over at those gathered around the bonfire that burned outside, and smiled at the sight of Schacna, who was sound asleep in his mother's lap.

#

Sleep was still in Jonathan's eyes when his young armor-bearer, Nahum, shook him awake.

"What is it?" Jonathan asked in hazy confusion.

"Three raiding parties are said to have been dispatched from the camp at Mikmash," Nahum replied nervously.

Jonathan leapt up. "And where are they headed?"

"One moves toward Ophrah near Shual, another toward Beth Horon, and the last heads to the borderlands by the Valley of Zeboyim and the wilderness."

Jonathan's shoulders relaxed, and he sighed. "While it's not great, I was afraid they were coming right for Gibeah. They must be probing our defenses, but we can withstand that better than a direct assault. Hopefully we will have another few days to prepare for that which we all know is coming."

He took his breakfast in solitude, though his mind was anything but peaceful. *What is the best way to stage a frontal assault on a sizable force?* he asked himself. *Will even the best of plans matter now that the prophet has gone home and said that the Lord has left our household?*

"For all I know, we could already be dead," he finally said aloud, but as no one was there to respond, he simply got up and left the rest of his food uneaten.

Next, Nahum followed him for a walk to inspect the few troops they had. It was a pitiful force in comparison to what was amassed beyond the pass at Geba. Jonathan resigned himself to the fact that he would be of better help examining the area around them for possible points of defense, leaving the shepherds and the other scant and scattered soldiers to Abner's direction.

As Nahum and he walked the land, Jonathan became distracted by his quest to find as many potential strongholds as possible. Hill by hill, he examined thickets, bending branches on them as reminders of their prospective use. As he moved on, he marked caves and dips in the land as prime locations for storing weapons or hiding soldiers to launch surprise attacks for when the Philistines passed through on their way to Gibeah. He was so intentional in his work that the morning hours passed by quickly, and so did the distance that he and his armor-bearer had traveled, so that Jonathan failed to realize how far they had wandered.

At last he lifted his head up and shaded his eyes from the sun with a hand to scan the horizon. In front of him stood a path with two cliffs on either side. The breath in his lungs seized when he noticed several Philistines on the one that faced north. The soldiers were dressed in armor, and their backs were turned to Jonathan and Nahum.

Jonathan pulled his armor-bearer into the shadows of the southern rock as he thought about how to get out of the area without being captured or killed by the lookouts. "If there are some up there," he pointed as he whispered to Nahum, "there are bound to be more of them walking around down here."

"Can't we go back the way we came?" Nahum shook in fear.

"Too risky," Jonathan explained. "We were lucky we were not seen before, but we won't be so lucky twice. They can see pretty far in all directions from that cliff top."

He rubbed his chin and thought on a plan, until at last an impish grin spread across his face. "Now that I think about it, I haven't heard any footsteps nearby. There does not appear to be too many of them after all." He turned to Nahum and winked. "And that cliff would look a whole lot better if our soldiers controlled it rather than theirs, would it not?"

"But what can the two of us do?" Nahum asked in great confusion.

"The two of us can't do much," Jonathan agreed. "But I'm thinking we have been relying on ourselves way more than we ought to."

"I could run back to Gibeah. I'm smaller and faster," Nahum offered.

"No, Nahum, that's not what I mean. We have the Lord on our side. So really, who do they have, other than a few soldiers on a cliff?"

Nahum shook his head. "I don't understand."

"It's simple." Jonathan smiled at him. "I think maybe we were led here rather than stumbled and bumbled onto this location all on our own."

"Oh, I see. You mean that we were meant to find it so that we can mark it on our maps as a place to avoid."

"I'm going to go out there and wave my hands at those men," Jonathan said energetically. He started to move out of the shadows when the armor-bearer put his hand on his arm to stop him.

"Why would you do that?" Panic began to rise in Nahum's voice.

"Listen to me. We have no one but old men and children. Our soldiers are weaponless. We are doomed to death, unless . . ."

"You just told me that we have been relying on ourselves, and now you are going to take on twenty fully armed Philistines by yourself?"

"Not alone, Nahum. Very much not alone. We will let ourselves be found, and if they say to us that we should climb up there, then that will mean that the Lord has led us here because he has already given them over to us. But if they tell us to stay where we are so that they can come down to us, then we will know that we should run away quickly and mark it on the map like you suggest."

"Hmm." The boy's brows furrowed. "Seems very risky."

"Think of it kind of like a game." Jonathan laughed.

"Well, I like games, so . . . sure, let's do it!"

Jonathan slapped Nahum on the shoulder, then stepped out of the shadows. "Hey," he bellowed as he cupped his hands around his mouth. "What is a pack of dirty hyenas like you doing on top of a cliff? We could smell your scent from ten thousand cubits away!"

Close to twenty men dressed from head to toe in bronze peered over the cliff's edge in wonder.

"Why don't you climb up here and find out," one of the Philistines yelled back, and the others laughed.

"Yeah," another chortled. "Come on up, shrivel-dicks."

Jonathan turned to Nahum and exclaimed, "They are ours!" But the boy only stared back with terror in his eyes.

"It's alright, Nahum," Jonathan soothed. "You are young and do not have to go with me. But know this—our God had the power to part the sea. Do you think a few Philistine fools are as powerful as one who has the ability to gather the waters?"

At this, the boy's face relaxed. "I will go with you. And may our God deliver these men to us, just as you have said that he will."

Jonathan slapped Nahum on the shoulder again and ran toward the cliff with a grin. "Here we come, you brainless dogs," he teased the Philistines.

Together, Nahum and he wandered along the bottom of the rock face while the Philistine men hooted and whistled from up above.

"This will be fun," one howled.

"The little one is mine," another said, licking his lips.

After a few paces, Jonathan spied a crumbling pathway that led directly to the top of the pass. He rushed forward and began to claw his way up, grasping onto rocks and exposed roots to help him step by step. Each time he reached a small plateau, he turned around and reached down to help Nahum up behind him.

As they traveled, they were no longer in sight of the Philistines. "Where did they go?" he could hear one of the men mutter from above, so Jonathan raised a finger to his lips.

"They lost us," he whispered. "Philistines really are dumber than field mice." Both he and the boy chuckled at his joke.

Then he turned back to the cliff face and mapped out the final steps. *The Lord be with us*, he prayed in his mind as he ran up the rock with a burst of incredible speed. Behind him came Nahum, and their sudden appearance sent the Philistines into a panic.

"How the fuck—" one started to say, but Jonathan pulled his sword from behind his back and sliced it across the man's throat.

A small dagger flew out of Nahum's hands and right past Jonathan's ear, where it landed with a *thwack* in the right eye of an approaching soldier.

The man screamed and turned around in distress. Then he lost his balance and tipped over the side of the overhang opposite the precipice that Jonathan and Nahum had traveled. From way down below, a loud thud was followed by the sounds of tens, then hundreds, and then thousands of men screaming and crying out.

"They are attacking us!" one voice yelled wildly in fear.

"The Israelites have us surrounded!" came another, until a cascade of swear words and screams began to ricochet up from down in the valley.

Jonathan looked back to Nahum in confusion and shrugged, then the two of them rushed forward into the foray against the Philistines that remained on the cliff.

Swords clashed and clanked, and men fell to their knees in agony and died, until, at last, only the two Hebrews stood victorious on the cliff. Every one of the twenty Philistines that fought them either lay dead at their feet or had fallen into the abyss below.

Heaving his lungs, Jonathan stumbled slowly to the edge and looked down. There, lying before him, was the sprawling Philistine encampment, spread out across the sweeping gorge. The number of men appeared to be countless.

Suddenly, the earth began to shake, and Jonathan fell onto his stomach and held on, lest he be thrown over the cliff face like the Philistines who had vanished earlier. There was a loud crack, and then both large rocks of granite and small pebbles of basalt began to peel off along the mountainside and roll to the ground far below.

The shaking appeared to toss the endless sea of Philistine soldiers to and fro, as if they were feathers lost on the sea during a storm. Blood-curdling screams of terror were unleashed from their mouths, and those on the furthest fringes of the gorge began to melt away into the forests and streams that edged the camp. Those who did not run away ran directly into each other instead so that the melee widened, and soon the soldiers had raised their swords and started to cut each other down. Philistine arrows flew out from the center of the encampment and peppered hundreds of their own fighters, who fell to the earth, while others were trampled by their fleeing brethren.

"What is happening?" Nahum shouted over the noise as he laboriously crawled up beside Jonathan on his elbows.

"I think the waters have just parted at Mikmash," Jonathan answered in awe.

A Thorn in Your Side

T he sun had long since begun its descent over the blood-soaked ground and now cast an orange glow on the faces of Saul's army as they worked their way through a forest of sycamore trees. Jonathan led these men, who had entered the battle against the Philistines once panic had ensued across their encampment. They had left their axes and shovels in the dirt and picked up the weapons that their hysterical enemies had dropped in panic.

Between twisted trunks and through the sporadic holes in the expansive canopy, the waning light fell down onto Jonathan. He now led the search for the last of the rival forces, who lurked between rocks and hid themselves in the glossy leaves of patches of young terebinth shrubs.

Weakened by the length of the day and the endless hours of marauding, he smiled with relief when he came upon a beehive tucked into a crease between two boulders. Without any hesitation, he grabbed a dead stick off the ground. From a distance, he stretched it out until it had passed through the angry mob of buzzing protectors and pierced into the gooey comb. He then pulled the stick back slowly and gently. Once it was free, he placed two fingers along the waxy blob on the end and scooped the fresh honey up. With an enormous grin, he placed them into his mouth and suckled deeply.

"Oh goodness," he moaned, as he felt life returning to his tired limbs. "This is so sweet and delicious." He turned to a soldier nearby. "You?" He offered him some of the delightful substance.

The soldier's face froze in terror.

"You look exhausted, and this sugar will revive your spirit." Jonathan smiled.

"What have you done?" the soldier cried out as he ran forward and slapped the honey stick out of Jonathan's hand and into the dirt.

"What did you do that for?" Jonathan barked. "If you didn't want any, I could have offered it to somebody else."

"It's not that, my prince," the man answered nervously. "It's only that . . . well it's . . . you see . . ."

"Go on and say it," Jonathan demanded. "There has to be some kind of explanation for your outright stupidity."

The man hesitated again but finally confessed. "Your father made us all swear we would not eat a morsel today until the sun has fully set," he explained with his head hung low. "That is why we are so weak and why I tried to save you from your mistake."

Jonathan's eyes scrunched up. "A mistake? To eat?" He was dumbfounded. "Why would my father ask the men for something like that? It doesn't make sense. That would be foolish, as anyone can easily see how this tiny drop of honey has enlivened me. From one small taste, I am ready now to cut down more Philistines than I already have done today!"

Dozens of other soldiers who had followed behind caught up with the two men and gathered around to listen to their argument.

"I'm not the one who said it," the soldier reminded him. "It was your father, and he is the king."

"This is true." Jonathan shook his head. "But I cannot believe he would deny his men the sustenance to wage war."

Second by second, more and more men arrived, until soon there were hundreds of spectators. Suddenly, Armoni and Mephibosheth burst through the crowd. They were followed by the king himself, who must have decided to go into the battle surrounded by all of his sons, as Abinadab and Shua were also by his side.

"What is going on here?" Saul demanded to know.

"Your son has eaten this honey." The soldier reluctantly pointed to the ground.

Gasps and whispers rippled through the group of men.

The king's eyes widened. "What have you done?" he cried out. "I promised that no one would eat today until nightfall." There was anger and grief on his tongue.

"Put him to death." Armoni gnashed his teeth. "The great Jonathan, the one who always scolds us and tells us we are wrong, has broken the king's commandment. He must die!"

Abinadab growled and ran toward Armoni with closed fists, but Mephibosheth jumped in his path and put his hand on Abinadab's chest to slow him.

"Armoni is right!" He grunted as he tried to hold Abinadab back. "Our father declared whoever ate today was to die."

"Do it." Jonathan raised his head defiantly into the air and took a step toward his father. "Our men have fought hard, but today we could have ended the Philistine threat for good had our men been nourished. Instead, they will ride back to their gentile towns only to continue to be a fly in our milk."

"Kill him," Armoni implored his father again.

Saul fumed at Jonathan. "You put me in a terrible spot, but what choice do I have?"

A wicked smile grew on Armoni's face, and the youngest brother, Shua, cried out, "No." He ran to Jonathan's side, where he put his hands around his brother's forearm and faced the crowd.

"You cannot kill Jonathan," he pleaded, but the king only let out a giant roar of pain in response.

"I must do as I said," he answered, "though it hurts me bitterly." Saul turned to two of his personal guards nearby and nodded for them to take hold of Jonathan.

After seeing Saul's instruction, many of the men who had gathered began to rush toward Jonathan. They took their places behind him and put their hands on the hilts of their swords.

"If it was not for Jonathan, none of what happened today would have taken place," one man called out.

"Yeah," cried another. "We all would have been killed by the Philistines!"

Another turned his back to Saul and thrust his blade into the air. "Jonathan will not die on our watch!"

The men rallied and shouted, and soon almost all of those who had gathered had raised their blades with grunts and nodded their heads in agreement.

Nahum emerged from among the others and went to Jonathan's side. "I was with Jonathan today," he told the king. "Your son killed the men on the lookout cliff out of faith, and because of that, God shook the earth and made the Philistines fall before us in their thousands. I believe we all must follow the king, but what about the Lord?"

At Nahum's words, the king's guards halted their approach and looked back at Saul for direction, as it was now two of them up against the many who had gone over to Jonathan's side.

"Wait," Saul told them with a sigh. "Let me think—"

But Armoni interrupted and stepped closer to his father. "You cannot think about this," he pressed. "A king's word is his word. Jonathan must die—you said it yourself."

"If only there was a way . . ." Saul lamented to the heavens, but then his face brightened. "Wait," he gasped with a smile. "Did I not bring a priest out with us today to witness the battle?"

A man in a fine woven ephod was pushed out into the clearing.

"Ahijah," Saul addressed him urgently, "are you not the grandson of Eli, our high priest, and do you not carry with you today the Urim and Thummim?"

"Yes," Ahijah replied with great confidence.

"Then you must cast them here and now between myself and my son," Saul instructed. "If it's the Urim, then Jonathan must die, just as I declared earlier. But if it's the Thummim, then my hand will be stayed by the will of God and the loyalty of these men." His hands spread out toward Jonathan and the many who stood beside him.

"You will look weak and your words will lose power if you do this," Armoni threatened.

But Saul could not be stopped. "There is only one whose word covers that of the king, and we will hear from him today," he admonished his son.

The muscles in Jonathan's neck began to pulsate, and his head began to ache as he watched the priest, Ahijah, cast his lots onto the ground. He held his breath until the answer was announced. "Jonathan's life is found to be spared," Ahijah informed the king.

Cheers erupted throughout the land, but not from the throat of Armoni, who gurgled in fury and stormed all the way back to Gibeah with his brother behind him.

"This day has been fruitful." King Saul waved his hands in the air to quiet the many voices. Once silenced, he declared, "On account of my son, Jonathan, and by the grace of our Lord, we have killed many. You all showed yourselves to be worthy of our calling as Jews—worthy to be his people."

There were nods of agreement and murmurs of satisfaction.

"Let us go now back to our camps, to our lands, to our homes, and let us eat merrily and drink deeply, for we have earned our peace," Saul continued.

Applause erupted, and the men hugged each other and clasped hands before they turned and dispersed in various directions, until all that was left was King Saul, Ahinoam's sons, the priest Ahijah, and a few of the guards.

"Now we ourselves will return to our home in Gibeah and take respite," Saul said to them all with a smile. He put his arm around Jonathan's shoulder, and Jonathan nuzzled his head into his father's neck.

"I knew you wouldn't kill me." He chuckled.

As they walked, Ahijah approached King Saul and Jonathan. "While the Urim and Thummim may have rescued Jonathan, the Lord is not happy with the house of Saul," he warned.

"But he just handed us a decisive victory," the king responded, confused.

"No," Ahijah stated firmly. "A victory, yes. But not a decisive one, though he would have had you had more faith."

Saul pulled himself and Jonathan to a halt. "What are you saying, priest?"

"The Lord has delivered all of the Philistines, your enemies, into your hands today. I will repeat it: all! However, instead of completely annihilating them as you were commanded, you have sent your own men back to their homes to rest. Did you not learn from your mistake with the Amalekites?"

"Surely many thousands are dead, the Philistines are no longer a threat to us, and they won't be for many years to come," Saul replied.

"You have again spared yet another king for what you believe to be your own needs."

"But is this not a great victory?" he asked.

"The Lord would have wiped this unclean people from the earth at your hands on this very day, but you have sinned and given respite where he offered none," Ahijah chastened the king.

Jonathan was so stunned by the proclamation that he could do nothing more than listen in silence.

"So know this," Ahijah continued. "The Lord has spoken, and the Philistines will rise back up after today. They will from then on until forever more be a thorn in your side. You and your household will never know peace from any of your enemies. They will swarm you like gnats from all sides, each and every day of your people's lives."

His prophecy pronounced, the priest turned from Saul and Jonathan and walked south, away from the group, who continued their path toward Gibeah.

The Harpist

It had been forty days since Ahijah departed from their company, but his words wore fresh on King Saul's nerves. He had spent the last forty days and forty nights red-faced and railing against everyone from Jezreel to Hebron so that not a man or woman in all of the twelve tribes escaped blame for the prophecy, except for Saul himself. Jonathan had listened to his father criticize and condemn soldiers and priests, the elderly and infirm, and even his wives and children to the point that everyone did their best to avoid his presence altogether, lest they too feel the lash of his bitter tongue.

"Why did you eat that damn honey?" he had shouted at Jonathan at least a dozen times. But Jonathan knew the fault lay with his father. It was he who had made the choice to starve his fighting forces and deny them the sustenance that would have ensured a far greater victory than was won. In fact, it was Saul himself who had initially angered their God years ago by not killing off the Amalekites and slaying King Agag immediately as instructed. Rather than challenge his father's misassignment of fault, Jonathan stayed in his quarters, away from the constant recriminations. There, with little to do of importance, he repeatedly bedded Judith out of boredom, until at last, one evening, she flat out refused him.

"No?" he asked with great surprise when she held him at bay by the palm of her hand.

"It wouldn't be a good idea."

Annoyance pushed its way up Jonathan's neck. Without sex, how would he occupy his time with her?

"Could this be Elim's daughter?" he chastised her loudly. "The one who relentlessly hounds me day and night for my seed?"

"Yes," she replied sternly. "And you have not been denied once, so I cannot understand your anger . . . or have you more of your father's temperament than I was aware of? Do we need to worry that you too will slip back and forth between fits and giggles?"

"Both your tongue and your sense seem to have escaped you, rather unexpectedly." Jonathan's eyes narrowed. "Do you forget yourself? Your duty is to serve me, not to offer commentary on my father and the state of our country. You are not a queen yet."

"I've made no comment on Israel," Judith said in great confusion.

Jonathan growled. "Are you *kesil* now, too? You cannot be so stupid as to not notice that you just said the country needs to worry about my mental capacity."

"I most certainly did not," she barked back.

"You said *we* need to worry! Or will you say that I am hearing things and have too become a victim of paranoia?"

She laughed. "Yes, I did say that."

"Then you are out of order," Jonathan snapped. "And your merriment dishonors you."

"I said we, my husband, because *we* do!" Judith lifted her hands up to her belly and rubbed it. "Your son and I do not wish to be saddled with a husband and father as unpredictable as the winter rains."

"You—" Jonathan started to shout in reply, but the weight of Judith's words sunk in and he took a step back, his eyes now wide with disbelief. "Wait . . ." he stammered. "Are you saying . . . Are you . . . pregnant?"

"I'm afraid it will be many months before you can bed me again," she told him as she reached back and rubbed her lower lumbar. "Not that I could at this moment imagine us doing it ever again, as much as my body currently aches."

"Oh, Judith . . ."

She sighed. "We did what was asked, and our families will both be happy."

Jonathan stepped forward and wrapped Judith up in his arms and squeezed her. "Thank you," he whispered.

She pushed him off with a groan. "Ugh, you pressed up against my swollen breasts."

"Oh?" One of Jonathan's eyebrows rose, along with something under his cloak. "How swollen?"

"I'm serious," she moaned as she gathered a shawl and threw it over her shoulders. "I will want to stay with my mother until after the birth."

"You mean you are going away?" His voice rose in confusion.

"Not away, just to my own family."

"You can't do that." Jonathan was firm. "You have a potential prince inside your body, and my own mother would not allow it."

"Well, I need help," Judith suddenly cried out. "I don't know the first thing about childbirth—or child-rearing for that matter." Her cheeks reddened, and her eyes filled with watery panic. "All I knew coming into this marriage was how to make babies, and we did that! I do not have the first idea on what to do with them once they come."

Jonathan laughed. "Your mother and anyone you want can come stay here at the fortress," he said. "We will find them quarters, and you will have all of the help that you require or desire."

"No." Judith sniffled. "I want to be in Bethel. At least there our child will grow inside me under the eyes of the priests as well as my kin. You can't protest that, can you?"

"If it's for spiritual reasons that you wish to go to Bethel, even my mother will not try to stop you. But you must promise me this: that you will return before the birth so that I can be the first to hold our son on the day he enters the world."

"I agree." She wiped her nose and stopped crying.

He continued, "And you must allow me to send one of my brothers to Bethel to look after your safety."

Judith rolled her eyes. "If you must, can you please make it Shua?"

"Why him?"

"All of my sisters and nieces and, well, even my grandmother swoons over his thick eyelashes."

Jonathan laughed. "Then Shua it is."

She threw her shawl off and sighed. "In that case, I think I will just go lie down."

Judith made her way to the bed and stretched her body out. "Can you stoke the fire? I am cold," she said icily as she reached for the covers. "Once you finish, I think I will need silence for a while. Would you mind leaving me?"

Jonathan made sure the embers were stirred before he turned back to his wife. "Wow," he commented. "They say women become melancholy when with child, but your change has come on quite rapidly, has it not?"

She lifted her head up and glared. "Don't you need to go talk to Shua about Bethel?" she hinted without humor, then threw her head down in a huff. "All of this conversation with you has left me weary."

Weary? Jonathan thought. *We haven't spoken but for a few minutes!* Then he realized that those few minutes were more time than they had talked seriously in all of their months of marriage.

"Alright," he relented. He left his wife to rest and went outside.

Once he was in the courtyard, though, he reconsidered his promise. Why should he allow his only child to be carried in a belly far away from his protection? The Philistines could raid Bethel, and he would be helpless to do anything about it.

No, he told himself. *Judith cannot go to Bethel—I simply will not allow it.*

He headed across the courtyard and was contemplating how best to break the news to her in the morning when something made him stop and turn. Through the latticework of a small open window in the dining hall wafted the most pleasant sound.

"I don't remember there being a special dinner this evening." Jonathan cocked his head to the side to take in the tune from the delightful instrument. "We must be entertaining a tribal leader, and I forgot."

Unable to abate his curiosity, his legs moved him to the large doors that led to the dining hall. When he entered, the only person he could see was his father, who was seated far away at the head of the table in a high-back chair. His eyes were closed, and a look of serenity lay across his face. Gone was the constant weight of worry that plagued him. Jonathan noted that his father looked at least a decade younger, and considerably more relaxed than he had in many years. There was no one else present—no tribal leaders, no special dinner guests, just Saul.

Beyond the table, back along the far wall, hung a set of deep-red curtains. They were pulled closed, but there was just enough space where they met for Jonathan to make out the shape of an arched bow harp. Its strings, which were crafted from the dried guts of animals, vibrated at the instruction of a set of slender fingers on a masculine hand that peeked out from between the scarlet drapes as they plucked away gently.

No wonder my father is at peace, he thought as he admired the skill of the musician who evoked such soothing sounds.

When the song came to a gentle close, Saul opened his eyes and smiled. "Absolutely wonderful," he gasped to the empty table. There was a scraping sound as he pushed his chair back and stood up. "I will thank my brother for bringing you to me," he declared to the unseen player. "And I simply must have you play for me as frequently as possible, for I feel better now than I have in many days."

With a great sigh of contentment, the king stepped toward the curtain, and without pulling it open, he said loudly, "Now that you have placed a balm upon my spirit, I believe that I will soothe my body in the cool waters of a cistern." He smiled at the divide that hung between him and the harpist for a second before floating his tall frame out of the hall.

Jonathan, whose father in his peaceful state hadn't even noticed, marveled at the power of the harpist. Desperate to thank the musician personally, he made his way over to the wall and pulled back the fine red fabric. There he looked down upon the back of a golden-haired stranger, who was placing his instrument into a large wooden crate.

"I must tell you that you have a truly remarkable gift," Jonathan said warmly. "My father has found great peace in your skill."

The musician turned around. "Thank you for your kind wo—" But he stopped speaking when Jonathan's jaw fell open.

"D-D-David?" Jonathan stuttered.

"Yes." He smiled.

"The David who slew the giant?"

"The very one." David laughed.

"You are the harpist?"

The once-boy from Bethlehem stood there, now a man, and he grinned through teeth that were as bright as sun-bleached stone. "Um, I'm not sure how else to affirm what I've already said yes to twice."

"What are you doing here?" Jonathan asked loudly.

David's forehead wrinkled. "I confess that I am more confused than you are."

"And yet here you are."

"I am." He looked around the room now that the curtain was back. "And I can tell you that here is a lot fancier than where I was before!"

"How does one go from war hero to shepherd to musician behind the king's curtains?"

David raised his shoulders and shrugged. "Seven plagues if I know."

"It's as if this almost isn't real."

"All I know is that I was instructed to perform for someone who had the demonstrations of an evil spirit. And my father agreed that I should go."

"Of all of the troubled souls in all of Israel." Jonathan shook his head in wonder.

"Perhaps we were simply destined to cross paths again," David offered.

"It simply is madness," Jonathan cried out again. He could not help but notice how the light stubble on David's firm jaw confirmed the maturity he now possessed . . . Or at least his body did.

"I've learned not to question things." David sighed.

"That's probably a good attitude," Jonathan said mindlessly, taking in the look of his strong arms, the biceps of which were now more defined than when they'd last met.

"No, seriously," David said more soberly, and that caused Jonathan to shift his focus back to his words.

"Oh?"

"Yeah. Ever since that Samuel guy dumped a jar of oil over my head, my life has pretty much been a desert storm of madness all around me."

Jonathan took a step back. "Samuel? Like, the prophet Samuel?"

"Yes, that's what my father called him, but all I call him is the old fool of silliness."

"Are you telling me that you were anointed . . . anointed by Samuel himself?" He looked around the room in alarm to make sure that they were alone.

David shrugged. "I'm not sure I'd call it an anointing."

"And when did the anointing take place?" There was a hint of panic in Jonathan's voice.

"Uh, I don't know. I was just a kid, and I'm certain he only did it at my father's insistence. He was always afraid that I would be eaten by wolves while watching the sheep in the fields. I guess he had the old man do some kind of blessing of protection."

"A blessing of protection?" Jonathan was becoming more and more concerned.

"Hey, it worked. I was almost mauled by a lion a few months ago, and I somehow managed to kill it with nothing but a notching knife," David shared without boasting.

"You did what?" Jonathan exclaimed. "The prophet Samuel visited you, and then you killed a lion with a tiny blade that barely can slice into bread?"

"Oh no," David explained. "That Samuel guy did that to me probably two or three years before you and I ever met or anyone had ever heard of something called a Goliath."

The realization that David had been anointed by the prophet Samuel before he killed both the giant Goliath and a lion hit Jonathan hard. After all, he was the one who had insisted to his father that David was not the one that would come next. He was the one who had convinced Saul to let David go home, and now he was back, in the fortress, having killed a massive beast with his bare hands?

He is clearly the one who is favored by the Lord. Jonathan felt a sense of knowing and awe, combined with worry for his father's reaction should he find out this news.

". . . but as I've gotten older, I have come to realize that strange things began to happen to me rather routinely after that one encounter," David continued.

Jonathan rubbed his chin and thought back to Saul's reaction to the women cheering for David after he had slayed Goliath. "It all makes sense now," he said, deep in thought.

"Yeah, you try to be a normal child after you get assaulted with a vat of oil that smells like a prostitute's tent." David chuckled.

At the joke, Jonathan focused back on him and smiled. "Well, we don't have giants or lions here," he responded.

"Um, okay," David said.

I am as giddy as a maiden, just like the first time we met. Jonathan shook his head at his silly words and tried to recover. "I mean, whatever did bring you here to Gibeah, I am glad for it." He extended his hand to David, who reached out his own.

As they shook hands, Jonathan took in David's firm grip. He looked into the Judean's eyes and felt as weak as he had when they'd kissed years back.

He probably doesn't even remember anything about me.

"It has been a long time." David grinned.

"The last time I saw you, you were still a boy—albeit one that did what a whole army could not. But now . . ." Jonathan said aloud as he eyed David's matured physique.

David's brow furrowed. "Do you know that I can barely remember much of anything about that whole experience?"

See? Jonathan chided himself.

"I mean, aside from the immense weight of the heavy sword that fell out of my hands and sliced through that thick neck."

"Oh," Jonathan remarked softly. "Then you probably don't remember much about me or our interactions in any detail?"

David's smile grew again. "That's the one thing I actually do remember."

Jonathan's face flushed.

"To be honest, it feels like I only just rode away to Bethlehem last night," he continued.

"Same here." Jonathan's heart leapt in wonder.

The two men stood in the silence of the cavernous room for a moment.

"Um, well . . . now that you have played for the king, where will you go next?"

"Oh," David replied, "I have actually been ordered to stay here in Gibeah by your uncle and to play for your father whenever he calls upon me."

"You're staying?" Jonathan's voice rose in excitement.

"Yes, but . . ." David shuffled his feet. "It's just that he made me swear never to tell anyone my real name."

The worry about the anointing came rushing back. "Ah, yes." Jonathan nodded in agreement. "I think Abner is more than right. I'm afraid my father was a little jealous of the attention you received in the past. There really is no telling what his reaction would be if finds out that you are here. And you must never tell him about Samuel . . . ever. Don't worry, I will guard your secret closely."

Just then, a woman servant walked in. "Your wife is calling for you," she told Jonathan.

"Wife?" David asked with surprise.

"She is complaining of sickness from the child," the servant continued.

Jonathan looked from the servant to David.

"Wow, I guess a lot has changed with you too since we last met," David stated.

"Yes," Jonathan said hesitantly, "and no."

"I want to hear all about it." David's mouth stretched into a yawn.

"You will, but clearly all you need now is some rest." Jonathan turned back to the servant. "Let Judith know that I am on my way. Afterwards, please make up the guest quarters nearest to my apartments. We have a special guest, and I insist that he is placed as close to me as possible."

"And who might I say the guest is to the other servants?"

"Um . . ."

He turned back to David, who said, "Gershom."

"Yes, Gershom, and in our house you will be most welcome. Go now and take rest, as you look weary. Tomorrow, we will meet and pick up where we left off, far, far too long ago."

David obeyed the order, and soon the servant had led him away and Jonathan stood alone in the silence of the room. The hairs on his arms were standing up from the electricity of the reunion, and he closed his eyes and smiled at the thought of being able to spend time with his friend, or whatever David was to him.

After a moment, his eyes opened, and he headed off to find Shua. True, Judith had asked for him to come tend to her sickness, and he would. But first, he needed to tell his brother to pack for Bethel.

Sticks in Their Hands

S ilence lay on the bed like the film on top of the goat's milk Jonathan's mother used to warm for him when he was restless as a child, only the stillness did not calm him. Judith had left with Shua in the early morning hours, so it was certain that by now she had arrived at the home of her father, Elim. But, instead of comfort from the peace of her absence, Jonathan found little respite in being alone, as his spirit was nervously aroused by the presence of another.

As he lay in the darkness on a bed of wadded wool, Jonathan could almost hear the gentle breathing of the man just on the other side of the limestone wall that divided his quarters from his guest's.

I wonder what he is wearing? he thought to himself. *Perhaps a linen tunic?*

He chewed at his lower lip as he imagined the tunic sticking to David's inner thigh in this heat. Though the sun had long set, a balminess clung to the air, and it moistened Jonathan's hand with sweat as he moved it past his navel and found himself.

Slowly he pictured David's lips, the ones that had touched him under starlight, moving against his neck. They traveled upward, and the tingle Jonathan remembered feeling on his mouth caused him to erupt quickly, with a nervous rush.

What are you doing to me? he wondered, but there was no answer, only the dewiness of reborn guilt that lay splattered across his bare stomach.

He reached for a soft cloth to wipe it away.

At first it came off easily, but he found himself rubbing the rag across his skin with increasing intensity, as if he could use it to erase his emotions. Yet no matter how roughly he applied the cloth, remnants of David still clung to him. This residue seeped down into his bloodstream and carried itself to his fingers and toes. It burrowed its way past his ribcage, then buried itself deep in the cavity in his chest, in that place where his heart touched the hem of his soul. There, as when he had met David the first time, the two became one.

#

"Gershom?" David laughed aloud to himself at the quick-on-his-feet answer.

What else was I supposed to say? Abner had insisted the word "David" remain unuttered, so now he had relegated himself to "the stranger" as a name. It would probably arouse more suspicion than if he had just stuck with his real one.

The lusty image he had held of Jonathan returned to his mind. It was one he'd returned to often during his alone time in the fields when there was nothing better to do than to rub on himself. There in the wet grass of morning, the vision of Jonathan's nearly naked body when he had given him his robe and tunic years ago provided the necessary impetus for David's enjoyment. Now, it came to him once more, only this time with Jonathan's more grown-up facial features.

I wonder what he would look like today if he were to offer his clothes to me again?

He tried to imagine Jonathan's matured body as he took off his tunic. Had it changed? His mind dwelled on the dark hair that decorated Jonathan's head as he traveled downward to consider if the same curls and waves gently encircled his manhood.

A small gasp escaped David's lips.

"Damn," he moaned.

All he could do was let his mind dwell on those thick, luscious eyebrows he longed to kiss. Oh, how he would nibble and peck his way over those eyelids and cheeks until he had reached those soft, full lips.

Another throaty groan erupted from his mouth.

"Whew." David exhaled loudly before he lay back and reveled in the feel of his release. He let the euphoric sensation spread out over his body. "Life is amazing!"

If being alive like this meant that he was wild and tempestuous, as his father had said many times, then so be it.

A thrill ran through him at the thought of the lion—how its mane had twisted around his fist as he dragged it to the ground. It was the same way he'd felt when the locks of Goliath's hair were wrapped between his fingers as he lifted the giant's head into the air. The blood had dripped out of its neck onto the hot desert sands the way David's love had just poured out between the powerful grip of those same fingers.

A familiar feeling of excitement surged through his body. Usually he was exhausted after an ecstatic climax, but now he only felt ready to go once more. *God has made me taste life, not run from it.*

He found his instrument, and played it to a rapid completion, whereupon he collapsed back onto the bed, exhausted. Spent, he quickly drifted into the world of dreams, where the name Jonathan carried on a breeze of whispers through his slumbering mind.

#

When Jonathan awoke in the early morning, he found his way to the spring just outside the fortress walls. There he covered himself in *borith* made from congealed ash lye and vegetable oil and used a sponge to lather himself up. Bending over, he lifted handfuls of cool water and released it all over his body in an effort to sweep away all traces of the night before. Yet his feelings would not be carried downstream, as they remained in his heart and wrestled with his mind.

By the time he had returned to the safety of the walls, breakfast had been served, and he made his way to the dining hall, where most of his family were already seated. It was not a formal setting, as it was too early for such things, but even still, the increasingly familiar stirrings of David's harp played from behind the damask wall hangings. No one spoke as bowls of figs and bitter biscuits, made from salt-boiled locusts that had been ground down and baked with flour, were passed around and nibbled on by drawn faces. Only King Saul himself seemed at peace, as both Armoni and Mephibosheth looked at each other and rolled their eyes. Abinadab appeared to be pale and hung over, and Abner's face was pulled taut, as if the Kings of Zoab themselves held a knife to Israel's throat at this very table.

When the last note sounded, they all sighed and cast glances at one another.

"I think I will have one more tune," Saul gleefully announced with a smile.

The servant who stood at the king's side began to walk away to tell David to continue to play, but Abner raised his hand to stay him. "Perhaps it is not wise to overplay the musician," he suggested gently. "We do not want him to be too tired when the time comes that he is most needed."

Saul eyed his brother for a moment before he nodded in agreement, so the servant instead went behind the curtain to dismiss the harpist for the rest of the morning.

After surveying the scene, the thought of sitting down at the table did not sound appealing, so instead, Jonathan tiptoed back outside. "I'd rather starve than sit with Armoni and Mephibosheth," he mumbled under his breath while he walked around to the side door in the courtyard. At that moment, David exited from the musician's entrance and nearly walked into him.

"Oh." David seemed startled by his presence.

"Good morning," Jonathan said awkwardly. The thought of what he'd done to himself last night with David on his mind caused him to blush.

"Hello there," David responded, seemingly unaware and unbothered.

"It is a beautiful day." Jonathan smiled as he tried to think of what to say next.

"Yes. Yes, it is."

"Would you care to practice spears?" he blurted out.

David shrugged. "I don't know how to use a spear."

"It would be nice to do something together today. Give us an opportunity to talk some more, maybe."

"I would like that, but . . ." David lifted his hand back toward the musician's entrance.

"Oh," Jonathan exclaimed. "I do not think my father will ask for you again today. He seems much at ease now, and I doubt if we shall see any fits or the visits of feverish spirits, at least until sundown."

"Okay, then," David agreed. "But I thought your weapon was the bow and arrow, no?"

"It is, but one should always know how to win using a panoply of weapons."

"I see. So you know I am mostly familiar with the slingshot, and yet you aim to take advantage of me and my lack of experience?" David teased.

"I would never do that." Jonathan feigned innocence, then chuckled. "Really though, since you are completely new to spears, we will use the ones with the blunt tips. After all, I don't want to send you back to

Bethlehem covered in bloody lacerations that healers have to stuff with horsehair, now do I?"

David played along. "Perhaps that's too much confidence against someone *anointed*," he said with a guffaw.

In a cloud of jolly jesting, the two made their way out of the fortress and down onto the valley floor, where there were all sorts of military training exercises going on.

"We have to always be prepared," Jonathan explained as they walked behind a row of archers to join a circle of spear fighters. He grabbed a long wooden pole off a cart. "Here," he said, tossing the six-foot stick into the air.

David caught it with some effort. "Wow, this is heavy," he exclaimed as he struggled to stand it up straight.

"Aww." Jonathan laughed. "Don't tell me the young man who dragged a lion down by its whiskers can't even pick up a little oak branch? Or was that just luck?"

"I'll show you luck," David said, squaring off his feet.

Jonathan grabbed another stick for himself and rushed toward him with a howl. "Let's see what you've got, then." He raised his pole with two hands and swung it down over the head of David, who quickly lifted his own long spear into the air to block it.

"I don't think I've got anything yet," he huffed, his lack of skills clear as he pushed up on Jonathan's stick with all of his might.

Jonathan panted as he stepped back. "All soldiers have some instinct they bring to the field." He spun his body and the stick around with all of his might, but David was too quick and blocked him instantly.

Wood clapped against wood like thunder, and Jonathan could see out of the corner of his eye that a group of spectators had formed a circle around them. The two men jousted back and forth as the crowd grew larger.

"What's happening here?" Jonathan heard a petulant voice say behind him. He turned to find Armoni at the edge of the crowd. "Oh, I see," his half-brother remarked smugly. "The great Jonathan cannot beat a peach-skinned novice who looks like he can barely hold on to his weapon with both hands, let alone wield it?"

A smattering of chuckles rang out, and Jonathan danced a few steps to the side as David lunged. His feet moved back, then forward again, and he thrust the tip of the spear toward David's feet.

The shepherd-turned-harpist leapt into the air and brushed his sparring partner's spear away, and the crowd began to clap.

David laughed through heaving lungs. "I guess this 'novice' learned quickly how to 'wield.'"

Jonathan stood up straight and rested the tip of his pole on the ground. David did the same, except he used his to hold on to as he leaned over and caught his breath.

"This actually is hard work," he panted.

"I'll show you a few of my favorite maneuvers next, but I wanted to see what you could do before any formal training," Jonathan explained as he stepped over and patted David on the back. "In no time you will be like me and be able to fight off multiple men at once using all of these different weapons."

"Is that so?" Armoni sucked his teeth in and stepped forward. "I hardly think that you should be the one training this new recruit. It's not like the spear is your gifting." He laughed.

"What are you on about?" Jonathan turned his head to face him. "No one asked you."

"It seems like Jonathan believes that he is the best at everything." Armoni turned to the crowd. "He boasts that he can defeat more than one man at the same time with a spear, and just about every other weapon." He put his hand on his chin. "Hmm, I have to ask the question everyone else is thinking, though. Have any of you ever seen the king's firstborn son look so clumsy as he did just now in this gentle sparring?"

There were some *oohs* and *aahs* before one person yelled out, "That sounds like a challenge to me!" This fired up the group, who all began to cheer and call for a match between the brothers.

"Piss off." Jonathan waved his hand in the air and turned back to David.

"Scared?" Armoni needled him.

Many eyebrows were raised at the question.

"Of you?" Jonathan turned back and stepped forward. "Nothing would make me happier than to slap the shit out of you with this rod,"—he rolled its point in the dirt with his hand—"but I made a promise to our father never to harm you, at least not in front of others."

More *aaahs*.

Armoni doubled over with laughter. "Harm me?" he asked in tears. He then abruptly stood up with a serious face. "I would love to see that."

The words fell heavy at Jonathan's feet, and he growled at them.

"Let's get the real spears," Armoni suggested, and the men nearest to him rushed away and brought back two battle-readied poles whose tips were made of sharpened iron.

"Do it!" an onlooker shouted.

Armoni took one of the spears and tossed it at Jonathan's feet. "Or are you too afraid it is you who might be hurt by me?"

Jonathan's nostrils flared at the smell of Armoni's blood. "You disloyal scorpion," he spat. "Always ready to strike at your own family."

The men in the circle began to beat their chests as Jonathan dropped the dummy stick behind him and bent down to grab the war spear.

Suddenly Abinadab rushed wildly out of the group, his arms flailing. "Don't do this." He stood between the two brothers and put a palm up to each man's chest. "Father would not like this display in front of so many, and one of you will certainly walk away from here weakened by the humiliation."

Jonathan's eyes looked past his full-blooded brother, as they were fixated on Armoni's. All he could see was the redness that would spread across Armoni's ass when he kicked it.

David stepped up to him. "Are you sure about this?" he whispered as he leaned in close.

"Hell yes," Jonathan declared loudly, and all of the gathered men erupted in applause and howls of enjoyment.

Armoni grabbed the other spear and rushed into the circle while everyone else cleared away.

The two men slunk around each other in slow rotation, until at last they each erupted with a guttural cry, raised their spear into the air, and rushed forward at their paternal enemy. Their rods were about to meet in midair when they heard a distinctive voice that sounded nothing like the men around them. "Stop this," its raised pitch commanded.

As Ahinoam broke through their ranks, the soldiers sucked in their breath. One by one, they ceased their shouting and bowed their heads in reverence at their queen. Jonathan and Armoni also froze in place and slowly lowered their spears.

"Shameful," she declared through pursed lips.

There was another sound, this one of swishing fabric, as Rizpah swayed her hips and also moved out from behind the crowd of men straight in the direction of her son. She walked up and slapped him playfully on the hand in reproach.

"No, you silly boy," she teased, and the men all burst into laughter.

Next, she turned to Ahinoam. Their eyes locked, but not for long, then Jonathan watched her stray toward David, who was standing just behind his mother. Rizpah winked at the Judean. "Oh pish . . . you know how boys behave when they get their sticks in their hands."

The men in the crowd roared again, but their laughter was mixed with catcalls and whoops of spicy language.

Ahinoam looked disgusted at their response, but recovered herself. "You will all disperse," she turned around and declared. "There have been enough military drills for one morning."

With sighs of disappointment, the men obeyed, and they turned and slowly walked away.

"What were you thinking?" Ahinoam turned back and rebuked Jonathan in a coarse whisper, but before he could respond, Rizpah and Armoni were at their side.

"You wanted to say something, didn't you?" Rizpah urged her son.

"I . . ." he hesitated, clearly pained. "I am sorry for this."

"There." Rizpah chuckled. "No harm done, and my son even apologized."

"We actually don't know what harm has been done yet," Ahinoam barked. "It could be weeks before we find out if this stupidity has hurt the standing of either of our sons, who each lead a portion of my husband's army."

Rizpah rolled her eyes. "Must you always be so dramatic?" She turned to David. "I am sure your attractive guest has better things to do than to hear women cackle and carry on so. Don't you . . . ?" She reached out her hand to him in introduction.

"Oh," David said at last as he rushed forward to kiss it. "Um . . . Gershom."

"Hmm." Rizpah looked at him curiously. "No, you don't look like a Gershom." She leaned in closer to examine him. "Aren't you that boy named David? The one who . . ."

A rosy color spread across David's face. "No—" he started to say, but Rizpah would not have it.

"Don't lie, boy," she flirted. "You are who you are, and that is . . . ?"

"Yes. I'm also known as David," he confessed.

"Wait," Armoni interjected. "Wasn't this boy tossed off by my father years ago as some kind of interloper?"

"Oh," his mother cooed, ignoring him. "In that case, I would love to have you in our quarters to hear all about how you managed to slay the giant. I found you such a fascinating boy back then, and I can only imagine how interesting of a man you are now. Would you take wine with me after dinner tonight?"

David bowed his head and smiled, his cheeks flushed. "I would be honored."

Now the heat rose in Jonathan's face as well, and it caused his mouth to twist with annoyance. "I'm afraid that won't be possible."

"Why not?" Rizpah squinted. "Oh, silly me." She opened her eyes. "You must not want people to know who you are, or you would not have used a different name."

"Um . . ." David hesitated.

Rizpah laughed seductively. "Don't worry, David." She batted her eyes. "Your secret is safe with me."

"Actually, we must be heading back to my quarters now." Jonathan stepped more firmly in between them. "David is staying with me, and it's getting too warm out to leave him here to gossip."

There was a taste of something Jonathan didn't recognize on his tongue, and he could see that the tone of it caused Armoni to raise his brow.

"What I mean is," he said in a calmer tone, "David is used to the sun in the rolling hills riddled with shade trees where he tends his sheep, not the open spaces of Gibeah with such little respite from its rays."

They all said their goodbyes, and Jonathan watched as Armoni and Rizpah went off arm in arm, but not without Rizpah looking back at David and sending him a sultry smile. Armoni also looked back at David, only his eyes were narrowed as if he were trying to solve a riddle.

"We will discuss this at another time," Ahinoam said sternly, interrupting Jonathan's noticings, then she too wrapped her arm around one of her son's and followed Abinadab up the path and back to the fortress.

"What was all of that about?" David asked incredulously now that it was just the two of them alone.

Jonathan sighed. "Your memory of the past does not extend to the machinations of my family, does it?"

"Vaguely," he confessed. "I seem to remember that you had two brothers who regularly got under your skin, but who was that woman? The one with the beautiful face and those . . ." He held his hands up at his chest.

Jonathan pursed his lips, annoyed by David's attention to Rizpah. "She's lower than a viper," he warned.

"I'd love to see her on her belly like one."

Jonathan laughed at David's joke. "Ew. Well, either way, you cannot break your acceptance of her invitation for tonight." His tone changed. "But I would remember to say little and fear a lot. Rizpah is always up to something, and I am afraid you are too green to the ways of our household to know when you have been taken advantage of until it is far too late."

"Take advantage, Rizpah. Please take advantage of me," David begged in jest as Jonathan led him back to his apartments to freshen up before dinner.

#

The table was not often set for the entire family, but Saul had insisted that tonight his wife, concubine, and all of their children join him. When his mood was elevated, he expected everyone else to be full of verve as well.

Closest to the king sat Ahinoam on his left side, and Jonathan, as heir, on his right. Next to Ahinoam was Abinadab and an empty space for Shua, followed by Saul and Ahinoam's daughters, Michal and Merab. On Jonathan's side was Armoni, Mephibosheth, and then Rizpah, who sat in the seat furthest from the front, glaring at everyone. Jonathan had one more brother, Ish-Bosheth, but he was still of an age where he ate with the royal nurses and thus was not expected to sit at the table.

When the last of the lentil stew had been lifted to the mouths of the diners, servants rushed in to take the empty dishes and replace them with bowls of freshly cooked peaches. Slurps and chews were heard in place of conversation, until finally everyone was satiated.

"I'm ready," Saul stated, and a male servant walked away briskly. Only a few seconds later, the first sounds of the harp began to ripple through the air.

"Ahhh." Saul sighed. "Is there anyone who can play as delightfully?"

"You know, I wonder who this musical genius is." Armoni turned to Jonathan. "Perhaps you should find out so that we might reward him publicly."

Jonathan's mouth tightened. "I think it is best that our father enjoys his peace." He dabbed his mouth with a cloth, then tossed it onto the table.

"Besides, I've made inquiries, and our harpist prefers to remain humble and unnamed." He pushed his chair back and stood up.

"You see, dear brother, not everyone desires recognition or riches. In fact, most have no desire to cause headaches. Some actually do things because they are the right things to do and because they live only to serve both our king and our Lord above."

"Oh really?" Armoni said, but Jonathan's rising caused the rest of the table to stand up. They began to depart quietly from the hall in various directions.

"Father." Jonathan bowed his head and made his own way to the door. Then he stormed off to his chambers.

There he sat and fumed over the fact that David would at this moment be visiting Rizpah and her toadish fools alone and not doing something with him. *Why does she want to meet with David?*

"She better not . . ." he started to say aloud, but then he wondered to himself what exactly Rizpah better not do, or more painfully, what she *might* do with David.

"I'm being ridiculous," he chided himself as he stood up and approached a table that held a pitcher of water. He lifted it and poured some into a cup. "I don't own him. In fact, this is someone I hadn't said a single word to in over three years before two days ago . . . and even now, we have only spoken but a handful of times since."

Though he tried to calm his concerns with the coolness of the water, in his chest he could still feel a smoldering, like old coals in the morning firepit, warm but not extinguished. It was then that he realized the depth of his feelings.

"Damn," he shouted at himself. Why couldn't he just be content having David as his friend?

He wondered what this feeling was that he'd had since the first time they met. He searched his mind for any memory of talk about attraction shared between two men, like the intense clawing he felt for David. All he could come up with were the ones who slept with other men who were prostitutes in front of their Asherah poles. But he didn't believe in idols, and he had no interest in sleeping with David under a tree as a prayer offering for fertility.

What he felt for this man was different. It was intimate. It was sacred.

"Ridiculous," he told himself.

But neither liquid nor laughter could dampen what still burned, so he switched his drink to wine. When it began to cloud his feelings, he stormed off with his cup in hand to find someone to entertain him in the absence of David—and Judith, for that matter.

This is nothing a good romp with a woman will not help me forget, was the last thing he remembered thinking that night.

Everything

"**W**here am I?" Jonathan said with a groan as he put his hand on his head to massage away the pain of a hangover. His eyes squinted against the light spilling across the unfamiliar bed he found himself in. He looked over to find a woman he had never seen before, naked and asleep on her stomach.

Quietly he swung his legs out from under the thin sheets and placed his feet on the floor. As he sat up, his toes touched fabric instead of dirt, so he glanced down and found that his clothing lay bunched up beneath his feet. He picked up his tunic and slipped it over his head, stood up, and strapped on his sandals.

The woman did not stir, so Jonathan made his way outside and found himself looking up at the backside of the fortress. He was surrounded by bedouin tents that sat under the protection of the king, and he wondered when he had left the fortress and how he had come to lie with one of the women in its shadow.

When he finally stumbled into his own quarters, all he could think about was a cool bath, so he ordered a servant to bring him a basin and a wash rag. At the table he sat down and sponged himself inch by inch, paying special attention to his genitals, in case his visit to the unknown had left him with more than a blank memory.

When he was cleaned to his satisfaction, he made for the full pitcher of fresh drinking water and downed it as quickly as he could. With liquid still dribbling down his chin, he found his bed and lay down across it.

"Knock, knock," David said as he entered the room. "I did not hear you speak at the table when I played for your father at breakfast this morning, and I wondered if you had gone off on some urgent business or had taken ill."

Jonathan closed his eyes and put his hands to his temples. "If only it was either. Instead, it's just the aftermath of a night of cheap wine and cheaper women," he confessed, opening his eyes to David's laughter.

"Why, you wanton lover!" his friend exclaimed, and walked over to the bed and flopped down beside him. "And here you were warning me not to drink too much around Rizpah."

"Well, what exactly happened when you went to her last night?" Jonathan asked groggily.

"Absolutely nothing," David groaned to the ceiling. "It was as boring as Sheol! She and her sons just peppered me with questions about the Philistine. But mostly they wanted to know the nature of our friendship and if you were the one who'd brought me unnamed to play for your father."

"Ah." Jonathan sighed. "Then what was boring to you was subterfuge to them. It comes as naturally as breathing."

"How could those questions be deceitful?"

"They are looking for any way to harm my father's image of me, and if I had snuck the one man the king had sent away back into his presence secretly, surely they would think to use that to advance themselves."

David shrugged. "Being royal sounds a lot more complicated than playing the harp."

Jonathan chuckled, but his mind moved downward to where he could feel the heat from David's leg pressed up against his own.

They lay in silence for a couple of minutes. Their breathing began to align so that when David's chest expanded with air, Jonathan's did the same. Inhale . . . exhale . . .

At last, Jonathan broke the stillness and asked nervously, "When you said the other day that you remembered everything about us, what exactly did you mean by *everything*?"

David rolled over so that he was propped up on one arm, and his eyes bore down on Jonathan like a sickle, ready to swoop in and slice the heads off stalks of wheat.

"I remember this," he said intimately as he lowered his lips onto Jonathan's and pressed.

Unable to control himself any longer, Jonathan pressed back until both of their mouths exploded open and he felt David's tongue plunge into his void with great longing.

They twisted and pulled at each other's faces with urgency until David leaned back and pulled his cloak off and threw it onto the floor. Jonathan smiled at the sight of David's taut chest. He lifted his head off the bed to find David's mouth again as he used his hands to stroke the outlines of his sculptured face.

Each one panted harder than the other as David tore off his undergarments. Jonathan's eyes widened at the sight of David's completely naked body. The tightness of his abdomen and the firmness of the member that jutted out toward him made Jonathan swallow hard in anticipation.

David laughed at Jonathan's wonderment, and he helped him out of his own clothing so that they were now both stark naked and wrapped in one another's arms.

David's voice lowered lustily. "I have waited for this moment for three long years."

"As have I," Jonathan responded.

They kissed more intensely than before, until he at last moved his head down across David's chest and followed the trail of light-colored fur down to his navel. He pursed his lips and blew out warm air against David's manhood. He responded with a moan, then Jonathan felt David grab ahold of his hair with his hands and pull him back up toward his mouth. They kissed once more, their lips smacking loudly.

Finally David's pupils dilated, and he rolled Jonathan onto his stomach. *What is he doing?* Jonathan wondered.

He could feel the full weight of the man who now lay across his back as David grabbed the backs of both of Jonathan's hands and thrust himself forward. A cry of both pain and delight escaped Jonathan's mouth, and he squeezed David's hands tightly with all of his might.

In this moment he felt as if he were David's instrument, and the music that they made together was warm and pungent.

With each pass, David's sweaty body slammed harder up against Jonathan's own in an increasing rhythm, a wild yet perfectly paced song, until at last the musician sang out in ecstasy and fell hard onto Jonathan's back.

There he lay, and he kissed the nape of Jonathan's neck gently over and over again.

"Wow," his lover exclaimed as he rolled Jonathan over onto his back. Then he used his fingers as if Jonathan was his harp until Jonathan released his own music into the air.

David lay down beside him and panted, "Next time, we switch."

All Jonathan could do was smile at the words "next time."

They lay there, their breaths heaving, until a feeling of safety and comfort covered Jonathan. He had never felt more at peace, so he allowed himself to slip under it, and he fell into a deep slumber.

#

When he awoke, David was gone.

The whisper of a male servant caused him to leap up onto his elbows. "He said in a quarter of an hour."

"What?" Jonathan asked. "Who said what in a quarter of an hour?"

"The king has asked for you to meet him in his throne room."

"Oh." Jonathan yawned and laid his head back down. "Thank you."

The servant departed, and Jonathan knew immediately that Rizpah had wasted no time. "She got whatever she wanted from David last night . . . slippery eel," he muttered to himself as he got up from the bed and exited his chambers.

Outside he found a place to piss against the wall behind one of the dwellings. As he relieved himself, he arched his back and stretched arms into the air so that his stream rose up in a steamy arc and sprayed against the stone. He thought about what had transpired between David and him, and he couldn't help but smile. It was better than anything he had ever experienced with Judith, or any other woman for that matter.

He shook himself dry and went to find out what trap his father's concubine and her sons had laid for him.

When Jonathan entered, his father's glaring eyes followed him along the length of the room. "What is this I hear about the boy who slew the giant being here in Gibeah, at this fortress?" he spat as he tightly gripped both sides of his throne.

"It is he who plays the harp for you each day and who has brought you great stillness," Jonathan admitted.

"Hah," Saul cried out. "How can there be stillness when the one I sent away has been secreted into my household without my consent?"

Jonathan had not seen his father this incensed in weeks, so he thought to tread lightly. "There was no malice in the act," he said.

"Is this not the one whom they sang about as if I were *his* servant? And now I learn he has come to the very place I lay my head, where he could easily remove it in my sleep—chop it off my body just like he did to the man-bear in front of thousands of cheering men!"

"I can assure you, he aims to do no such thing—" Jonathan started to explain, but his father cut him off.

"You can assure me?" he hollered, raising a pointed finger in accusation. "How can you assure me of anything when you keep such secrets from me?"

"Father, it was only so as not to upset you and—"

"But upset me you have. How dare you bring him here without first asking me? Surely I have more loyal sons than this whom I should consider as my next in line, or even as my confidants."

"It wasn't him," Abner stated firmly as he entered the room from a door behind the throne. "I cannot allow Jonathan to take the blame for that which I myself did."

"You?" Saul's eyes widened. "Is there no one whom I can trust in this family?"

"I searched the land far and wide, and David was the best musician alive. I knew you would find his strings soothing but his face distressing, so I told him to always play behind curtains and to never tell anyone his real name," Jonathan's uncle explained.

Saul stopped yelling. "But why would you make a fool out of me?" he asked in confusion.

"It was neither Jonathan nor myself who made a fool of you, but whoever exposed his secret," Abner said. "David could have gone on playing for you as long as you had a need and then been returned to his home in Bethlehem without anyone's knowledge. No harm would have been done to your person, but now you are more agitated than had this small act of concealment not been revealed."

"I suppose," Saul said softly as he bent over to think. "But either way, it is known." He shifted in his seat as if to find a more comfortable position, then he sat up straight. "And now that he is here, it must look as if I myself welcomed him into our home and into our family." He seemed to be speaking more to himself than to Jonathan or Abner.

Jonathan smiled brightly. "I knew you would be gracious." He had hoped his father would allow David to remain. A rush of excitement surged throughout his body at the thought of running out of this throne room to share the news and find himself entwined once more in David's arms.

Judith will not return for months. He grinned from ear to ear.

"So I will announce to all this evening David's marriage to Michal."

Jonathan's mouth fell open. "Wh-what?" he stuttered, a sudden dryness seizing his throat.

"What did you need me to clarify?" Saul asked in annoyance.

"Marry Michal . . . my sister?"

Saul stood up. "Do you know another Michal?"

"Why would he want to do that?"

"It is a great gift to be given the hand of the king's daughter. And if you recall, I had publicly declared that whoever killed Goliath would marry one of my daughters. With this David's return, you have all forced my hand, and now I must fulfill this promise."

"Do you not think that we should ask him first?" Jonathan said.

"Your friend will be thankful that I didn't put him in irons instead," Saul growled. "I must keep David close to me now that he has returned, and I can think of no better way to watch his every move than to chain him to Michal. She is her father's most dedicated servant if ever there was one, and dare I say that had she been born with a peen, she might be the next king and not you."

Nothing Jonathan said from this point on mattered to his father. Within minutes, a dispatch was ordered to ride out for the house of Jesse so that all of David's family might attend the royal wedding of their son to a princess of Israel.

#

The days and nights were filled with plans and preparations. When the women met to discuss fabric and table settings, Jonathan and David would steal away to Jonathan's quarters, where he would tell his servants that no one was to enter without warning, not even the king himself.

It was there in the quietness of the bedroom, the air heavy with the scent of sweaty bodies, that they discussed their turn of fate.

"You were always to be married," Jonathan said, in an effort to convince himself more than David that his disappointment was unwarranted.

"Me marrying your sister at least ensures I will be close to you always."

"Sure. But I think sleeping with one's relation is far worse than anything we are currently doing." Jonathan chuckled at the thought.

David sat upright and sternly corrected him. "We are not, nor will we ever be, related by blood. However, we will always be related by spirit. In this way, what we do is more sanctified and much more special."

These words sunk deep into Jonathan's heart, and he knew it to be so. David was closer to him than his brothers, and even his wife. David was the rising to his falling. The sun to his moon. No person could stand in between them any more than they could stop day and night from kissing twice a cycle, even if they were each formally wed to another. Both men knew in their spirit that they were a kind of first spouse to each other, the women in their lives simply a custom. This was not adultery, as their connection had come before either of them had ever heard of their wives.

Even my father has more than one person that he is pledged to, Jonathan told himself. And this was no different, and yet different all the same.

Neither he nor David could walk away from the expectations placed upon them by their families for issue and heirs, but the unspoken truth screamed out across the land that they were bound to each other for all of eternity. This bond was their true covenant, and the rest were mortal ties.

Together they honored their never-ending connection as often as possible, in both small and large moments, but mostly in the sight of others, who suspected nothing beyond a friendship. A knowing look, a brushed hand were as forceful of reminders that their souls were tethered as their nights of unconstrained passion. But love did not stop time from moving or the hour from calling. Now it seemed as if Jonathan's head had only spun once, and yet it was already the night before David's wedding to Michal.

"It will be more difficult to meet like this after tomorrow," Jonathan said sadly. He hovered over David's chest, kissing it before he rested his head.

"Especially now that my father and all of my brothers have come," David replied. "Though they are euphoric that my actions have brought them so close to the king."

"Oh." Jonathan pushed himself out of David's arms and sat upright, his face gone to stone. "Speaking of your family, there is one thing you must make sure that they all remember to forget. We probably should have discussed this earlier."

"Hey, calm down." David smiled. "You suddenly seem so worried."

"Because there is something to be worried about. You must make sure that no one, absolutely no one, says anything about the prophet."

"I am not sure that I can put a dog's muzzle on my father," David said.

"You will if you do not want him, you, and all of your brothers to die."

"Huh?"

"What else do you think my father would do if he found out that Samuel anointed you?" Jonathan said sarcastically.

"It was just a child's blessing," David argued.

"Maybe, but to King Saul it will be a direct challenge to his throne, and I would not be surprised if all of Judah suffers harshly should this secret ever get out."

"I had not considered that before." David pulled Jonathan back into his embrace. "But I will go shortly and speak to my family about your warning."

Jonathan sighed in contentment hearing those words. But as he lay there, in the comfort of David's arms, he thought he heard the soft shuffle of feet on the other side of the wall.

It's just one of the servants, he told himself, but a terrible feeling scratched at the edge of his mind.

#

The air was oppressive in the small sanctuary that sat under the throne room. There were no windows, only floors made from the same matte limestone that covered both the walls and the ceiling, so that one could not help but feel closed in and stifled. While it was cooler than the floors above ground, the lack of ventilation made being in it feel as if one had died and been entombed.

It was there that Jonathan stood as he was forced to watch his sister marry the man he loved. He lifted his fingers to his neck and clawed at it gently, feeling suffocated by the ceremony.

"You look almost in panic," Armoni leaned over and whispered.

"Not panic," Jonathan countered. "Only worry for David, as even you can agree that Michal is a taste that few desire."

At this, Armoni laughed aloud, and those in attendance all turned around to stare at the half-brothers, who were normally engaged in argument, as they unnaturally smiled at one another.

Michal was several years younger than Jonathan, but she walked with the air of a queen. She never did believe that girls and boys should do different things, and even as a little girl, she had followed her brothers around unrestricted until they chased her from both bedroom and barracks alike.

Not that she will be unattractive to David, Jonathan thought as he admired her beauty while she stood in front of the priest. Yet she could be insufferably demanding, and worse, an incurable tattletale. Now that she was in her late teens, the tantrums from not getting her way involved words instead of the kicks and punches she used to hurl at her siblings, but she had yet to grow out of her need to report everything back to their parents. Between her wants and her spying, David would have many difficulties finding equilibrium with Michal.

At least this meant he was unlikely to develop a close relationship with her. Who could be close with an informant who was as prickly as a porcupine? He laughed once more, then bowed his head as his mother shot him a firm stare.

After the ceremony, both families ate and drank in the hall, but there was little merriment in Jonathan's heart. At times he thought he caught David looking over at him, but he did not let his eyes linger on his brother-in-law for fear that he might cry out and that all would know the pain he felt inside.

It was not solely due to the marriage that he hurt, but also for the change in his father's rapidly altering disposition. The soothings induced by the harp had given way to agitation and an almost maniacal need to counter an ill-perceived threat. Convinced David had his crown at the forefront of his mind, Saul had falsely concocted an image of David as a stealthy usurper, and this image ruled his thoughts. Jonathan was glad his father did not know about David's anointing, as it would only have confirmed his worst fears. In the end, though, David seemed to have little interest in what Saul thought of him, and was more concerned with fun and living in the moment. It was exciting to marry the king's daughter; the rest, he'd repeatedly said, he left in the hands of their God.

"I am no more meant to be the next king than the pharaoh is meant to convert to Judaism and curse Horus in public," he would say when Jonathan tried to explain why Saul must never know about Samuel. "But, if the Lord wills it, then Thutmose himself would stand at the Temple of Hatshepsut at Deir el-Bahari and declare the Egyptian gods stone idols and throw himself on the ground as a vassal of Israel."

Jonathan could only agree. After all, who were any of them to counter whatever their Lord had decided would be?

In his most secret of places though, Jonathan had decided that if he himself were not to be Israel's next leader, then no one would be better than David. There was an air of authority and confidence about him that would serve him well. But for now, Saul was alive and ruling, and so Jonathan kept the anointing to himself and cautioned his lover to be careful of his father's suspicions.

Out of nowhere, Saul had made his first move against David by altering the original bride-price only a few weeks before the wedding. Rather than accept the agreed-upon shekels of silver and herds of sheep, Saul had insisted that David provide him instead with the foreskins of one hundred Philistine soldiers.

"This is madness." Jonathan had begged his father to reconsider, but the king was resolute. "Why are you so pressed to move against him after only just extending him a way into our family?"

Saul laughed heartily. "Let's see if they sing any songs about him after he tries to remove the skin from the cocks of those barbarians."

David himself seemed unbothered by Saul's demands. Jonathan tried to convince him to break off the engagement at this ludicrous requisition and instead return home with his family.

"Don't you see that he desperately wants you dead—and quickly?" he pleaded.

"If I could kill their most prestigious soldier when I was but a child, I hardly think a hundred *arel pin* will prove too difficult to harvest," David joked.

"It's not funny," Jonathan snapped, but David could not be stopped, and to Saul's regret more than anyone's, David returned in less than a day with a bloodied sack of more than two hundred dickheads, double what the king had asked for.

"Does he mean to mock me?" Saul fumed.

"He only did as you asked, and to please you and show you that he is your servant, he killed many more of your enemies," Abner had said as he tried to calm his brother, but Saul's suspicions would not be eased.

Then, one evening, everything changed yet again. Jonathan was seated on a lounge in one of the fortress's rooms listening to David play for him when he heard a loud crash and a cry. He turned his head back to the door and saw a young servant covered from head to toe in wine, a broken clay vessel lying shattered at his feet. However, the boy was not the one who had screamed. Instead he lifted his shaking hand to point in the direction of David. The king's golden war spear wobbled from the wall it was stuck in, just above David's head.

Jonathan leapt up and ran out into the hall, where he found his father, his face reddened and his fists tightly gripped at his sides.

"I aimed to kill him," he howled in madness.

"But why?" Jonathan cried. "David has not harmed you in any way!"

"I know what he wants," the king said as David came into the doorway, Saul's weapon in his hands.

"If I meant to kill you, wouldn't I do it now?" David said coolly as he thumbed the tip of the spear.

The king looked at Jonathan and then back to David. He gulped in air in what Jonathan assumed was the realization that nothing stood between him and death at David's hands, as he did not have any soldiers at his side to rescue him.

"Then do it already," he challenged David. "That is why you came."

David calmly walked over to Saul, who shook with nerves and eyed the spear as David raised it up. Then he flipped it around and placed the handle into Saul's shaking hands.

The king gasped in disbelief. "You do not want to murder me?" he asked with great surprise.

"Of course not." David smiled. "You are the king the Lord has chosen, and I am only here to serve you, whether that be as your musician, your soldier, or even as your son-in-law."

Saul seemed embarrassed as he departed back to his chambers, and he kept mumbling aloud, "He didn't kill me," in disbelief.

Though his father had spared David's life and decided to allow the wedding to move forward without any further incidents, Jonathan continued to beg David to give up the idea of marrying his sister. "Please just go home," he said over and over again. "I will find a way to see you frequently, and then one day, when one of us becomes king, we will live in each other's household unfettered."

But his pleas were ignored. The day arrived, and the priest had blessed them as husband and wife while all smiled and rejoiced at the reception that followed. However, Jonathan only drank.

He did this freely, both to calm his nerves and to numb his heartache, until at last he remembered nothing but the taste of *yayin* and the touch of his brother Abinadab's hands as he laid him gently upon his bed to sleep, lest his nakedness be exposed. At last there was slumber, lined with the fading smack of fermentation and distress on his tongue.

Saul among the Prophets

Over the weeks after the wedding, Saul's paranoia crept back in as he returned to his state from before the incident with his golden spear. His first move was to have David assigned to lead a group of men in the most elite and lethal section of his army. This provided an excuse to send him out repeatedly on the most daring of missions. Each time the king thrilled with anticipation awaiting news of his son-in-law's demise, while Jonathan would chew on his nails and look out over the valley below. Over and over again, the dust from the sandals of a thousand soldiers would appear on the horizon and David would return, each new victory greater than the last. This only infuriated Saul more, and the cycle would continue in what felt like a sleepless dream for Jonathan, who would sit up at night and worry.

"You are only making yourself more of a target," he'd warned David during one of the few times they had managed to be alone.

"How so?" David's chest swelled as he bragged of all of his battles and the number of Philistines who had fallen at his feet. "It's your father who asks for the impossible, but it is I who makes it possible."

"That may be so," Jonathan countered, "but even Moses eventually died, unless you liken yourself to Enoch and plan to ascend to heaven without tasting death?"

The air blew out of David's inflated lungs. "Okay, perhaps that was a little too boastful."

"Ultimately, I want my father to accept you as an ally, not constantly seek to make you out to be worse than the gentiles."

"Eventually he will."

He is always so sure of himself—unbothered. Jonathan shook his head in mild annoyance.

At last their time together at Gibeah boiled over like honey that had sat on an open fire and thickened into syrupy *dvash*. Only here, none of the sweetness remained, only the bitter taste of burnt sugar.

Jonathan was coming down off the wall, where he had been standing guard for the evening, when he noticed a group of the king's attendants marching in formation toward the quarters where David and Michal were living. They held their hands on the hilts of their swords and approached with menace on their faces.

Jonathan rushed in front of them. "Why are you headed to the home of my sister, and in such a hurry?" he asked, but they kept the pace of their thunderous approach, so he was forced to step aside or be trampled down.

He followed them to the doorway of David's chambers and watched as they barged inside. There in the main room stood Michal.

"David?" one of the men inquired, and she pointed to another room. In it was a bed that appeared to hold a sleeping man.

"Get up," the king's guardsman commanded, but the sleeper did not stir.

The guard leaned over and yanked off the covers only to discover a wooden idol with some goat's hair that lay propped up under the sheet.

"Where did he go?" Saul appeared from behind some of the troops. He screeched as he pushed past his men. "You said he was in here, Michal, and I cannot believe that you would lie to me!"

"He threatened to kill me if I did not let him down the window," Michal cried. She pointed to the open hole in the wall and a tangle of sheets, which were joined together and fastened to a pillar.

"He can't have gotten far," Saul roared.

He gave new orders to his attendants, and they all rushed outside, where they were joined by a larger group of men who rapidly filed out of the fortress and into the night in search of the escaped man.

#

They will never catch me. David crossed the plain in the darkness as he moved quickly over rocks and tree branches alike. In his hand he held the spear that Jonathan had taught him to use, but he had no need of it, for he felt invincible.

Saul will realize that I am no threat to him, and I will return to Gibeah, to both his daughter and to his son, he thought to himself.

Though the moon was only a sliver, he found his way, as he was light itself.

When morning came, he strolled into a small town, where a group of men were prophesying.

One of them came out of a trance and approached him. "You are he."

"Who do you think I am?" David asked in confusion.

"The Lord says it is He who makes the streams flow and causes the wheat to grow. It is He who raises men up and tears them down. He plucked you from nothing, and to nothing you could easily be returned."

David could feel a stinging nip at the hairline on his neck.

"It is good to be afraid," the prophet told him.

"I am." David trembled.

"The Lord says that you are to go no further. King Saul is coming to kill you."

So David stopped his journey and sat and waited as the unfamiliar feeling of fear gripped at his throat for perhaps the first time.

#

By the next afternoon, word had returned to the palace that David was among the prophets at Naioth in Ramah.

"We will ride out at once," the king declared, and Jonathan too, dressed in armor, joined the troops that set off with the group.

As long as I am there, I can stop my father from killing him, he thought.

As the rooftops of the city of Naioth appeared over a hill, suddenly the men closest to the city began to throw down their weapons and prophesy.

"What are they doing?" Saul shouted, but the question had hardly left his lips when he also slid off his horse and tore at his clothes so that all that remained on him was his ezor.

Jonathan followed behind and watched in wonder as his father, nearly naked, walked on foot to the great cistern in the center of the city. There he lay down on the ground and ranted and raved in the Spirit along with the other prophets who were present.

"Isn't that King Saul?" one of the townsmen inquired, and another shrugged in confusion.

Saul could not be moved and remained prostrate for many hours. The heat of the day gave way to the coolness of the night, but each time Jonathan tried to cover his father with a blanket, he tossed it off in a fit of agitation. Concerned about Saul's welfare, Jonathan sat several cubits away and guarded him from the multitude of passersby who gathered to see the king of Israel, asking one another in great surprise, "Is Saul among the prophets?"

As the horizon changed from the blackest pitch to orange to pink and then to blue, Saul's fits slowed, and by the time the top of the sun had broken the skyline, he was at last calm. "I need rest," he announced, and tried to stand up only to fall back into the dirt.

Jonathan rushed to his father's side and helped him off the ground with great effort. Once on his feet, Saul lifted his arms up, and a look of bewilderment spread across his face as he looked down on his naked body.

"Quick—cover me!" he commanded, and Jonathan wrapped a blanket around him and led him to the first dwelling they passed that had an open door, where a young couple eagerly ushered them both inside and offered their bed to the king.

"I have been wrong to that boy," Saul declared weakly to his son.

"Did I not tell you?" Jonathan whispered in reply.

"God forgive me," Saul cried out as he fell onto the mattress and wept bitterly.

Jonathan turned and bowed his head to the couple. "Thank you for your kindness."

The woman and man left them alone and insisted that they wait in a relative's house while the king rested.

After Saul was comfortably asleep, Jonathan stationed two guards at the door. He decided to walk around the city, where he inquired as to the whereabouts of David. A baker told him that the man he sought had left a message to be delivered to the king's son only. Once Jonathan was able to convince the baker of who he was, the message was passed. He was to meet David at an old well, two mils and a stadion to the east.

Jonathan made haste and found David there. He was pacing frantically back and forth in front of the dried-up water hole.

"I have made your father angry . . . I have made the Lord angry, too. Saul has come to kill me, and I fear that, at last, he will succeed," he confided, and for the first time, Jonathan could see that the seriousness of the situation had finally become clear to David.

Jonathan's forehead wrinkled. "How did you know to flee Gibeah to begin with?"

"Your sister," David said.

"M-M-Michal?" Jonathan sputtered.

"She told me that she overheard your father in his throne room tell a guard to wait until nightfall, then go to my room and arrest me."

"Wait, Michal told you what my father said and not the opposite?"

"She said Saul would have me killed the next morning for treason," David continued, but Jonathan's head spun with thoughts of his sister.

"I guess she must love you." His jaw opened wider at the thought.

This made David stop in his tracks. "Well, I don't know about that." He chuckled. "She said it would not help her standing to have her husband killed for subterfuge."

"Now that makes better sense." Jonathan shrugged and grinned.

"Now I must figure out how to reconcile with the king."

"I've been telling you for some time that you were in danger. Yet it seems that things have changed drastically for both you and for my father."

"What do you mean?"

"I suddenly do not think he wishes to see you dead any longer."

"You mean he came all the way here with a band of armed men just to forgive me?" David raised an eyebrow.

"No. I mean he did come to kill you. But apparently, whatever happened last night, it did something to him. I believe he no longer sees you as a threat. You are safe now. Let's just go back to Gibeah and get on with our lives."

David's eyes widened. "For weeks on end you have been telling me to flee for my life, and now you are telling me to stay?"

"It's not every day that the Spirit of the Lord falls on you."

David's feet began to pace again "The prophet told me he came to kill me . . . You told me he came to kill me."

"He did. The prophet wasn't wrong, and neither was I. But now he won't."

David stopped abruptly. "No," he said. "I cannot go back."

"But it's clear you are protected from—" Jonathan began, but David raised his hand.

"The only thing clear is that you have been devoted to me, and I to my pride," David confessed. "I can see why the Lord has been disappointed, yet he lets me live, and so I know now deep inside that I cannot go back to Gibeah without a sign from above."

"Then what can I do?" Jonathan said. "Tell me. Whatever it is you ask, I will do it."

David reached out and pulled Jonathan up into his arms and squeezed. He began sobbing gently. "Just hold me."

Jonathan leaned into the embrace and hugged David back firmly.

"As surely as the Lord lives, you were brought into my life with great purpose, Jonathan." David's voice broke. "What would I do without you? What would I have been had I not met you?"

They stayed together for a moment in silence, then unwrapped themselves. As they pushed away from each other, David wiped his eyes and nose on the back of his arm.

"I guess I'm not as strong and tough as I have pretended to be."

A smile crept across Jonathan's face. "None of us ever are," he replied. "What now, though? Ask and I will do."

"Tomorrow is the new moon fest. I was originally supposed to have dinner with your father. Instead, there is a field of barley just to the south of Ramah, beyond these trees. You cannot miss it, as it is hemmed in by a grove of olives on either side. There I will wait."

"I know the field nearby, as we confronted a raiding party close to it that came from up north near Mizpah last year."

"Go to your father and say these words to him. Tell him that David wishes permission to go home to Bethlehem to offer a yearly sacrifice with his family. If the king grants permission, then I will know that he is no longer against me and that I am safe. But, if he loses his temper and refuses the request, then it will be clear that he has not changed his disposition toward me. Then I will know for certain that I am still in danger."

"All will be well." Jonathan tried to assuage his fears.

David squinted, pain in his eyes. "Forgive me, but I must ask you this. Haven't you yourself, as the faithful servant to your father, sworn to kill his enemies?"

"Of course." Jonathan was confused by the question.

"Then if I really have done King Saul wrong in any way, won't you take out your sword and slay me now?"

"Never!" Jonathan was repulsed by the accusation. "If I knew my father wanted you dead at this moment, I would protect you, just as I planned to do when I rode out with him only yesterday to Naoith."

David beamed. "Then it is true that we have entered into an eternal covenant of love, for you have placed me above all others—even your king."

Jonathan pointed his chin to the field they'd spoken of moments ago. "Let us walk this way."

As they neared the expanse of barley, they approached a large stone that everyone called Ezel near its edge.

"I will ask my father in the exact way that you told me, then return here the following evening. You are to hide behind the Ezel stone, and when I return, I will shoot three arrows in its direction. When I send my servant to collect the arrows, if I say to the boy, 'Look, the arrows are on this side of you,' then you are safe and God has mended my father's heart. However, if I say to the boy, 'Look, the arrows are way beyond you,' then you will know that God has sent you away from here, as you are in danger."

"If you love me, then you will swear again to me now that it will be exactly as you say it. Swear it here in front of our Lord," David urged him.

"I swear it before our Lord. May he strike me down dead if I do not warn you of my father's plans against you if hatred still lurks in his heart."

David grabbed hold of Jonathan's hands. "We are bound together by this covenant."

"Always," Jonathan agreed.

The Stone of Ezel

T he smell of fresh-baked bread filled the room. Some loaves were covered on the outside with seeds and spices that danced before the eyes, while others had delectable fillings of savory meats or sweetened dried fruits that dazzled the tongue. Dry and sweet wines sat in swollen goat skins that hung along the walls, and the servants walked around the room and filled up the vessels of the king and his guests frequently, and without demand.

Abner was seated next to Saul while Jonathan sat at the opposite end of the table, as befitting the heir on more formal occasions. In between were his brother Abinadab and his half-brothers Armoni and Mephibosheth. None of the women of the family were present, as they ate their own supper in another room during the moon festival.

"When will Shua be back?" Abinadab asked.

"Not long now," Jonathan replied. "Judith is to return before the birth."

Everyone talked among themselves for a few moments before Saul silenced the table and called out to Jonathan, "Where is your brother-in-law, David?" His tone was icy. "Was he not supposed to join us for the festival?"

Jonathan trembled, knowing the moment had come, and he could only hope that his father remembered the words that he'd spoken on the morning when he reemerged to himself after his long night of prophesying.

"He was unable to make it this evening, but he did ask if the king would be so kind as to grant him permission to attend a yearly sacrifice with his family in Bethlehem," Jonathan replied.

"Are we not his family?" Saul's voice began to rise.

"We are. As one family member to another, he asked me to present his cause."

"Should he not be here to ask for himself instead of sending you, my own son, to speak for him? He is family, and yet a stranger to our household, and already he wants to go away from us to his father's land?"

"David's brothers asked for his presence so that they can worship together and—"

Dishes and vessels of wine crashed across the table and into the laps of those nearest Saul as he leapt up from his chair. "You son of a worthless harlot!" he screamed from across the table. "How dare you shame your mother into the name of a whore by siding with the son of Jesse and not the husband she lay with."

The lids on Saul's eyes had disappeared so that only his pupils, surrounded by shrinking pools of blue, stared out wildly at his son. "Ever since that troublemaker came into our lives, you have licked at his toes," he hollered.

There were gasps from servants and family members alike.

"Blindly you have followed him around, and you fail to realize that as long as he lives, you will never be king! After he kills me, what do you think will happen to you?"

"David would never harm you or me," Jonathan protested.

Suddenly Saul pulled his golden spear out from under the table, where he had rested it, unseen by all. "You . . . shall . . . die!" he shrieked. A primal yell escaped his lips as he lifted the weapon into the air and threw it with all of his might directly at Jonathan's head.

Jonathan could see the tip of the spear as it spun its way closer and closer toward his face, until it slid right past him. There was a thud and then the sound of metal as it crashed to the floor behind him.

"Have you completely lost your mind this time?" He lashed out in fury. "It is not enough that you tried to kill the one person who saved our entire nation from slavery, but now you also try to kill me, your own son?"

"You have . . . kept his secret . . . from me . . . all along," Saul stammered, his voice starting and stopping in staccato measures, the timbre erratically rising and falling with each syllable.

"What secret?" Jonathan asked.

"He was anointed!" Saul screamed, and everything seemed to stand still.

Jonathan swallowed hard at the accusation, which had poured out onto the table like blood upon an altar.

"I did not want to upset you," he tried to explain, but the king was not to be reasoned with.

"Get out!" Saul shouted, and his voice ricocheted around the room so that it sounded as if a hundred judges were pronouncing a death sentence.

Jonathan's eyes scanned the space looking for help from his uncle or his brothers, but all he was met with were blank stares and the slightly up-turned mouth of Armoni, whose eyes glistened with delight.

"It was you!" Jonathan lunged at him as the soft sound of sandaled feet he had heard on the other side of the wall when he lay with David returned to his memory.

There was little time to think or act further. Jonathan had barely made it halfway to Armoni's neck, which he aimed to snap in two, when a few of Saul's attendants raced to his side and escorted him out of the room, one holding each arm.

"The next time we all see David, it will be on the end of a spike," were the last words he heard from his father as he was dragged away.

#

David sat behind the stone of Ezel. The coolness of the rock against his back calmed his restless spirit enough to while the hours away, but not enough to completely stay his mind. It would have been better if he had his harp—then at least his focus might have been on its strings—but unsure of Saul's intentions for him, he thought it best to remain unheard as well as unseen.

He could have his guards searching the area for me now, for all I know, he thought as he crouched down and slowly peered out from behind the large rock. Off in the distance he could see that someone was coming, so his eyes followed them with trepidation, until at last two men appeared close enough that he could see their faces.

It's Jonathan at last. He jumped to his feet, and his heart thumped in anticipation.

There was a servant with him, so David pulled his body back so that just a piece of one of his eyes could see past the rock. He watched as both Jonathan and the young man slid from the back of the horse they had ridden together.

Optimism surged throughout David's body. *Maybe it is just as Jonathan had said to me, and the king truly favors me now.* He clenched his fists with excitement. *I look forward to going back to Gibeah.*

At last, Jonathan nocked his bow with a single arrow and shot it across the field toward the large stone. David held his breath as the young boy ran out to retrieve it.

"The arrow is beyond you. Go . . . run . . . don't stop!" Jonathan shouted.

At those words, David's heart fell to the ground like harvested wheat, his dreams of reconciliation the chaff that blew away on the wind. He could hear the sounds of the servant fetching the arrow just behind the stone, but David had pulled back so that he remained unseen. There he leaned back, his head against the hard rock, and wept.

"Return to the horse and pack away my bow and arrows," Jonathan directed. "I must relieve myself, and I will need a few minutes alone."

When David saw Jonathan round the corner, he immediately rushed to him, and they fell into one another's arms.

"It is even worse than before, I'm afraid," Jonathan informed him. "You must leave this land and go far."

David nodded in acceptance, and between sobs and snivels, he said, "I love you."

"As do I," Jonathan replied, his voice cracking from the strain.

"Where will I go?" David worried aloud. "I will be hunted throughout all of Israel now as the king's personal enemy. Nowhere will be safe for me, and for what, I do not know."

"Wherever you are, remember this: I will always be there." Jonathan pointed to David's chest, then he grabbed David's hand and placed it on top of his own. "And you will be in my heart whether you are in Dan or Beersheba . . . or even as far as Egypt."

David broke his hands free, then used them to grab Jonathan's face. He drew him in quickly and kissed him deeply, lips moistened by tongues and tears. "You are mine forever," he whispered as at last he let go.

"No." Jonathan tried to grab him again.

"Hey." David forced a smile. "Somewhere out there, there must be a man who will actually teach me how to use a spear, unlike the soft son of a king who plays with bows and arrows."

He winked, but as he turned away, he could see Jonathan lift a hand to his mouth to suppress a cry of pain. By the time it erupted from his mouth, David's feet had already moved with all of their might so that he was now far into the grove of the olive trees and on his way to the unknown.

THE SACRIFICE

The Cost of a Bad Decision

The morning light reflected off the beams of acacia wood, which had been overlaid with sheets of hammered gold. The pieces of the structure's frame were held together by sockets of polished silver and separated by pillars that had also been wrapped in a brilliant yellow metal. Its roof was layered with seal, ram, and goat skins, and the deepest of purple curtains draped its inner core.

It was there, in the heart of the sanctuary at Nob, that David's tired feet had finally stopped their forward movement.

"Why would the husband of the king's daughter be here in Nob alone?" Ahimelek, the priest, asked suspiciously.

"Saul has made me vow to tell no one, not even you. The purpose of my journey is so secret that no one knows of my whereabouts," David said firmly.

He wondered if the priest did not already know that he was a wanted man. But thankfully, Ahimelek played along, not seeming to have any desire to be caught between the current king of Israel and the whisperings of the new one to come.

The priest sighed. "Well, I have little to offer you."

"I do not need much," David told him, though his growling stomach said otherwise.

"I see." Ahimelek pretended not to hear it. "I have yesterday's consecrated bread." He raised a brow and pointed to a table. "So long as you have not had any sexual relations since the last nightfall, you are welcome to eat it, though I cannot say it will be particularly tasty. It was baked yesterday morning and by now is more than likely stale."

"It's perfect," David replied all too eagerly. He grabbed four loaves and placed them in the shoulder bag he had managed to bring with him when he first fled for Naoith. One loaf still in hand, he tore at it with his mouth.

He could feel the priest take in his pitiful state before he hesitantly asked, "Do you not even carry a weapon on this secret journey of yours?"

"The king sent me out so rapidly that I did not have time to even grab a sword," David said between chews.

"Hmm," Ahimelek said in thought, then he scanned the room and walked to the other end. He took out a large item wrapped in cloth from behind a piece of furniture and awkwardly handed it to David, whose body buckled at the unexpected weight of the gift.

"It's yours, though our Lord has allowed us the pleasure of holding this treasure since you first used it," the priest said.

David's eyes widened as the cloth slipped off, leaving the glistening bronze sword of Goliath in his hands.

"Thank you." He marveled at its craftsmanship. He had not held it himself in years, as his father had given it over to the priests when he first returned home to Bethlehem. He lifted it high and remembered it being much heavier than it now felt. True, it had weight, but not the kind of weight that had nearly tipped him onto his backside the last time he held it. Instead, he felt a sense of control as he gripped it firmly and tested it against the air.

"And now, you must go." Ahimelek suddenly herded him toward the entrance. "Even a high priest cannot remain behind curtains all of his life and must eventually come out and face whatever the Lord has placed upon him."

David knew that he was being sent away before Saul came down on either of them for this interaction.

They left the inner sanctuary and came out into the walled courtyard. A man standing nearby gaped as the others moved around him with haste to their duties. David searched his mind for who this was and where they had met before, but by the time the vague memory had a chance to surface, the man had receded into the shadows and Ahimelek had walked him to the gate.

"Peace be with you, David, son of Jesse," the priest said. "And may the Lord shine favor upon you, whatever path he has chosen."

David had barely enough time to offer his thanks before the priest turned and made his way back to the sanctuary. He stood there in the dust for a moment and looked down, watching his toes wriggle in hopes that they would have an idea of where they should move next. At last, the corners of his mouth slowly turned upward.

"Only a crazy person would do that," he said to himself. He felt a tickle in his stomach as he grasped the helm of the sword and headed southwest into the hills and down to the plains of the long valley, which ran on for days.

#

"Kill them all!" Saul's voice rattled with fury.

Jonathan watched the flesh on his father's cheekbones flicker between tense jaws as he raged from his throne.

It had not taken long for him to get back into his father's good graces. In fact, when Jonathan returned from warning David at the stone of Ezel, he had found the king sitting in his quarters waiting for him.

"You have and will always be my closest confidant," Saul said as he embraced his son. "I have acted foolishly, and I ask both your and our Lord's forgiveness. Never has there been a more faithful son."

Jonathan patted his father on the back as he quietly sobbed. "It's alright." He comforted him as if he were a child who had been reprimanded for disobedience.

"I know that you would never do anything to harm me, my son, and yet in blind rage, I almost harmed you," Saul whimpered.

"Let us put it behind us now." Jonathan pushed his father away gently. "David has gone away, and you can focus on ruling the nation instead of your relentless anger toward him."

"Gone away?" Saul's tone darkened. "How could that be so? One does not go away without the leave of their majesty."

Jonathan was about to respond to yet another shift in his father's personality when a servant burst into the room, out of breath, and gasped, "It's a boy!"

Jonathan froze in place, though the hairs on the back of his neck stood up. "A b-b-boy?" he managed at last. "How could that be?" He remembered that Judith had promised to make her way back to the fortress prior to their child's birth.

Saul beamed as he slapped Jonathan on the back. "I am a grandfather at last!"

"Judith will take leave from her father's home in two days and return to her husband in time for the circumcision. She asks that you wait until she can present the child to you here at the fortress, rather than for you to come to her," the servant continued.

"She doesn't want me to see our baby?" Jonathan was confused. "Why was I not summoned earlier?"

"This will allow time to plan a proper celebration," Saul announced with glee. "Go to the kitchen and tell them that the king has ordered a dinner in honor of his grandson tonight, then find the prince's mother, Ahinoam, and tell her the good news."

"I don't know why Judith didn't return before our son was born," Jonathan said to his father.

The servant departed, and Saul laughed. "There will be plenty of time to talk about the doings of Judith, and even David, for that matter. For now, though, let's you and I get drunk on new wine, because today you are a father, and now you will forever know both the joy and the anguish that come with having a child of your own."

Saul grabbed the back of Jonathan's neck and squeezed until merriment burst out from all of their muscles. They reveled the night away in celebration, though the happiness over the newborn lived within the fortress for only a few short hours. By morning, joy was as empty from their hearts as the drinking vessels that lay on the stone floor were from wine. Mirth and fermented fruit alike had spilled out like piss that had been dumped over the fortress walls.

"Treasonous!" Saul railed from his throne, his voice scraping the inside of Jonathan's wine-soaked ears. Though his head and body ached from dehydration, he was glad that for once it was somebody else who his father was screaming at.

Before them stood a room full of priests. Saul had ordered them to walk by foot throughout the night to face his wrath once word had arrived of their doings. At the king's side stood Doeg, the Edomite, who leaned over and whispered in his ear, a great grin of fortune on his face.

"It is treasonous at the very least to permit my enemy to pass through the sanctuary unharmed, let alone eat the consecrated bread!" Saul's voice rose with disgust.

Jonathan stepped forward. "Should we not let the priest speak, rather than simply take the word of a man who spends more time with sheep dung than with the divine?"

I really have come to despise Doeg, he thought. The chief herdsman stood up and glared in his direction.

It was not simply the fact that the man was an Edomite, though that would have been enough for most of Jonathan's kin. After all, these were a people who were often at the neck of the Israelites. Jonathan had not understood at first why his father had given Doeg such a high position among his ranks.

"This is how one builds stability," his had father explained. "It is imperative that we have peace with the Edomites at this time, so a strategic agreement to bring the son of one of their most prominent tribesmen into our fold meets an important objective for our nation."

He cautioned Jonathan that the key to a successful reign lay in the ability to maintain a delicate balance and told his son to take heed and do everything he could to build trust and comity between himself and the man he'd chosen to be his chief herdsman.

"Wars will come and go, so a king's allies must exist both within and outside of his immediate sphere, especially when a kingdom is as new as ours," he had elaborated.

Jonathan followed his father's command, and though it was awkward at first, he treated Doeg as if he was one of the other Israelites. He even let him run around with him and his brothers. After all, Doeg wasn't that much older than Jonathan himself. Over time, they became something akin to friends—that was, until everything happened during the standoff with the Philistine army.

The Israelites had been camped on the hill opposite the great horde, them with their howling behemoth who would come out and mock the army every morning. This was in the days just before David burst out of nowhere, when the men of Israel sat idle day and night, and each waited for the great battle that never seemed to arrive.

One afternoon, Saul had demanded an animal for sacrifice and had sent Jonathan to find the Edomite so that he could bring him a lamb without blemish. He could have sent one of his own servants to the makeshift pens that sat on the far side of the encampment, or into the fields to the west where the rest of the herds pastured. But Saul was insistent that Jonathan himself go and help Doeg select the perfect animal. The outcome of the war with the Philistines was uncertain, and the king wanted to seek favor with their God through a sacrifice so that he would in turn be merciless against their enemies.

Jonathan had searched for Doeg among the other shepherds, but none had seen him. At last he'd made his way to the Edomite's tent, where he walked in unannounced only to find the chief herdsman on top of the back of one of his male servants.

"Oh," Jonathan exclaimed in disbelief as the Edomite jumped up and wrapped himself in his robe. The servant, who screeched, rolled under a divider and disappeared from their sight.

"Forgive . . . me," Jonathan stammered. He had seen Doeg bed women before but had never considered him the type that also lay with men. Unsure what to say or do, he just blurted out that his father needed a lamb.

Doeg, whose cheeks had not blushed even the slightest, simply replied, "Alright," and led Jonathan into the sunlight to find the right animal as if nothing had happened.

As they worked their way through the pens, examining each lamb for the slightest of imperfections, Jonathan could not get the image of Doeg's naked body pressed up against his male servant out of his head. The act had aroused as much as terrified him, so much so that he did not know whether he should report the incident to his father, pretend that he'd never seen it at all, or run to the darkness of his own tent to touch himself.

He was considering all three choices as he and Doeg squatted in the wet hay. They were pretending to admire the white-and-black fleece of a perfect beast when Doeg finally asked, "Have you never been with a man?"

"No," Jonathan replied softly, his eyes locked on the sheep, though he could see Doeg's hand in his peripheral as it stroked the animal's coat. "I . . . I don't think we're allowed to be."

"Would you want to if you could?" Doeg's hand came closer with each petting of the fur.

"I . . . I'm not really sure." A lump formed in Jonathan's throat. He wasn't used to such forwardness, at least not when it came to this topic, and though he did find himself attracted to some men, Doeg made him feel awkward in this moment, so he just wanted it all to go away.

At last the herdsman's hand brushed up against Jonathan's. "We could try," he suggested, but Jonathan recoiled at his touch.

"No," he said sternly. "I don't think so."

They both stood up quickly.

"Forgive me, but I have seen the way you look at some of the soldiers," Doeg said.

Jonathan felt denuded. "I . . . perhaps . . . but—"

"Is it because I am an Edomite that you reject me?" Doeg accused.

"No, but . . ." Jonathan tried to collect his thoughts in order to form a cogent answer. He wanted to say that he had grown fond of Doeg over time, that he regarded him as something of a brother, even. He might have told him that while he did find some men physically enticing, just as he did some women, he usually preferred some type of emotional connection before there was any sex, but he had no time.

Suddenly the man he had known for years interrupted his thinking and launched at him with a surge of unexpected bitterness. "You practically tongue-fuck those Jewish men that carry swords with your eyes," Doeg spat. "But you think you're too good for me!"

"Huh?" Jonathan started to say, but the herdsman grabbed him by the robe at his chest and pulled him in.

"Well, at least try it before you say no." His mouth landed on Jonathan's, and the hairs on his beard scratched up violently against Jonathan's smooth face.

Jonathan tried to resist, but his mouth was forced open by Doeg's tongue, which had plunged inside and filled his own mouth with the taste of garlic and leeks from their midday meal. A hand came up roughly under his robe, and callused fingers pushed their way into the folds of his ezor until they found his flaccid member and gripped it tightly.

Unable to breathe, Jonathan pushed him away in a surge of panic. "Stop," he yelled, anger burning at his throat. "Why did you do that?"

"Because I wanted you to feel how incredible it could have been to have me as a lover, if only you had been able to pull the silver chalice of princehood out of your ass."

"A lover?" Jonathan was confused. "Lovers don't force themselves on each other. They let each make the decision to join together."

"Well, you just made a bad decision," Doeg spat.

"You took my right to a decision away altogether."

"Either way," Doeg growled, "don't even think of telling your father or anyone else about this. King Saul needs my family's support."

"I hadn't planned to—"

"We will go on like nothing ever happened, but any sign that I have been treated unfairly or that I might be removed from my position," he threatened, "and I promise you that the Philistines will be the least of Israel's worries."

At last Doeg stormed away, and Jonathan was left stunned by everything that had happened. Things were never the same between them, and Jonathan always made sure to keep a healthy distance. His last words to Doeg had been when he dragged David away from his presence in his father's tent.

It wasn't that Doeg was unattractive, it was that he was not attractive to Jonathan in that way. Jonathan wanted to tell him that he wished to remain friends, even after the unwelcome advance and his bitter words, but instead Doeg only glared whenever he saw him. Over time, the herdsman became just another bitter presence in his father's company. One of the many who floated close to the throne and waited for that one moment when opportunity would present itself, much like Jonathan's half-brothers and his father's concubine. Only now, Doeg's moment seemed to have arrived.

"And to hear Doeg tell me now that you let David take the sword of Goliath with him! That's just great. Now he has a powerful symbol to wave in the air and declare a rebellion, a rebellion that you yourself will have encouraged." Saul pointed his fingers at the priest in accusation.

Jonathan thought he saw Doeg wink at him ever so slightly, and he wondered if all of this stemmed from his rejection many years ago. He worried there had been whisperings and insinuations about himself and David, and that perhaps Doeg had heard of these and was jealous. But he and David had taken extra care not to tell anyone about their physical attraction. Jonathan had even paid his servants handsomely to keep their mouths closed, and he knew they would not betray him. But still, something about the look in Doeg's eyes gave him pause.

"Your son-in-law said that he was on a secret journey—that he was acting on your behalf," the high priest tried to explain.

"Any fool would know that that was a lie, especially one such as you, Ahimelek, with priestly tools you could have used to decipher the truth. Instead, you aided and abetted a pretender to my throne."

"How can one pretend to be chosen by our Lord?" Ahimelek asked. "One is either anointed at God's will or not." The room went still.

"Kill them!" Saul jumped up from his throne and pointed his finger at the priest again. "You heard him," he bellowed. "He has confessed to supporting another. He claims that David was anointed to succeed me, and this is blasphemy!"

There were gasps everywhere as the guards looked at the king, then at their commander for direction on what they should do.

"Kill them all!" Saul repeated, this time more wildly.

The leader of the king's guard paused for a moment before he stepped forward and looked up at Saul on this throne. "I'm afraid we cannot kill the Lord's priests, your majesty," he said with his head held high. "We are loyal, but we too fear the Lord before all men. We simply cannot kill them."

"But I can."

Jonathan turned his head around to see that Doeg had walked up behind Ahimelek, the high priest, in all of the confusion.

"This is the cost of a bad decision." The Edomite smiled, staring directly into Jonathan's eyes. Then he lifted his hand, reached around the priest's neck from behind, and slit his throat with a small dagger.

Ahimelek fell to the floor, and the priests who had come with him cried out in terror, but it was too late, as Doeg had already pulled his sword from his back. With a single swoop, he sliced open the stomachs of all who wore the priestly garments.

As their guts poured out onto their feet, King Saul declared Doeg as the general of one of his fiercest battalions over the screams and cries of the dying men and shocked armed guards.

"You will no longer herd sheep but men on my behalf," he boomed. "And I will have you bring to heel anyone who seeks to supplant me as the king of Israel, including the one man who you *will* kill in my name!"

#

"Tempestuous and impulsive fool," David's father chastised him loudly.

It had been many months since Saul had had the priests of Nob killed in cold blood. During that time, David disappeared, until at last, he had returned to Judah. Here in a large cave, he gathered a group of men, fierce fighters who were loyal to him and to his safety, and after several weeks, he called for his parents to be brought before him.

David had just explained to his father how during the months prior, while neither Saul nor any of David's own kinsmen knew of his whereabouts, he had crossed over into the Philistine lands. There he became an unnamed wanderer, a stranger who moved from town to town until he found himself at last in the great city of Gath.

Once inside its walls, he begged daily at the city gates and listened to the Philistine men who discussed the latest gossip from home and abroad. David, in rags and covered in dirt, bided his time in hopes of news that would indicate that King Saul had forgotten his anger. Once he was certain, he would return to his homeland and seek peace with the Israelite ruler, who he hoped would welcome him back into his household and return him to his station. Then he could have access to the one he loved more than any other.

David was remembering the feel of Jonathan's kiss when he overheard a couple of men talking by the cistern. "Isn't that the boy who killed our champion, Goliath, several years ago?" one of them said to another.

This made David emerge from his daydream back into the dust.

"It's the hair that makes me agree," the other responded. "We don't have many with that shade here in Gath."

David had hoped to remain unnoticed but knew the risk he assumed the minute he left Israel behind. An effort to save one's life sometimes meant having to chance it, or so he told himself, but now that his identity had been discovered, he wondered if this was one of his most ill-conceived ideas.

Several hours after the men departed, trumpets sounded and a small horde of soldiers approached the well.

"Show me this boy who killed our giant," Achish, the old and wrinkly king, roared as he came down from his palace to look at the one they called David face-to-face.

A chill went up David's back when he saw the menacing look of the time-hardened ruler and the dozens of armed guards who surrounded him. Without thought, he let the drool trickle down from his mouth until it hung in a long line from the edge of his beard to the ground.

"Whatta-hoop-hoop," he called out, and then he rolled his eyes to the back of his head and jerked his body this way and that way with spasms.

"This man looks insane," the king pointed out, and made a face as if he had eaten a bite of meat that had gone rancid in the summer sun. "This cannot be the one that they say killed tens of thousands to the Israelite king's thousands!" He laughed so hard that all of the men around him shook with convulsions as well. Finally, the king turned and lumbered away, until they had all departed back to the palace.

The skin on David's arms shivered at the thought that the king might reconsider his decision, so he leaned on a stick and pretended to hobble away into the desert. Once he was far enough from the city of Gath, he threw the stick down and ran for his life.

For three days he did not slow except to slumber briefly, until at last he found a cave near the town of Adullam by the forests of the Canaanites.

There he hid until a lonely shepherd boy wandered by. David called the child to him to talk and then sent him away with a message for his brothers.

Before long his brothers came, and they brought many others with them, as David's name elicited the utmost respect and loyalty from the tribe of Judah. Soon he was surrounded by a large band of men, and they worked day and night to build shelters in the cave. From there they hunted and fished in an effort to feed them all, and before long, the cave was almost a village unto itself.

Once David had regained his physical strength after his foray into the land of the Philistines, he sent for his parents to join him at the cave. They arrived at once, but instead of an embrace of gratitude for their son's safety, his father arrived with a long list of rebukes.

"It would have been far worse to be a prisoner of the gentile king Achish than to have died at the hands of a Jew such as Saul," Jesse admonished.

"So are you happy that I am alive?" David asked.

"Of course I am. But I worry, as always, about the amount of thought that goes into any one of your decisions."

"Well, then you might not like my next one," he said cautiously.

His father sighed. "I'm afraid to ask."

"You and my mother will go to the land of the Moabites. There, you will wait until things calm down between Saul and myself," David instructed.

"Why would I go to the Moabites for help?" Jesse was incredulous. "No, I will stay here in the land of my fathers."

"I'm afraid that's not possible. At least the Moabites are kin, whether you like to admit it or not. Your great-grandmother Ruth was from Moab, and as such, the king there has guaranteed me your safety."

"But why would you send us away?" Jesse whined. "We are not a part of whatever is happening, and I know that Saul will soon forget this whole thing. You are married to his daughter, after all."

"Saul's intention to harm me does not seem to be fading. With both my mother and you tucked away in Mizpah, there will be one less way for him to hurt me. He will not be able to capture you both and use you as bait if he cannot find you."

Jesse's shoulders slumped in defeat.

"You will leave tomorrow, but I have already been told by a prophet that I am to remain here so I cannot travel with you," David said. "Whatever is to become of me, it is all in the hands of the Lord. Either way, you will be safe until I am either restored or dead."

His father furrowed his brow and he looked closely at his son's face. "Those are the words of a future king." Jesse turned his neck and looked around at the many men of Judah who were at David's side, and his chest grew and his head rose tall on shoulders that no longer sagged.

"Forgive me, my son," Jesse said as he put a hand on David's arm. "I did not realize until now that the Lord had made my restless child into a man, and even into a leader. I can see now that you are different and that you are no longer the boy who chased after frogs in the river near our tents."

David beamed at his father's words.

In the morning, he waved goodbye as a small group of men led Jesse and his mother away toward the land of the Moabites. When they were gone, David squatted down onto a stone and thought about the love that his parents shared. His mind wandered back to Jonathan, wondering what his brown eyes with the bushy brows were looking upon at this very minute, and smiled.

Milkweed Wraps for
Soiled Bottoms

"I will not name him Mephibosheth!" Jonathan protested loudly on the day of his son's circumcision.

The thought of his child sharing a name with his fat amphibian of a half-brother turned his stomach, but Judith insisted. Three years ago, she had lost her eldest brother to a Philistine raid, and it meant more than anything to her that her first son be named after him.

Jonathan relented, but from the time the priest made the incision, he only referred to the boy as Sheth.

During the months after the ritual, Sheth became increasingly precocious.

When he was just over a year old, he discovered that if one grabbed hold of something higher than the ground, one could use it to pull oneself upright. Once on two legs, one could then will one's feet to move.

And move, Sheth's feet did. From the waking hour to bedtime, he used them to run this way and that way. Sometimes he ran to grab something on the table and throw it down onto the floor, like food or full cups of wine. Other times he ran so that his nurses had to sprint to stop him from leaving the fortress or falling off the edge of the stone walls down into the valley below.

No matter what Sheth did with his feet, Jonathan could not bring himself to do anything other than smile and laugh. Never did he reprimand him for the terror his newfound freedom inflicted on those around him, nor forbid him from doing as he pleased.

"He'll be a wild goat if you don't discipline him as any father would," Judith scolded, but Jonathan didn't care.

"Let him run free, Judith," he would tell her whenever she brought it up. "There will be plenty of time in his life to stand still, when the world will force him to be idle or his spirit to be confined. For now though, let him be a child."

Judith would roll her eyes and storm off in a hurry.

Since her return, their relationship was nothing like what it had been prior to her pregnancy—not that it was much of anything then either. The important task of succession completed, Jonathan and Judith spent as little time as possible together beyond what was necessary for the care of their son. Gone were the nights of intimate contact with little conversation, and in their place were milkweed wraps for soiled bottoms and little desire to make small talk about anything other than the best way to nurture Sheth.

Jonathan was thankful for his son. He had provided the answer to so many nagging questions.

For one, there was the issue of what to do with his time. He could have spent it worrying over where David was or anticipating the return of Doeg from the wilderness with David's head in his hands. Instead, his idle hours were filled with nuzzles and kisses on his baby's neck and giggles and cries of fascination at each of Sheth's bowel movements.

Then there was the fact that Sheth was a source of great happiness for his parents. Saul still wanted David dead, but a grandson was such a welcome distraction that at times he could go days without mentioning his son-in-law's name in anger.

Jonathan's mother also doted on the child's every move, and this warmed Jonathan, because he knew that being the wife of a king brought constant duties and, at times, unrelenting attention. Her little cherubic Sheth, though, would save his grandmother with many moments away from the scheming of the concubine Rizpah or the work of running a demanding royal household.

During one of those moments, Sheth was teetering on the balls of his feet with the king's crown in his hands while Ahinoam tried to coax it away with a ripe, red strawberry. Just then, Doeg entered the throne room.

Saul looked up from where he sat on the floor among carved donkeys and soldiers that he and his grandson had been playing with before the child had grabbed the golden circle from off his head. Jonathan's peals of laughter at the way his son had reduced his parents from royalty to common nursemaids faded abruptly.

"He is at Keilah," the Edomite announced proudly.

"Keilah?" Saul asked in confusion. He held on to the throne and used it to pull himself upright. "The pretender to my throne disappeared for over a year only to wind up in an inconsequential village over by Hebron? But why?"

"Apparently the men and women of Keilah were being attacked by the Philistines, and David showed up with five hundred men and drove them out of the city's gates."

"He commands an army?" Saul's voice began to rise, as it often did when the subject of David was brought up.

"I would hardly call a few hundred men an army, but nevertheless, many men of Judah have rushed to his side."

"Damn those Judeans and their weak loyalty to my crown. And you say David and these men are in Keilah now?" Saul somehow seemed taller, Jonathan thought as his father's voice filled out.

"At this very moment." A sinister look spread across Doeg's face.

"Then the Lord has delivered him into our hands, as Keilah is a tomb from which there is no escape," Saul said. "Prepare my guard. We leave in an hour."

All of the joy that Jonathan had felt with his son over the last many months bled out onto the ground, just as in his mind he saw a vision of David's blood pouring out once his father caught him in Keilah.

He did not wait to be invited. Instead, he jumped up and told his mother to return Sheth to Judith, then ran out of the room. With no time to waste, he threw on the king's armor and joined his father's guard.

He rode in their midst for two days until they had reached the walled city of Keilah. At the main gates, they learned that David had fled the city only a few hours before.

"How could he have known that I was coming?" Saul growled and looked in his son's direction with accusation.

Before Jonathan could deny that he had warned David, a simply dressed priest emerged from the walls.

"Abiathar, son of Ahimelek, the priest who you had killed for his actions at Nob, rides with David, and he carries the Ephod," the priest informed them all, though his tone was more indictment than explanation.

"One of Ahimelek's sons lives?" Doeg asked in surprise.

"He fled your bloody welcome when the other priests of Nob were treated so uncharitably, and now Abiathar uses the Urim and Thummim to advise David on behalf of the Lord."

A chill ran up the spines of all who listened, as until now, only Saul had been advised in such a manner. The king's face twisted violently, and he cursed the priest as he turned his horse around and thundered across the plains back to Gibeah.

#

A mournful cry rang out across the moonlit terraced hills that sat above the lowland valley near Keilah. Saul had forced his army to return only a few days after he rode back to Gibeah. He felt he had left too soon and blamed all of his generals and men for not stopping him. By now, all traces of David were gone, and there were only the haunting cries of what some insisted was a lilith. Even the fiercest of Saul's warriors quaked with fear, and swore that, indeed, this was a night spirit who foretold that they too would become graveless ghosts if they did not abandon their quest to pursue God's other anointed. But Jonathan knew the sounds were only the titterings of a screech owl, who hunted for prey just before the sunrise.

All of his brothers—Abinadab and Shua, Armoni and Mephibosheth alike—were gathered to break morning bread with their father, and to receive his orders on where they were to lead their men once the sun was high over the hills.

Jonathan was mid yawn when a group of bedraggled farmers were brought before them.

"Who are you, and why do you disturb my breakfast?" Saul asked as he sipped on a broth made from the bones of old ewes.

"Forgive us, our king, but we are Ziphites from the south of Hebron," one of the three men said with his head bowed low.

"That answers the who," Saul muttered, "but not the why." His eyes moved to Jonathan's, and Jonathan knew that his father meant for him to either hurry them up or to hurry them out.

"State your business," he urged them. "Afterwards, we will see that you are fed and clothed before you are sent back on your journey to Ziph."

"We are not on a journey." The man raised his eyes to look at Jonathan. "We have only come to tell the king that we have the man named David hiding among our strongholds near Horesh."

Mouths stopped chewing, and Jonathan looked over at his father, whose eyes widened.

"Where is this?" he asked with sudden interest.

"He hides somewhere near the hill of Hakilah, just outside of Jeshimon," another of the three men interjected.

"You have only to tell us when, and won't we, the Ziphites, go up and capture this man for you?" said the third.

Saul's brow wrinkled. "Yes," he said, "I think you will." He placed his cup down onto the table loudly and stood up.

"You will go back to the land of the Ziphites and find out the exact location of David's camp. My men and I will follow two days behind you, so as to not startle David and scare him away. On the second day of your arrival home, you and your people are to surround the hill from all sides. At the midday hour, we will arrive and ride up onto this hill of Hakilah and I will slay David with my own hands. Then you and all of your people will be rewarded handsomely. For it is no small matter to protect your king, and that is what you have done today."

After they received Saul's orders, the three Ziphites happily left to return home, and Saul demanded that each of his sons secure their own troops and ready them to depart in exactly two days.

Jonathan grew frightened that this siege of the hill of Hakilah would be an inescapable noose around David's neck. He conspired a plan, and his hands shook as much as his voice when he confronted his brothers with direct orders.

"I must ride ahead and assist the Ziphites in their preparations for this trap," he told Abinadab and Shua.

Shua raised an eyebrow. "I did not hear our father give you such orders."

"Nor did he." Abinadab slapped Shua on his chest. "You always were the stupid one of us three, or can you not see that Jonathan means to warn his friend of our father's plan."

"You can't do that," Shua protested. But then he seemed to sense that he would only be arguing with himself, so he sighed and asked, "But you will anyway, so what is it that you need your brothers to do for you while you are away?"

"I will split my men into two groups, and each of you are to take half as if they were a part of your own. What you command, they will obey."

145

"Oh really?" Armoni rubbed his chin as he and Mephibosheth stepped into Jonathan's tent.

"If you have any love for me as my brothers, you will turn your heads and allow me to do this unopposed," Jonathan pleaded with them.

"And why should we?" Amoni demanded resentfully. "When have you ever once done anything to show love for either of us?"

"Yeah," Mephibosheth agreed.

"No," Armoni said. "In fact, I think I will go to our father now and tell him that you mean to betray him so that you can lie at the foot of another man's bed."

"Then if you cannot step aside, I'm afraid you will have to be pushed aside." Jonathan's voice grew menacing.

A quick glance at his brothers told them all they needed to know. Armoni and Mephibosheth had barely any time to yell out before they were both gagged and tied up. Once secured, Jonathan had both men rolled up into carpets and placed onto the back of an ass. He paid a servant a fistful of silver to deliver the irritable goods to Gibeah.

"You are not to unfurl these carpets until you are in the fortress, and then only at the feet of our mother, Ahinoam. Tell her that she is to pay you again for your service to me, and then you are to run off into the heat of the day or coldness of the night before either of the snakes that are wrapped in these rugs have time to strike back."

After the servant rode away, Jonathan called for his uncle, Abner, who agreed to take control over each of the twins' regiments of men. Abner also saw no point in David's death, and though he knew their actions would enrage his brother, he told Jonathan that it was "better to be an honest man before God than a wealthy liar among kings."

Once he was convinced that his plan was secured and that his father wouldn't notice his or his half-brothers' absence, Jonathan mounted his horse and rode it until sweat lathered its coat and the hills near Ziph were in sight.

#

"There's a man," yelled one of the lookouts.

High on an outcrop, David crawled on his belly and peered down into the valley below.

"That is no mere man," he replied. "It is Jonathan, King Saul's son."

146

"Alone?" the lookout asked.

David stood up and whistled to the left, then pointed below. Two more men stood up, and one responded with hand gestures before they both made their way downhill.

David returned to the camp and stood in the center of his several hundred soldiers, who were all lined up in formation. A woodfire smoldered at his feet as a horse with his rider appeared over the ridge, flanked by the two lookouts that David had sent down to retrieve him.

The eyes of the man that stared back at him were dark and wide. He slid down from his saddle, and his neck turned from side to side to examine the armed men surrounding him.

"The harpist who couldn't so much as hold a spear now commands an army such as this?" Jonathan teased as he approached.

David smiled. "A year and a half on the run changes a person."

"David." Jonathan grinned back.

The two clasped hands, but then David pulled Saul's son into a brief but not overly familiar hug.

"We will share more later," he whispered into Jonathan's ear before he pushed him back. He shouted out to the men, "Here is a friend, and no greater one! He has come with the latest news from our king, and we will receive it. Then we will do what we do best—drink!"

The men nodded and cheered.

"Now go to your duties," David commanded, and they obeyed and broke formation.

"I'm not used to seeing you like this," Jonathan confessed as they walked to David's tent. "But it shows me what I have known all along."

They were alone now in David's dwelling, and Jonathan grabbed his hands and squeezed. "You will be king one day," he affirmed, "and I will be at your side."

David recoiled and stepped back at Jonathan's words. "I never asked to be king. I do not seek to supplant your father, or you for that matter, as the next in line," he protested, but Jonathan had already approached and taken his hands again.

"It matters not what you seek or what I want. This is the Lord's doing," he affirmed.

"Did the Lord's doing will you to approach my camp alone?" David asked. "My men could have easily shot you with a bow and arrow had they assumed that you were a mere scout for your father."

"I do not presume to know the will of God," Jonathan responded, "but I come to warn you that my father will have you in a death vice by this time tomorrow."

"How so?" David asked. He had been very particular about his place of hiding, but clearly if Jonathan knew where to find him, so did Saul.

Jonathan explained to him the plan for the Ziphites to surround the hill come the morning and for King Saul to ascend with two thousand men so that he could freely kill David himself.

David listened intently before he got up and walked outside. He called over a grizzled man who served as the second leader of the men and ordered him to prepare for their immediate departure. "We are to pack and move out in one hour. We will sneak down the back of Hakilah and make for Jeshimon before we turn into the Desert of Maon."

Saul will never find me among the araba and stones of that sunbaked land.

David knew the location of a craggy canyon with a hidden spring where they could live for months or even years unseen. Life in the desert would be harsh, but it would be better than death.

When he returned to the tent, Jonathan grabbed him by his shoulders and pulled him into a warm embrace. "I have missed you more than words," he said softly. Before David could reply, Jonathan had closed the small distance between their two faces and kissed his lips three times in quick succession.

Surprised by Jonathan's actions, David leaned his head back and chuckled. "There will be time for that later, but now we need to move."

This required the breakdown of the entire camp, but first there was his own tent. He instructed the handful of servants he had acquired over the months in Judah what to pack and how.

"Well aren't we the sort," Jonathan remarked as men came in and out of David's presence, seeking direction and responding to his orders.

"What do you mean?" David asked. He helped one of the servants wrap a sword in a small rug and placed it in a chest for transport to the desert.

"I mean that when we first met, it was I who gave orders to men and you who couldn't wait to bed me," Jonathan explained.

"Oh really?" David raised an eyebrow.

"Now it is you to whom men answer, and it is I who cannot wait to feel your flesh against mine." Jonathan's voice became husky, and he reached out and touched David around his waist.

"Nuh-uh," David cautioned him as he turned his head to make sure that no one else was present. "My men must only see the seriousness with which I take their service to me. They cannot know about you and me, so that means no fun until we are far away from here and everyone is safe from your father's forces."

"See what I mean?" Jonathan wrinkled his brow. "Somehow only you went out into the wilderness, and yet we both came back different people."

#

Dozens of small fires burned in patches. The circles of glowing embers were surrounded by groups of men who pulled cloaks up over their heads and leaned in toward the warmth. Along the periphery, a half dozen were still awake and standing with bows and swords, ready to sound the alarm and launch the sleeping men to their feet in defense of their leader.

Jonathan admired the loyalty that seemed to bind this group to David. He pulled his head back into the one tent that had been erected at the center of the fires, pulled its flaps closed, and tied them tightly.

"They appear to love you," he remarked, turning to David, who lay naked among furs in the middle of the tent's floor. Jonathan walked over and squatted down by him, his face right next to David's. "What I am trying to figure out is why."

David laughed, then reached his bare arms up out of the animal skins and threw them around Jonathan's neck and pulled him down on top of him with one movement.

"And none of them have even had the pleasure of my having made love to them," he whispered as his mouth found Jonathan's and bit down upon his lower lip.

Jonathan gasped at David's chew, and he could feel his eyes roll back into his head, unable to control themselves—like the rest of his body. "Uh," he moaned when David's hands found his ezor and pulled them down over his hips. Like the army outside, he was ready for David's command and would obediently follow his every order.

"I have missed you," David said, and when he stood up, the furs fell off his body.

Jonathan felt air beneath him as David lifted him into his strong arms, and the night passed in a series of caressed limbs and mind-numbing eruptions, until it was almost time for a new day.

Jonathan laid his head on David's chest at the realization of dawn, which tugged at his mind. "I do not think I can bear to be separated again," he whispered.

He was certain that they must be, regardless of how he felt. It was one thing for the king's son-in-law to be on the run, but a whole other for the king's own son. *No.* He reminded himself that he must return to his father and brothers.

In his heart, Jonathan had accepted long ago that being royal really meant doing whatever was good for the country. This did not mean doing what one wanted for oneself, unless what one wanted aligned with the role. He was very clear on the fact that, until the day came that Saul was no longer king, it was his unquestionable duty to follow him, to support his father in all things. Except, no matter what, he would have no active part in the killing of David.

However, staying here with David would be a way bigger step than just warning him of an impending attack. Staying would mean Jonathan would not only be disloyal to his father, but disloyal to God's anointed. While he loved both of these men, he loved God most of all, and accepted that whoever prevailed was the one the Lord willed, especially as it was clear now that both had been chosen.

Beyond this reasoning, there was the simple fact that, as the king's son, Jonathan's continued presence would probably put David in further danger. A prince would not be easy to hide for long, wherever they ran to, and staying at David's side meant making him an easy target throughout the rest of Israel. Like the Ziphites, others would seek to betray David for their gain. Then there was the threat beyond the borders, as David's force was not big enough to defeat an army of invaders from any one of their gentile neighbors, who would delight at the thought of capturing Saul's firstborn son and holding him for ransom.

Any way Jonathan looked at it, this meeting must end, and he must return to his family and the protection of the fortress walls in Gibeah. But the sad thought about when he might have another opportunity to hold David in his arms like this again caused tears to escape his eyes.

"Did water just drop onto my stomach?" David used a hand to wipe himself dry.

When Jonathan lifted his head, David pursed his lips and pulled Jonathan toward him.

"Don't cry, my love," he comforted him. "One day we will be together once more, and nothing will ever separate us again. There will be not only you and I, but all of our various children—by our many wives—will run around, and the endless days and nights will be filled with nothing but the love that we share."

"If only it were that easy." Jonathan sighed. "To love in the light instead of the shadows. In real waking hours and not in dreams."

He squeezed David with both of his arms and felt the warmth in his heart at his lover's words. He confessed to himself that, while he did not know what the future would hold, the life David described sounded like heaven.

There was a call like a morning bird, and he felt David's body tense up.

"That's the all rise," David explained sadly as he sat up straight.

"Oh, David." Jonathan's lip quivered. He threw his arms around David's neck and sobbed. "Why must we be filled with so much but be denied by so little? My father's anger could be pushed aside and we could all live in harmony if only he would choose to do so. I mean, after all, I am the one who should be upset by your anointing, and I am not! I am the one who will not be king when all is said and done. My father could go on and live the rest of his life in his position, then pass the crown upon his death to you, but instead he has gone completely mental, as if killing you will somehow lengthen his life and make him a king forever."

David patted Jonathan on the back and tried to soothe him. "It would be difficult for any man to accept that his legacy will end when his life does," he tried to explain, but Jonathan choked back his tears and lifted his head.

"Being a runaway has made you into someone even more special than you already were," he said with soaked lashes and dampened cheeks.

"And you, my dark-haired prince." David at last stood up. "You have always been more special than either you or anyone else has ever known."

Jonathan looked up at the incredible form of David's body as it towered above him. *This is a king*, he thought to himself.

He pushed up from his knees until he had stood up as well, and the two threw their arms around the other and leaned their heads onto one another's shoulders.

"May God grant you safety, and may all of your days and nights be filled with beauty and happiness until we meet again," Jonathan said as he lifted his head up and looked into David's eyes.

"Beauty and happiness have already filled my life because you have been in it," David replied, then they kissed as if all of creation found its source in their mouths.

David released Jonathan and walked to the edge of his tent, where he pulled on his clothing. "I must go now," he said, before he turned and abruptly walked out of the tent.

Jonathan stood in silence, naked and alone.

A Foul Air

There was a foul air that lingered in the darkness of the damp cave. Saul had pursued David through the desert of En Gedi, and it was there, near the Crags of the Wild Goats, that he had finally come close to achieving his mission.

Learning of Saul's proximity, David took a small band of men with him to find out firsthand just how many soldiers had marched with the king. They peered over the edge of a canyon as the sound of endless feet thundered by in unison.

Fearing that they might be spotted, David led his men into a cave, whose entrance was hidden by a dangling mass of wispy maidenhair ferns. As they pushed into the darkness, the men lit torches in order to search for bats and predators. Once they were satisfied that the void was clear, they sat around close to the cave's opening and joked about the ineptitude of Saul's thousands to cheer themselves up.

"They don't look like much more than well-fed fortress guards, not hardened men like us," one had assured, bringing the others to laughter.

David broke in and rebuked them. "Do not let me ever hear you disparage the army of Israel again."

Faces fell and silence rested on lips.

Suddenly a voice broke through the vegetation on the outside of the cave. "I need to piss," announced a baritone stranger.

"Yes, my king," another responded. "I will take your horse and wait by that patch of trees."

Footsteps grew closer, and the jostling of undergarments grew louder.

"It is King Saul," one of David's men whispered to him and to the others.

Another tried to persuade him to strike. "God said that he would deliver your enemies into your hands. Now is your chance!"

"Yes," implored yet a third. "Take your knife and slay him here and this will all be over!"

There was excitement and bloodlust in their eyes, and their words motivated David to seize the moment. He crept over to the mouth of the cave and peered through the ferns. There he found Saul, bare-assed and pissing. One arm held onto his robe, which he had gathered up and lifted above his hips. The other directed his stream to prevent any wetness from touching his clothing.

This is it! David encouraged himself as he grasped his knife with his right hand. He pushed it through the maidenhair until its point stood just a breath away from the king's back. All he needed to do was push it forward in a quick motion, and Saul would be dead. The blade would pierce through his back and rupture his heart.

This seems a terrible way for the first king of Israel to die—dick in hand and ass to the world.

The thought of Saul found in a heap in a state of extreme humiliation caused David to hesitate briefly. But if he didn't strike now, he knew that it was Saul's blade who would be at his back before long, so he urged himself forward. His muscles tightened as he pulled back his arm to add force to his impending thrust, but as he struck out into the air, concern for Saul's status once again worried his heart.

Though he despises me thoroughly, I have no hatred for him. That realization spun through David's head so that when he slashed forward, he turned his wrist back. On his recoil, a small corner of Saul's robe sliced off and fell to the ground.

"Ahhh," David heard the king say as he jiggled himself clean. He watched through the ferns as Saul bent down and pulled up his undergarments, then dropped his robes back around his body and walked away unharmed.

David kept his eyes on the king as he crouched down and slowly pushed his right hand back out into the air. He felt along the ground until he grasped the piece of Saul's robe that had remained behind. With a yank, he pulled it into the cave and turned to face his men.

"Why didn't you do it?" one asked with wild eyes.

"This was your moment to kill the man who wants you dead, and you let him go?"

Each man protested and shook his head in disbelief, but David held up his own to quiet them all.

"You are right," he agreed. "I could have killed King Saul right here—and easily, at that. But is it for me to kill God's anointed? Am I anyone to cut through the back of the man who our Lord, whom we worship, has made the ruler of all Israel?"

Skin tightened across the faces of his followers, who gave him looks of confusion and anger.

"No," David insisted. "None of us are. Only God can call for such a man to fall, and I am not God, just a poor wayfaring stranger in a land that already has its king."

At these words, the heads all of his men—including David's own—fell to their chests in humility. "You are right, David," one of them whispered. "We only mean to protect you."

"And I so greatly appreciate you all for it." David's heart felt full, but guilt covered over the warmth. "But I cannot ask you, or even myself, to go on hiding day after day and year after year for something that I did to anger our king . . . Even if I still do not know what it is that I did. No, I must release you from your vow to stand behind me and allow you to return to your homes."

"You are Judean, and you are our brother," a man responded, and the others nodded their heads. "We will not go home so long as you are in danger. No, we will follow wherever you flee, even to our graves in battle, if that is the Lord's will!"

They rallied around David, and he felt their love. Yet in his heart, he knew that he could not allow any of these men to die for him, so he squared his shoulders and marched right through them with purpose in his step.

"Where are you going?" his men shouted after him as the last of the maidenhairs fell from his face. "You will be killed!"

David's head pulsed and pounded.

This must come to an end, he told himself forcefully as he ordered his feet to march onward.

Once he reached the top of the hill, he looked down at the massive formation of Saul's troops and gasped. A small voice inside told him to run, but he quieted it quickly. He lifted his head into the air and called, "My lord! My lord!"

Down below, all noise ceased and all eyes moved upward.

"My king!" David shouted when he spotted Saul in the crowd.

The king turned his horse around and squinted at him. "David?" he asked in disbelief as he slid off of the beast and stood in the dust.

David's mind went blank, and his legs moved impulsively and his feet carried him down the hill with all of their might. Soldiers all around grabbed the hilts of swords and lifted blades into the air to protect their king, but David rushed forward before any of them could stop him. Instead of attacking Saul, he fell face first at the ruler's feet.

"My king," David cried, and his tears fell freely on Saul's skin.

"My son?" There was confusion in the king's voice.

"Why do you listen to people who say I want to kill you, when I love you?" David wailed.

"You love me?" Saul's voice twisted in response.

David did not look up but clung to Saul's sandals with his hands. "You are the only king of Israel, and I would do nothing to harm God's anointed."

"Would you not?"

A hand fell on his head, so David leaned back onto his knees and looked up. Then he lifted his arm and opened his palm. "Look here," he said through tears as he thrust it forward. "If I wanted to kill you, I could have done it before, when you were alone and unarmed and up on that hill."

"How did you get this?" Saul asked warily.

"There up on the hill, when you stopped to relieve yourself. I was to your back, inside a cave where you could not see me." He pushed his hand closer to Saul. "I lifted up my knife and cut the hem of your robe so that a corner fell off it, but not a hair on your head did I harm in any way."

Saul's eyes widened, and he used his hands to pull up his robe and shift it around quickly to examine it, until at last he found the spot on its back hemline where a piece was indeed missing.

"I have never tried to hurt you, even when I could have, yet day and night you seek to kill me. For nothing—for absolutely nothing!" David's voice grew louder.

"For nothing?" Saul appeared to be as baffled by their quarrel as David was. "But . . . I . . ."

"King Saul, I do not want to harm you. I never did. But may the Lord judge between you and me right now, because I have not sinned against you or Him in any way on your account."

Suddenly Saul's knees buckled. He fell to the ground next to David and wept as well. He hung on David's shoulders, then grabbed ahold of David's hands and begged him repeatedly, "Forgive me . . . forgive me."

"Of course," David reassured him softly, and hope filled his heart. At last he was no longer a hunted man, and this brought a fresh round of tears to his eyes.

When he had regained his composure, he pulled himself up and bent over to help Saul to his feet.

Saul put a hand on one of David's shoulders. "If you were truly my enemy, you would have killed me today, as clearly God delivered me into your hands by the cave. But you spared me, and now I know that you are a righteous man, David. You *will* be king one day."

Gasps rippled across the canyon.

"All I ask is that, when the time comes, you spare me and all of my descendants," Saul urged him. "Promise me that you will not kill any of my family yourself, even though you will supplant them."

"I would never harm any of your household, my lord, as your family is also mine," David assured him.

Saul threw his arms around David and hugged him tightly. When he released him, he returned to his horse and climbed up on its back.

"I will go now," he announced. "There are true enemies of Israel that this army must fight. And you, David, you are welcome to go wherever you please, as I will no longer seek to kill you or harm you in any way. May our Lord grant you peace and safety."

Saul kicked his horse and trotted away. He was followed by the rhythmic sound of three thousand pairs of feet that also stomped a dusty retreat out of the desert and away from David's life.

The sound of thousands of broken hearts bled into a stone structure that sat on a lonely hill just outside of the city of Ramah. The prophet Samuel had died two days earlier and was quickly buried there in a chamber under this home. His body had been lowered and sealed in a hollow in the ground, but his memory lingered. It was in honor of this that men and women traveled across Israel to pay their respects to what had been one of the most important men in all of their lives. From leper to lord, all knew that their God spoke through this prophet. Now he was no more, and a sense of worry permeated the air. They grieved his descent but also shared a common anxiousness over who, if anyone, would fill the old man's sandals.

Though Samuel had not spoken to any of them in ages, Saul insisted that all of his family ride out to Ramah with him, and it was there that Jonathan studied the troubled profile of his father's face.

"It seems like only yesterday that he told me I was to be king," Saul said softly when the chants and cries ended and the masses turned around and began their journeys home.

"Perhaps the time of the prophets has ended," Jonathan mused aloud.

"Why? Because there are princes?" his father asked in annoyance. "There will always be a need for those who can tell us what we cannot hear otherwise."

He began to walk, and Jonathan followed along beside him.

"I know I can certainly say I often disregarded Samuel's words, and look at the troubles it has brought me," Saul continued.

"But I thought all was settled now and that David was free to return to Gibeah after your encounter with him in the desert of En Gedi," Jonathan said.

"Return to Gibeah?" Saul stopped and shook his head. "Why would he ever do that?"

"He's married to your daughter, is one good reason."

"Ha!" Saul laughed. "Michal, at her own insistence, was given away in marriage again, but this time to Patiel, son of Lash, only two weeks ago. Why do you think she is not with us today?"

"I had assumed she was preparing for David's return."

"Michal is decisive. She would never be kept by a husband who did not maintain her father's favor," Saul muttered. "Unlike the king's other children."

He started to walk again, but Jonathan hurried and stepped in front of his father so as to stop him. "Did you or did you not make peace with David?" he demanded.

"You cannot make peace with a serpent," Saul answered bitterly.

Jonathan became exasperated. "You yourself came back and said that he could have killed you if he wanted to but that he showed you favor and devotion!"

"As I said, all snakes are slippery. They lie on their bellies and slither their way out of danger until you find them poised to strike you even harder on the neck."

"So in other words, we hate David again?" Jonathan threw his hands in the air. "It is impossible to keep up with you. One day he's a hero, the next he's a usurper, then he's a son-in-law, next a hunted criminal, then a friend, then a foe yet again. When will this ever end?"

"When the bones of either he or I have been gathered to our fathers, and for once I am clear whose bones they will need to be," Saul avowed. He pushed Jonathan aside and stormed away toward the rest of his family, who stood in waiting.

"Oh, David," Jonathan groaned. "Will we ever know peace together?"

He wandered the opposite way from his father, and when he reached the stones around Samuel's hill, he sat down and sighed. Then he fell to his knees and threw his face into the dirt and prayed.

"Most righteous Father," he entreated his creator. "I humbly throw myself before you and ask for wisdom and for mercy, not just for myself, but for all of those that are in my life. For my father, the king—would that his spirit at last be settled. For David—grant him safety and security. May he come into his own, at the right time, and not suffer harm at the hands of my father. Oh fearsome and gracious God, is it wrong to love them both? To be loyal to my own as he was called forth by you yourself, and to be loyal to the man who walked into my life and seized my heart? I ask again, is my love wrong?"

He lay there on the ground in silence until the soft patter of feet approached his body in the setting sun.

"Rise up, son of Saul, and follower of the one true God," a voice called down to him.

Curious, Jonathan lifted his head up very slightly from the dirt to see who was speaking. While he had never seen the man who towered above him before, or heard his voice, something about the timbre made his hands shake and his heart tremble.

"The Lord hears all, sees all, and knows all," the stranger proclaimed.

"Who . . . who are you?" Jonathan managed to say.

The figure was outlined in red and orange against the sky, and the fading light at its back was just enough to blind Jonathan from seeing his face.

"It is for your father's sins, not yours, that the house of Saul will fall to the ground, and all of his sons with it. For it is he who failed to obey the Lord's commands."

"How . . . how do you . . . ?" Jonathan struggled from the dust to speak as questions swirled through his mind.

"You are not rejected because of the love you hold inside, for the Lord sees you and knows even the hidden spaces of your heart."

Love? Is he speaking of my father? Or perhaps of David?

"Did not Moses tremble from the cleft when he looked upon the Lord's presence?"

"I am afraid too," Jonathan at last cried out.

"How much more so should the kings of Israel fall down in fear? It was there on that rock that all firstborns, including those of men, were claimed. And though for five silver shekels, you were bought back from the hands of Aaron, all men belong to God—especially the sons of Saul. For it was He who made them kings at all who told Moses that He is slow to anger, and that He abounds in love and faithfulness."

"Go away from me, I beg of you." Jonathan lowered his head in terror.

"The Lord forgives, yet He will not let the guilty go unpunished, even to their children's children. It will be as it will be. And though the head of the family is cut off, even the hand will pull the body along the ground by its fingernails to find a way back into the Lord's presence, for did not the hand remain strong?"

At those words, a light breeze blew over Jonathan's own hands, and just as suddenly, the air went still and all of his fear was gone. After a moment, he pressed his palms into the ground and used them to push his body up with great effort until he was stood up on wobbly knees. He quickly dusted off his tunic. When he'd finished, he looked up to ask the stranger more about who he was and what he had said to him, but he found that the man was gone.

The sun's glow was at last snuffed out by the horizon, and Jonathan was alone in the darkness, where all was silhouettes of ochre and violet. To his left in the distance, he could see the light from a lantern that swung on a pole. It was held by a servant who was leading his family back to the caravan they had joined to travel here from Gibeah.

Jonathan pivoted back toward the darkness and strained his eyes once more for any signs of the stranger. With a sigh, he turned again and headed for the caravan himself. As his feet moved along the earth, his mind raced over the words that had been spoken to him, and he wondered what it all had meant. There had been something about his father, and there was much about the Lord, yet it was the stranger's sparse words on love that lingered.

Yes, in Jonathan's heart he at last understood that it was not the love he had for David that was odious. For when God had removed his hand from Moses's eyes, he'd commanded that his people should not prostitute themselves in front of their false gods. No, Jonathan and David's bond was not about idols, but instead was abounded in love and faithfulness, just like the Lord they both worshipped.

#

"Oh yes, I love you too," David moaned to Abigail, his new wife.

He was sprawled out across a mass of cushions, where he lifted his arms and put them around the narrow waist of his beautiful goddess, her firm, ripe pomegranates shaking ever so enticingly in front of his face.

Abigail purred, "Ah, my husband," and David felt her body shake as her waters mixed together with his in a pool of newly established matrimony.

They both panted and smiled as she rolled off him and onto her back alongside his body. There he could feel her breathing slow before it fell into that steady lull that came with deep sleep. David was ready for another go himself, but he recognized that his new wife's exhaustion was to be expected after all that had transpired over these last few days.

He had not anticipated that he would ever be wed again, as he was not sure he believed in second wives. That, and the fact that he deeply loved Jonathan and wondered how adding another wife might affect him. But when he thought more about it, he kept asking himself why that love had to stop all other relations. After all, he needed release as much as he needed to procreate and to have children. So he decided that there was no harm in adding another to his fold, though admittedly, when he rode out to Carmel three or four days ago, it had been the last thing on his mind.

Saul had removed his foot from his neck, but David still needed to feed the nearly six hundred men who had stood by his side day and night over the last two years. Hunger didn't dissipate just because the king decided to let you live.

When he heard that the rich man was shearing his sheep, he'd known it was the perfect time to claim payment. It was David's men who had protected his herds in exchange for meat while they hid near Carmel. So, seven of his best men rode out from the wilderness to at last collect, but when they arrived, the rich man, whose name was Nabal, refused them.

"Who is David?" he asked, as if he had not benefited from the strength of this very man's security. This was the man whose shields and weapons had managed to scare off the Philistine raiders that regularly poached Nabal's herds and ran off with his best goats and sheep.

"The bread and water I have here is for my own shearers. It is my men who will eat all of the meat we roast, and not some band of ruffians that have no homeland of their own."

David's delegation were dumbstruck at the response, as they had anticipated a warm welcome. When they returned to David, despondent and empty-handed, David became enraged at both Nabal's words and at his treatment of his men. He wasted no time in gathering up four hundred of his men, and he urged them to prepare for battle.

They marched hard toward Carmel, and they were storming like thunder onto Nabal's land when they unexpectedly stumbled upon a beautiful woman who sat alone upon a donkey, waiting for them. Behind her were another five donkeys, each loaded with heaps of goods tied onto their backs.

"Whoa." David slowed his horse as the woman climbed down and bowed to him. "What do we have here?" he asked curiously.

"Forgive me, my lord." She stood and looked up at him in grave concern. "I was not home when your men came to my house and asked for comfort."

"Are you the wife of Nabal?" David asked in surprise.

"I know the Lord protects you," she said with great passion on her tongue. "My husband is a foolish man, and he does not know that I am here before you now, begging for your forgiveness."

A bemused smirk turned up the corners of David's mouth. *What kind of woman rushes out to protect her foolish husband in this manner?* he wondered.

"A good one," he then answered himself aloud.

"Huh?" the woman asked.

"Um, I meant . . . what is your name?"

"Abigail," she responded.

Hearing it aloud stirred something in him. David climbed down off his horse and approached her.

"I have brought food and wine," she explained quickly. "May I find favor in your eyes, and may you and your men spare both my husband and myself for his foolishness."

Her begging aroused David, and he found his head spinning with thoughts of her lips, wondering what her mouth might taste like. *Honey?* He raised a brow.

"Go home in peace," he said aloud, though inside he wanted to ravage her. He would take her right here on the back of her donkey, he decided.

"Oh, thank you," she cried, and the vision of her naked faded away.

David raised his head up. "On your account, everyone in your husband's household, including Nabal himself, will live."

Abigail fell at David's feet and wept until he lifted her up by that perfect chin. She thanked him again, then ran up the side of the mountain and turned back to look at him once before she went over its crest.

"Now that is a woman any man would be proud to call a wife," David said to his nearest riders, and they all nodded in agreement.

They led the donkeys back to the camp and to the rest of the men, who had waited behind to guard their supplies. As they unloaded the bread, meat, and wine, word came back that Nabal had died instantly when he heard of his wife's actions.

At this, David left his men alone to their ample feast and rode to Abigail's side as swiftly as he could. There he stayed until the widow's husband was buried. Once mourning was completed, David hoisted Abigail into his arms and pushed her up onto his horse, leading her back to his band of brothers.

Then he sent for the priest, Abiathar, who married them before the Lord under a tangle of nearby grapevines. David led his new wife into his tent and made love to her across the pillows on the ground, upon which she now slept soundly by his side.

Heady with lust, his mind wandered from Abigail back to Jonathan. He lingered over the last time, in this very tent, their own love juices had been poured out together. In the darkness of the firelight, he imbibed freely on the memory and let himself become intoxicated from this wine.

#

"Pour me more!" Armoni ordered the servant who was leaning over the table with a skin of fermented grape held over Armoni's cup.

"What sorrow are you trying to drown?" Abinadab asked, sucking his teeth.

"The one where I was born into this mess of a family," Armoni snapped back, and Mephibosheth snorted.

"Boys," Ahinoam interjected. "Please stop it. It is tiresome, all of this constant bickering. Your father insisted on us all eating together this evening and I, for one, would like to do that in peace for a change."

"Funny," Rizpah grumbled. "I didn't hear anyone actually ask what you wanted."

"Stop!" Jonathan slammed both of his fists onto the table as he stood up. "I agree with my mother. Why can we not ever get together without it turning into a fight?"

Shua, who was at his side, erupted into hysterical laughter. "The veins in your neck look like they are about to burst," he howled, wrapping both arms around his stomach.

Jonathan sighed. "I give up." He fell backward into his seat and dropped his head into his hands.

"You always were so quick to give up," Armoni chided him. "It is quite a womanly quality. Makes me wonder if all of that talk about you and David being a little *too* close"—he tipped his hand at the wrist—"is more than just gossip."

Abinadab sprung from his side of the table, nearly knocking Jonathan's chair over. "Don't you ever say something derogatory about my brother." He stabbed his finger into the air. "You wish that you were half the man he is."

"Oh please." Rizpah giggled.

"Now, don't you laugh at my son." Ahinoam's voice rose, and it was so unexpected that Jonathan lifted his head again to see that her face had gone as red as sacrificial blood.

Suddenly every single one of them was on their feet screaming, each louder than the next. Arms were pumped into fists, and fingers were pointed into faces in hot fury and baseless accusation. Jonathan stared in disbelief. The cacophony of voices had become so deafening that he could no longer hear any single one over the others.

When the long shadow of a tall figure grew across the length of the table, one by one, each family member swallowed their words in fear. At last, only the voices of the two who were seated farthest from the head remained.

"... and now everybody believes that Jonathan lies with David as if he were his own wife!"

"... so the witch said that your sons will never be kings!" Armoni and Rizpah shouted from separate sides of the table into the deafening silence that spread out across the room.

"Oh," Rizpah said suddenly in great surprise, lowering her eyes and bowing her head. Her son saw his mother's actions, and when he understood why they'd come about, his face turned ghostly pale. He closed his mouth and stood, silently staring at the far wall behind Jonathan.

"What?" Saul suddenly screamed with violence as hot as the burning sulfur that had destroyed Sodom and Gomorrah.

Jonathan had never heard him erupt so loudly before, so he clenched his fists in anticipation of the dense smoke that would rise up from this red-hot furnace.

"Who says this about my Jonathan?" Saul roared with righteous indignation. "I will tear the limbs from their dead carcass myself."

Not one of them dared to respond, even to attempt to calm the king down.

"And you—" He seethed at Armoni. "If I ever hear you say such a thing about your brother again, I will feed you to lions bit by bit, as I will not have any one of my sons be a Cain to another's Abel!"

"Um . . . yes . . . Sorry, Father," Armoni replied weakly.

He next turned his face to Rizpah. "Wicked woman. Is it any wonder that your son speaks like this? He crawled out from your poisonous loins on his belly and now slithers on the ground alongside his forked-tongued mother."

The concubine's eyes began to pool with water, but Saul would not be stilled. "It is sinful that a Hebrew woman, who was blessed to have sons with a king, has turned to a medium in vile disobedience of our laws. Where is this witch?"

A sob from Rizpah's mouth grew into a throaty wail.

"You will answer!" Saul pounded his fist so hard onto the table that Jonathan had to catch a cup of wine to keep it from falling over the table's ledge. "Who but God dares to proclaim to know what will happen to my wife's sons?"

"Endor," Rizpah answered weakly. "She lives in Endor, near the edge of the Jezreel valley."

"You are right to tremble," Saul growled. "How dare you seek out a spiritualist! It isn't any wonder that I did not make you a wife, for my Ahinoam would never have stooped to consort with mediums."

Rizpah ran over and threw herself at Saul's feet. "Forgive me, my lord . . . forgive me," she sobbed.

"Be gone from my sight," he said in disgust. "And take your useless sons with you. I have done all that I can to make worthy men out of them, but I have failed. It was impossible for me to counter your unholy influence."

"No, my lord," she begged.

"Go." His voice dripped in disappointment. "Do not appear in my presence again until you have made right your sins. Sacrifice a thousand bulls if you must, but do not ask to return to this fortress, or into my presence, unless you have been sanctified and cleansed from all of your unrighteousness."

Jonathan could not believe his eyes when Rizpah and her two spiteful sons, the ones who had haunted all of their lives day after day, crept out of the room in disgrace. Never had his father rebuked any of them so fiercely. The fact that it had happened in public, where servants as well as family could bear witness, made it clear that Saul wanted them out of Gibeah immediately, and potentially out of his life forever.

Once they were gone, Saul sat down in his chair as if he had just returned, exhausted from a great war. "As for you, I expected better." His voice was soft and low now as he addressed Ahinoam.

He motioned to the boys. "Go and take your mother to her quarters. She seems to have caught a spirit from Rizpah, because the wife I married—the one who I have known all of these many years—has never once raised her voice the way that I heard today. I believe she must be overwrought and in need of rest to help her recover. Hmm, hmm." He stroked his chin. "I believe she will need at least two weeks before she can come out into sunlight once again."

Abinadab and Shua leapt up and helped their crestfallen mother to her feet, but as Jonathan pushed his chair back to join them, his father commanded him to stay. "No, not you," he said firmly. "I will speak with you alone once your mother and her other sons have left."

Jonathan sat back down slowly while Saul dismissed the many servants who were lined up along the walls to attend to the family this evening. At last he whispered instructions to the final man, who nodded and left at once.

What will he do to me? Jonathan worried now that Armoni had put his secret into his father's mind.

Soon the cavernous room was completely empty of everyone except for father and son. They sat in uncomfortable silence for a few moments.

What is he waiting for?

But they both remained lost in their own thoughts, until Aber appeared at the door.

"Do you have the soldiers with you?" Saul demanded to know.

"Yes," Abner replied. "They are just outside."

"I want them to have a cage made. I do not care about its beauty or craftsmanship. I want it fully completed by the morning according to my designs," Saul told his brother, who nodded. "Then have those same men gather dozens of rocks, large and small. They will place the cage and rocks in the center of the courtyard. There will be a stoning at this fortress."

Jonathan swallowed quietly, but his mind loudly raced to unpack what he was hearing. *He plans to kill me in front of everyone.* He trembled within.

"And as for you, Abner," Saul continued. "After you send them away with my instructions, you are to wait outside, as I will have another task for you shortly."

Jonathan braced himself as his uncle left them alone again. Tension rose up his throat like bile as his father forcefully dropped both of his arms onto the wooden tabletop with a loud thump.

"It's an abomination!" Saul screamed in rage. Over and over again, he slammed his forearms and fists against the table, his eyes wild with a savage madness.

Without thought, words flew out of Jonathan's mouth just as tears flew from his eyes. "It was uncontrollable," he cried out. "I really don't know how to explain it, but from the first second I met David in your tent, I fell in love with him, and—"

Suddenly, Saul stopped his banging and looked at Jonathan's face. The king's intense and narrow eyes widened in wonder and surprise. His whole body began to shake, until at last it erupted with hot laughter that spewed uncontrollably from his mouth.

"Not that," he hollered heartily between guffaws.

"Huh?"

"Not David." He held onto his sides.

"But you said it was an abomination . . ." Jonathan cocked his head to the side in confusion.

"No." Saul eased his laughter into a lighter chuckle. "I really don't care who you fuck."

"You don't?" Jonathan's mouth fell open.

"What men do in their own tents is no concern of mine." Saul flicked a tear away from his eye, then sobered up. "What I mean to say is, ordinarily I would not care at all, but the truth is that when one of the men is a prince of Israel and the other seeks to supplant him, I do care some. Maybe I even care quite a bit. But that is a conversation we will need to have at another time. There are things that must be attended to now, and together we will have many years to reflect on your poor decisions. Perhaps we can even find you a man more fitting to take to your bed."

As ever, Jonathan was thoroughly confused by his father. "Then what were you screaming about and calling an abomination?"

Saul's face turned to stone, and his voice simmered. "That the mother of my own sons would ask a medium to tell her my future . . . and yours!"

"Surely you do not plan to kill Rizpah with stones?" Jonathan gasped. Even though he could not stand her, he did not wish to see her killed in such a brutal manner, and in front of the family she had been a part of for so long.

"Of course not," Saul bellowed. "You and Abner will ride out from Gibeah this evening with a thousand men. Together you will find this witch of Endor and bring her here to me. She will answer for her sins with each rock that is hurled at her wretched body, until she is nothing but pulp and mash."

Another figure came through the door.

"You summoned me, lord?" Doeg bowed his head.

Saul continued to look at Jonathan. "Now go and ready yourself. I have my own plans that I must attend to."

Achish II

A pile of stones lay around a cage in the center of the courtyard. Jonathan eyed the rocks as he passed them by.

What a way to die, he thought as a shiver went up his spine.

He had only departed the fortress two days ago with Abner, to search for the soothsayer as his father had commanded. When they made it to Bethel, word had come that they were to turn back immediately with the one thousand men and head straight to Gibeah.

"But he just ordered us away?" Jonathan asked in surprise.

The messenger replied, "The Philistines have sent a party to raid from Ekron, and the king commands your return to protect the fortress."

Jonathan wondered why his father had called them home if it was merely a raiding party. Abner and he had taken less than a third of the men that were stationed at Gibeah.

"How large is this Philistine force?" he asked the messenger, who joined them on the ride back home.

"I'm not sure, but the fortress lay unprotected, as your father sent his other two thousand men out yesterday morning with Doeg at their helm."

"For what purpose did they ride? Was there another raid in a different location?" Jonathan pressed.

The messenger hesitated, then confessed, "The king sent the Edomite south to find and deliver the man called David to him."

Irritation tore through Jonathan's mind, but he'd kept his composure and ridden on.

Now, as he passed by the pile of rocks, he wondered if they'd ever really been for the witch at all, or if his father had sent him to Jezreel as a distraction. Perhaps he had planned to bring David back to Gibeah while

Jonathan was away up north, and have David killed by these stones right in front of everyone.

Saul smiled when Jonathan found him in his quarters. "I am glad you have returned." He was lounging on an embroidered couch with a cup of wine.

"Are we to head to Ekron to defeat the Philistines?" Jonathan asked with a furrowed brow.

"What Philistines?" His father hiccupped before he took another sip.

"The ones that crossed the border and are raiding our lands?"

"Oh." Saul flexed his bare feet, which extended out from beneath his rich robe of golden threads. "It turned out to be false information." He sat up and patted the cushion next to him. "Sit down."

Jonathan obeyed his father. *He must be drunk.*

"Have some wine. In fact, my new cupbearer is young and muscular."

"Wait . . . what?"

At that, a strapping man in a short tunic came out with a wineskin and a cup. He approached Jonathan with a toothy smile.

Saul winked at Jonathan, who could feel his entire body flush with embarrassment.

What is he thinking? he asked himself in horror, but to the room he said, "Uh, no thank you."

Saul tilted his head to the side and raised his shoulders. "Not your type?"

"Oh my goodness." Jonathan sighed in exasperation as he tried not to look at the cupbearer.

The king waved the servant away, then took a sip of his wine. "You are a prince of Israel and can have any man . . . or woman, for that matter. In fact, maybe a new wife might interest you instead?" He raised his eyebrows.

"A what?"

"One son is not enough," Saul explained. "If you have grown tired of Judith, I am sure there is more than one match I can have your mother make for you. Perhaps two or three new wives will keep you too occupied to worry about anything but babies."

Jonathan stood up.

"Oh, piss," Saul chastened him. "Don't be like sour wine. There are benefits that come with being royal, and you, my son, need a distraction to take your mind off other things."

"By other things, do you mean David?" Jonathan's voice grew tense.

There was silence for a moment, then Saul cleared his throat and followed it with another sip of wine. "Do not say that name in my presence," he muttered.

"I will not even ask what changed your mind this time," Jonathan said. "I know about Doeg and his mission. All I know is that, for whatever reason, whatever spirit has been put upon you will not rest until David, or all of us, are dead. But know this: you can send ten thousand chariots out from this fortress, and not even they can stand against the word of God. So I implore you one last time, as someone who deeply cares about you, not just as my king, but as my father, leave David alone."

Saul's head fell to his chest in shame.

"Years and years of all of our lives have been wasted in pursuit of this one man—time stolen by your own hands—and we have all suffered because of your own fear," Jonathan said.

"He frightens me." His father whimpered like a child.

"That may be so, but he has had ample opportunity to strike out and has never done so. Yet you have made it the mission of all of our lives to harm him, only the cost has been to us, perhaps more than to you. Now, this time, if and when Doeg returns empty-handed, I beg of you—erase your hatred of David from your mind and let us all live in peace!"

As Jonathan stormed away, he could hear his father hiss for more wine.

Outside he ordered two guards to hastily dismantle the rock pile and have the precious iron from the cage taken to a blacksmith and made into weapons.

He walked to the fortress edge and moodily stared out. *Was all of this worth it?* he asked himself as he thought of David. Perhaps it would have been better had he never appeared out of nowhere and killed the giant. Then they wouldn't have met in his father's tent. Then he would never have known what it meant to be connected to someone so deeply. To know the pain and the passion that was love.

"Ugh," he muttered aloud.

All he wanted to do was to be with David, and yet at every turn, they found themselves further and further apart.

It was then that the cupbearer's firm thighs entered his mind.

He was attractive. He laughed to himself.

Since becoming physical with David, Jonathan had scarcely lain with another person. A few months back he had tried to visit one of the women of the tents, but he'd found himself flaccid and uninspired.

"Perhaps you have another taste?" the prostitute had suggested, pulling back a curtain to introduce two naked men.

Though their forms were enticing, Jonathan remained disinterested. He decided to leave and told himself that if he ever were to get intimate with a man again, other than David, it would need to be with one of his own choosing. He did not just want to lie with a random person.

He had chosen someone only recently, but he ultimately had not been the one.

There was a member of the king's guard whom he had repeatedly caught eyeing him when he would visit his father in his throne room. Giddel was his name, and Jonathan had laughed to himself when he first heard it. He wondered how someone called "grow" had gotten such a moniker, and whether this was from birth or something earned in adulthood as the result of some kind of magical appendage.

I'll have to find out, he vowed.

One evening, Giddel had been leaving Saul's service when he approached Jonathan as he came down from the fortress wall. "Shalom," Giddel greeted him, and somehow that simple salutation led to them being alone and naked in Jonathan's bed.

Quickly he confirmed how Giddel had received his nickname, but when it came time to do something more than stare at it in wonder, David crossed his mind and all thoughts of frivolity vanished.

He had been the last one of either sex to share Jonathan's bed, and none had stirred an interest at all since . . . until he'd seen the cupbearer today.

It was not that he didn't crave sex. It was that he craved the connection he had with David more. The spiritual aspect heightened the physical for him, and in David's arms he felt each layer of his being cover over the other. From body to soul to spirit, no one else elicited anything close to the feelings that he had for David, and that left him alone in a desert of celibacy during all of this time that they had been forced to be apart.

His mother crept up behind him. "Someone on your mind?" she asked in a sweet tone. "Only another can make us grin like that."

"Oh." Jonathan turned around. "Mother."

Ahinoam put her arms around him and squeezed. Saul had released her from confinement, and now, wrapped around him, her faint smell of oil and spice made Jonathan feel safe.

She released him and stepped back. "I know about everything now," she confessed.

"You know about—"

She put a finger over his lips. "One thing that women teach each other is that all men have three parts when it comes to their beds, but not all receive them in equal measure."

"What do you mean?" he asked her gently.

"There is duty, there is lust, and there is love."

He shrugged. "I don't understand."

"Most men accept their duty, all men are fueled by lust, but few men ever find love, though all yearn for and seek it out. Count yourself blessed, my son, for you have experienced all three."

"Oh." Jonathan flushed with embarrassment.

"I know Judith was not a love match for you, but duty has been ful-filled. Lust you found in the women of the tents as well as the men in the fields of battle. Your father, as unstable as he can be at times, only sought to assuage that part of you by presenting his cupbearer. How many sons could say the same about their own fathers?"

"Not many . . . I guess?" he replied in more of a question.

"Love came for you in an unexpected person, as love does. You did not ask for it, nor did you deny it, as love in its purest form comes from a place that is foisted upon us without permission. Love, true love, is a blessing and a gift from heaven. Be proud that you have tasted its wine, even if it was a single drop that was poured out into your desert-parched mouth. For your thirst has been quenched more than many who have lived before you, as most are not as fortunate to taste such sweetness."

Ahinoam stood on her tiptoes and kissed Jonathan on his forehead. As she walked away, he returned to his thoughts and felt confident that it was indeed all very much worth it after all.

He quietly meandered back to his quarters and had hardly even gone inside before a servant announced that his brothers had come to speak to him.

"Let them in at once," Jonathan instructed the man, who left and re-turned quickly with Abinadab and Shua. After he'd led them into Jonathan's room, he departed again, and the two men found seats that they plopped down into.

"You weren't gone long, were you?" Shua joked.

"Long enough I guess," Jonathan mumbled.

"Long enough for what?" Abinadab pressed him.

"I would rather not talk about it." Jonathan sighed.

"Ohhh . . . You are worried about Doeg and David," Shua said, as if he had just invented the wheel.

"You chittering hyena," Abinadab huffed at his brother. "You weren't supposed to say anything."

"I just think he would want to know," Shua protested.

"Know about?" Jonathan asked.

"But you always do that," Abinadab said. "I don't understand why you can't ever keep your mouth shut about things."

"About what?" Jonathan was irritated now.

"Why does this family have to have secrets, though? See, I find that much more aggravating than simply telling the truth," Shua barked back at Abinadab.

"What would I want to know about?" Jonathan screamed out, and both his brothers stopped their argument and turned to look at him.

"That we took care of it for you," Abinadab confessed.

"I am already in a mood, and the two of you have me completely vexed. Say what you mean or get out and leave me to my rest," Jonathan snapped.

Shua giggled. "Calm down, Jonathan. You are always so uptight . . ."

"It's alright." Abinadab put his hand up to stop Shua from saying anything more. "We sent a messenger to warn David about our father's plans for him."

"You did?" Jonathan asked. "But why?"

The two brothers looked at each other, then back at their eldest brother.

"The simple fact is—" Abinadab started to explain.

"That we know you love that damn guy," Shua blurted out.

Mouths fell open, but for different reasons.

"Did you have to be so indelicate?" Abinadab chastened Shua.

"Wait. You do?" Jonathan asked.

"Of course." Abinadab stopped glaring at Shua. "You love him, and let's face it—we love you."

"Yeah." Shua shrugged. "So we couldn't let our father kill this guy without warning him, or else we would have to look at your sulking face for the next fifty years!"

Jonathan laughed, then rushed at them both. He threw his arms around the men. "You're not just my brothers, but you are my dearest friends," he cried in laughter.

"Okay . . . enough," Shua protested with a chuckle. "We know you love him, but for the sake of us all, please do not think that we want to be covered in your sloppy kisses too."

They all laughed together.

#

"Again?" David fumed. "How many more times will this man forgive me only to take it back?"

He dismissed the messenger, who had ridden from Gibeah with news that Doeg was on his way at Saul's command to attack him, as he had done before. Only this time, the Edomite knew exactly where David was to be found.

"If we leave this land for good, maybe Saul will finally give up searching for me," he said to Abigail, sighing.

"As long as we are together, I do not care where we go," she said plainly.

Once his men were packed, David led them into the land of Gath.

"Are we to slay or to live among the Philistines?" one of them asked as they came over the horizon and saw at least a thousand swordsmen and archers waiting for them.

"Perhaps both." David said with a smile. He instructed his men to wait while he rode out alone in the direction of the amassed army.

"Is he crazy?" he heard one of his soldiers ask another. "Won't they kill him the second they learn who he is?"

But David kicked his horse forward. He believed that God had made clear his path, and not so much as an eyelash quivered on his body as he approached.

He could smell the musk from the unwashed Philistines' bodies as he slowed his horse to a stop and slid down to the ground. There, from among the sea of stern faces, one man stepped forward.

"I am Achish the second, son to King Maok and grandson to the former King Achish, who came first and said you were insane when you once came before him in our land," he announced.

David bowed his head.

"Why has David, the slayer of many, returned to our lands? Are you cured from insanity, or do you still suffer from madness and hope to burn Gath to the ground so easily?"

"I come in peace," David said on approach. "I have become a stench in the nose of the king of Israel. Day and night he pursues me. Let me and my men settle peacefully in one of your country towns and I will in turn be your servant and fight your battles for you, even against Israel itself."

"I have heard how odious you are to King Saul as I have also heard of your many successes in battle," the man replied.

David waited while Achish stepped back to discuss the matter with others, then came back and said, "I welcome this arrangement."

David sighed in relief.

"I will give you Ziklag, and it will be yours—if you and your people come to my aid when called."

David agreed. He waved for his men to come forward, and they were led by Achish to the town of Ziklag. There each ran to lay claim to one of the stone homes that stood empty.

Within weeks, all of David's men had sent for their families, and in Ziklag, a community began to thrive. Over the months, the country town became a city, and all who lived and dwelled there became satiated with food and wine.

In time though, Achish called upon David to fulfill his promise. "Go back now into the land of Judah," he commanded. "I have a list of towns for you to plunder. Your people hate you, so why should we not together raid them and take all that belongs to them and make it ours?"

"We will dance on their bones," David exclaimed as he led all six hundred of his men out of Ziklag.

"Surely we will do no such thing as to kill our own brothers," he told his men once they were far away from Achish's ears and had crossed into the Negev of Judah.

Turning to the north, David led them in a circle, until they were far behind the Philistine cities and well into the land of the Geshurites. There they came upon a town, and David ordered his men, "Kill every man, woman, and child here. No one must live and escape who can go back and tell Achish what we have done. And when we are finished, we will take every bit of treasure and return to the land of the Philistines as if we have obeyed their lord's command and sacked our fellow Hebrews."

The soldiers obeyed, and they surged forward for battle, cutting down every living person until there was not even a servant or a slave left that could tell who had raided and destroyed their people. Soaked in blood, all six hundred returned to Ziklag with scores of donkeys and camels, each one laden with satchels of goods.

When Achish heard of their return, he rushed to David to collect his share of the spoils. "Yes." He rubbed his hands together as he salivated over the heaps of gold and herds of cattle, which they separated into two. "You have done all that I have asked. Together we will become a plague on the Jews, until they curse both of our names in the same breath."

"Ask again and we will ride out at your command," David assured him.

For months he led his men into the desert as if he were on his way to kill many Hebrews, just as Achish expected. But David always took them in a wide loop until they were far behind Gath.

Village by village they would burn to the ground, killing all of the Geshurites, Girzites, and Amalekites that they came upon. Afterward they would return with their sheep, cattle, camels, and clothes, just as they had done the first time, and they would laugh behind Achish's back for believing that they had killed their own people.

One evening, after walking for many days to return home from a far-away raid, David saw smoke over the horizon.

A bedraggled woman ran out to his side from behind some bushes. "My lord," she said. "They attacked us while you were away."

Some of his men rushed past David upon hearing her words.

"I am the only one to escape," the woman cried after them.

David hoisted her onto the back of his horse and rode into the ruble and ruin.

In front of the smoldering remains of a home, they slid down from the beasts' back.

"Who has done this?" David pressed.

"It was a group of Amalekites." She sobbed and her tears spilled a path over cheeks darkened by soot and sorrow. "All are gone. My children . . . and even your wife, Abigail."

Anger surged throughout David's body. "How long ago was this, and which way did they travel?"

"It has been two nights, and they went that way." She pointed east.

"It is because of you that our wives and children have been stolen," one of the men shouted out. "If we had not moved to the land of the Philistines, our families would still be alive!"

There was a clamor, and all of the men beat their chests and raised their fists in anger at David.

"Wait," David shouted in indignation over the din, and the men hushed. "It is true that you have followed me, even as far as into foreign lands. For that I am grateful, but let us not forget that we have one weapon that even the Amalekites do not possess—God!"

There was uncertainty and hesitation in the air, so David called out for the priest Abiathar, the son of the murdered high priest Ahimelek.

"Bring out the ephod, Abiathar," he commanded. "Inquire of our Lord. Ask him if I am to lead us out into the land to go after this raiding party."

"Yes," Abiathar answered. "You are to ride out, for you will surely be successful and will restore what you have lost."

"See," David chastened his soldiers. "Where all is lost to men, it is found to those who trust in the Lord."

In a roar of revenge, the six hundred men rallied and poured behind David as he led them en masse in the direction of the Amalekites.

After a day's march, some of them became exhausted. "We have been traveling on foot for many days," they said. "We cannot go any farther."

So David left them behind in the Besor Valley, and with the four hundred men he had left, he pressed on.

Later that day, a soldier dragged a dark-skinned man by the arm to David's side. "Look what I found."

"Who are you?" David asked him. "And why are you here alone in the wilderness, far from any towns?"

The man fell on his knees. "Have mercy on me, my lord." He trembled. "I am a servant to the Amalekites, a slave to my master. We went out from our home to raid the Negev of the Kerethites, the land of Judah, and the Negev of Caleb. After great success, we turned to go home and found the unprotected town of Ziklag on the way, which we burned to the ground, and we took all of their women and children."

"And why are you not still with them?"

"I became ill, and my master left me behind and told me that I was not worth his trying to save. For a day I have sat alone by a pool of water, too sick to move until now, when the sickness has all but left me. All that remains is hunger and exhaustion."

"Do you know where this raiding party went?" David asked forcefully.

"Yes," the slave answered. "I can show you, but only if you promise me that you will not give me back to my master, as he has treated me poorly."

"Show us where they are and you will be one of our people and live free," David assured him.

The slave wept at his words, and David had mercy on him and called for his men to feed him.

They walked on until the sun was setting. As David peered out over the crest of a mountain, the slave squinted and hissed, "That's them. I can see my master from here."

Down in the valley, David could see campfires being lit among the Amalekites. He counted close to a thousand men, most of whom were eating, drinking, and laughing as they plopped down around the flames and reveled in their success. At the center of their camp, in makeshift pens, he could see hundreds of women and children who were tied up and guarded.

David turned back to his army and gave orders. "Descend this mountain as if you ride into the very heart of Sheol. Take back what is yours, for the Lord our god has given these pagans into our hands today."

A great roar rang out from the mountaintop, as if it were a volcano signaling its eruption, and with cries of battle, David and his men flew down into the valley in a stampede of righteous fury.

The Amalekites were unprepared for this onslaught, and many of their men fell to their deaths by the Hebrew blades within minutes. Yet, as they greatly outnumbered David's men, the fighting lingered on until the sun broke over the land anew. This was when the last of the Amalekite men in the camp fell to the ground.

David stopped to survey the scene in the sunlight. Before him, countless bodies lay broken and bloodied, but in the distance, he could see a small group of young men who must have escaped in the darkness. These figures receded quickly before they disappeared over the horizon.

"Let them go." David shrugged. "They can go back to their homeland and warn their people that never again should the Amalekites be as foolish as to try to take what belongs to David."

His men celebrated their win with war cries and shouts of jubilee. Reunited, they hugged their wives and children and urged everyone to gather up all of the spoils that the Amalekites had planned to carry home. Together, man and woman alike, they made their way back through the Besor Valley, while each carried silver and gold or led great herds of sheep and goats. There they found the two hundred men who had stayed behind. Rather than deny them any treasure for not having had the fortitude to carry on and attack the Amalekites with the rest, David swore that everyone would share in the great treasure, whether they'd fought or rested. At last they continued westward and made it back to the smoldering embers that were all that remained of Ziklag.

The Witch of Endor

*A*bner pointed to a map made of papyrus. "There," he grunted. "At Aphek."

Jonathan peered down and considered the terrain.

It had been one year since Doeg had come back from his last mission to kill David, and to Jonathan's delight, he'd been empty-handed. Afterward, word of David's whereabouts had gone silent, like a desert night just before dawn. It was almost two months later when Jonathan heard that he had moved into the land of the Philistines near Gath.

At first Jonathan's heart dropped, as he realized that David was now even farther away from him. If this information was true, he was in a place that Jonathan could never visit. A prince of Israel couldn't just ride into the land of King Maok and expect to return alive.

It was true that he could not blame David for his decision to flee there. Perhaps somehow he would find safety with the Philistines. He knew God had caused stranger things to happen. Besides, the move seemed to calm Saul, whose attention at last turned back to his archenemies, the eternally promised thorn under his skin.

"Our reports are that they have already amassed more than ten thousand men there, with many more on the way," Abner continued.

Of course David's move into Gath pained Jonathan nothing in comparison to the news that he had taken a new wife. How could he?

He sulked in his quarters, but once he had calmed, he remembered David's words to him when he was about to marry Michal. David had reassured him that both of their marriages to women were just a part of their commitment to progeny and that no relationship would ever compare to the eternal love that he and Jonathan shared.

This warmed Jonathan, and it placated his jealousy, as what hold could any woman have over a man with whom he shared a part of his soul?

"It seems to me like we should head for Jezreel and set up camp there," Shua piped in.

Abinadab came up behind him and put his hand on his shoulder and nodded. "I agree," he said firmly.

Jonathan looked at his two brothers and wondered where the years had gone. He remembered them being brats when they camped across the valley from their first battle with the Philistines many years ago. Now they were grown men, each offering advice on how best to repel one of the largest forces to have ever threatened all of Israel.

As for Armoni and Mephibosheth, they remained with their mother, who had returned to the home of her father, Aiah, when Saul had thrown them out of his household. Though it was rumored that Rizpah had secretly visited Abner on more than one occasion in an effort to get him to persuade Saul to allow for her return, Jonathan had not personally seen any of the three.

"Then to Jezreel we shall go," King Saul stated confidently as he approached the map. "It is time that we do to the Philistines what I should have done to them in Mikmash way back when."

Abner nodded and rolled the map up.

"Call up all to arms," Saul commanded. "Let not any man of age stay behind, as this may be the final battle, where we at last eliminate the Philistine threat and dwell in our land in peace forever."

All of his children and their uncle nodded, and each went out to rally their men and to send messengers off to gather any that were able to fight for Israel from far and wide.

It took less than two weeks to assemble the greatest force the nation had ever seen. Jonathan rode at its head alongside his father, and the land shook and dust flew into the air as thousands of men, both young and old, marched out from Gibeah and north to the Jezreel Valley.

#

The cloud from the mass of footprints floated high into the air. *If only these feet were Hebrew,* David thought to himself. However, they were the soles of men from Gath who were headed to Shunem. Along the way,

Achish had made David his personal bodyguard and told him that he was as much a Philistine as any other.

"There has been no one more loyal to me than you," Achish lauded David. "I have sent you out dozens of times into the land of your fathers, and like a faithful servant, each time you have come back to me having destroyed the Jewish towns and villages, small and large alike. Not once did you return to me empty-handed, but you have plundered your people as if they were the Canaanites themselves."

"I upheld my promise," David replied sternly. "I am still bound to it and will destroy King Saul as if I were one of your own spearmen."

"I relish in the thought that King Saul's own son-in-law might be the one to stick an iron point into his eye on behalf of the Philistines," Achish said.

Yet the other Philistine leaders did not agree. They were wary with distrust. "Why do you allow this man and his army to march out with us?" one commander asked as David listened nearby.

"David has been with me for more than a year and has shown himself to be more faithful than your own brothers are to you," Achish told them.

The commanders did not want to hear it, though. "Surely when the time for battle comes, he will side with the people of his blood," they cried out. Then they demanded that Achish send David away. "He is still the one who killed our greatest soldier ever," they said, and they told Achish that they would never trust him, regardless of Achish's assurances.

"He is the one they sang about across their land and said that he slayed more men than Saul. Why would we want him behind us with swords and shields?"

Achish was disappointed.

"You have heard them, so what can I do?" he explained to David. "Tomorrow morning, you and your men must get up early and return home. Do nothing along the way to upset the Philistine rulers so that they do no harm to you after our battle with Saul has finished."

When the morning came, David and his men departed, going back in the direction of Ziklag. Along the way he contemplated just lying back unseen for a while. Once the battle began, he could double back and attack the Philistines from behind. But Abiathar, son of Ahimelek, told David that the Lord meant for him to return home and wait for his instructions from there. So David dragged his feet in the dust toward Ziklag, though he turned his head back over his shoulder to Jezreel again and again. Each time, he prayed that Saul would prevail, and also each time, he could not help but to worry about Jonathan.

May the Lord protect you. He urged it to be true in his mind. David had already decided that, while he must obey God's command to return to Ziklag, he would finally return and go back to the land of Judah soon. He no longer wished to be estranged or to be far away from his fellow Israelites. Once he was back in Judah, he would send for Jonathan.

It has been too long. He smiled at the thought of holding him in his arms and rustling the mass of dark hair that sat on his head again.

"And this time," he assured himself, "not even Saul will separate us."

#

From the crest of Gilboa, Saul looked out upon Aphek and shivered. "They are like the sands along the sea." His voice cracked in the harsh wind that blew across the mountaintop.

Down below, across the Valley of Jezreel, an uncountable number of Philistines had gathered.

"Do my eyes deceive me?" Saul asked. "Even with all of our men, there is no way that we can stand up against a force such as this one.".

"We cannot, but remember how the ground shook at Mikmash?" Jonathan said in an effort to encourage his father. "We do not know the will of our Lord, as he can open the ground and swallow them up in a single moment, if we have faith in Him and His ways."

At once, Saul called for a priest. "What does the Lord say?" he begged the man, but the priest told him that there was no answer from above.

"Bring me a prophet," Saul demanded next, but he was told that no prophet would answer his call.

Finally, Saul sent a messenger to the house of Aiah. "Bring my concubine, Rizpah, and my two sons Armoni and Mephibosheth. Tell them that they are to enter my tent on their knees. For today, if they obey me, they might be restored to my good graces."

When they arrived, Jonathan stood at his father's side and wondered why Saul would forgive them now.

"Enter," Saul thundered, and as Rizpah approached the throne, he stood up. She was wearing a torn garment and had ashes on her forehead as she crawled along the carpet on her hands and knees.

"Please," she begged him. "Restore my children and me as you once promised you would if I had humbled myself for your sake and for theirs."

"Have you?" Saul asked.

"Yes." She trembled. "I have sacrificed and prayed to the Lord on our behalf."

"Good," Saul said as he looked down at her. "You may rise, then, but take heed to obey my commands, lest you and your children be removed from my presence again, but this time forever."

"Yes, lord," she promised as she stood up.

She glanced Jonathan's way, and he could see that behind the feigned look of meekness, a lioness still lurked. Perhaps she was more deadly than before because she had been uncovered in the weeds.

This is only a setback, the angle of her neck seemed to suggest. And her pupils seemed to call forth as if to say, *My next move will be deadly.*

Jonathan did not have time to dwell on the thoughts of this woman. *She will always be a burden, until death.* He half chuckled inside. *But alas, she will at least never be anything more powerful than what she is now—a disgraced concubine.*

He shrugged and listened in on the conversation between his father and Rizpah.

"I can put your sons in positions of power today at the snap of my fingers if you obey," Saul continued.

"Yes, my king." Rizpah found her rhythm again as she smiled coquettishly at him. "I will do anything to see them, and myself, in your good graces. Just ask it of me."

"Good." Saul nodded. "If this is true, then you must do one thing for me."

"Anything." Her voice grew husky, and Jonathan watched as the taut lines in his father's face softened.

"I remember well why you have always been a favorite of mine," Saul all but giggled as he became entrapped in her trances. She held a hand up to cover her mouth and giggled in reply.

"Oh, Rizpah." The king smiled sweetly. "I will come to your bed this evening, if first you tell me the name and the location of the witch who you once consulted in this region."

"What?" Jonathan gasped aloud.

Rizpah shot him a look as if to silence him, but Jonathan could not be quieted.

"Why would you want that information?" he asked sternly. "Certainly you do not mean to—"

His father slammed his foot on the floor. "The name and location," he boomed over Jonathan, and at this, Rizpah turned her gaze back to the king and bowed her head.

"Of course I will," she cooed. Then she stepped forward and stood on her tiptoes to whisper into the king's ear.

"Ahhh . . . yes." Saul smiled. "And now, make yourself ready, for I will come to you late in the night. Perhaps you will bring me good luck on the eve of this battle and carry away from this war a new son. The ones you have already given me are now restored. I will have them each put in charge of men on the field against the Philistines. For they too are sons of Saul, and that makes them worthy of honor."

Rizpah backed her way out of the tent, and when the flaps closed behind her, Saul faced Jonathan and commanded him, "Call for a servant to bring us the clothes of the common man."

"Whatever for?" Jonathan was puzzled.

"We cannot ride out to meet a medium dressed as a king and a prince, can we?"

There was little time for protest—not that his father would have listened. Frustrated but obedient, Jonathan changed into the dingy robes of a shepherd. Under the cover of darkness and disguise, he as a herdsman and his father as poor farmer, rode away into the evening and out across the Valley of Jezreel.

By the time the night was deep, they approached the spring just outside a walled city. There, by the fountain, they used a few pieces of silver to buy directions to the medium's home. A few winding streets away, deep inside of Endor, they came upon a small stone door.

"Who is at my door?" a frail woman's voice rattled.

Jonathan's father opened the door and peeked his head inside. "We have come for guidance."

"Come, come," she said, and Saul grabbed Jonathan by the arm and led him through the doorway.

He could make out the outline of something thin sitting in a chair near the fireplace. "Come closer," she rasped in a voice as old as time itself. "I am long in years, and my sight is not what it once was."

Jonathan followed Saul closer still, until the two had sat down by the fire as well.

"We have traveled far to see you," Saul said sweetly.

"Me?" the old woman asked in surprise.

"You must call up a spirit for me, for I have heard that you are able to do this, and what I need is of great importance," he urged her.

The woman cleared the cobwebs from her throat. "I cannot call any spirits," she replied coyly. "The king has forbidden all mediums in this land, and I, being only an old lady, would not dare to defy the king even if I could call up these so-called spirits, as you claim."

"You will not be punished for this." Saul's voice grew stronger.

She laughed, and Jonathan wondered if it would not be best if they just got up and left now.

"What assurances do I have that you could stay a king's hand from cutting off my head?" the woman cackled. Her guffaw turned into a cough, which progressed steadily until she was hacking and gasping as her eyes bulged out of her head. Then, just as suddenly, she recovered and sat back in her chair in great solemnity.

"The assurance that you seek is here in my personhood." Saul stood up and reached into his robe. He pulled out a handful of silver and gold pieces and threw them onto the ground.

The old woman looked down at the scattered coins, which glimmered in the firelight, then widened her eyes as their worth registered. At last, she looked up and gasped. "Why did you deceive me?" she cried. "You are the king himself, are you not?"

"Yes," Saul affirmed, but then he lifted his palms up to show he meant to do her no harm. "I do not seek to injure you in any way, old woman. I just want you to do as I have asked, and all will be fine for you."

"I am afraid," she wailed, but Jonathan could see his father's patience was nearing its end point.

"Call up the spirit for me," Saul ordered menacingly.

At this command, the fire in the pit suddenly blew out. Only the light from a small oil lamp was left, and it burned dimly along the far wall, its wick flickering violently in some unknown wind.

"I see a body coming up out of the ground." The witch's voice rose in fear.

"What does he look like?" Saul implored her.

"He does not look happy." Terror sang on her breath before she settled into something of a trance.

"Tell me more."

"His frame is of bones, over which he wears a robe of crimson," she said.

"Are you certain?" Saul pressed.

"Look for yourself," she told him. "For he is right there." Then she lifted her bony arm, and with her wrinkled finger, she pointed to the ground where Saul had tossed the coins.

Jonathan's skin crawled when he saw a ghost suddenly rise up from the earth. The figure glowed as if the firelight still shined from the hearth, and the room grew colder than any night he had ever spent unprotected in the desert. All warmth of spirit dissipated at this figure's presence, and the room itself became quiet as a tomb.

A cavernous voice displaced the air. "Who disturbs me?"

Saul threw himself onto the ground. Jonathan felt something tug on the hem of his shepherd's robe, and he looked down in panic to find that it was Saul, urging him to fall to his knees just like he had already done. Fear spread through Jonathan's chest, so he dropped to the floor next to his father and lowered his head.

His breathing shallow, he gently lifted his eyes to find the pale, glazed orbs of the prophet Samul staring back at him.

"Why did you call me up?" Samuel demanded, and Jonathan felt as if this form of death could see directly into his soul.

"It was me," Saul quivered, and Samuel turned his gaze to the king. "I have called on you, Samuel, as I am in great distress!"

The prophet then closed his mouth and said nothing further, and his figure began to fade.

"Oh, please," Jonathan's father begged from upon the ground. "Tell me what to do!"

Samuel disappeared no further, though his eyes began to slowly close.

"The Philistines have gathered in great numbers, and the Lord will not answer me by priest or by prophets or even through dreams—nothing! I do not know what I am supposed to do!"

"You fool." Samuel's image became clearer as his words thundered. "Why ask me when you already know the answer? The Lord has departed from you, just as I told you he had. Likewise, he has handed your kingdom over to another."

"Tell me this is not true," Saul begged again. "Tell me what I can do to save myself and my sons."

"Nothing." Samuel's voice turned to a whisper. "Tomorrow, the Philistines will deliver you into the hands of your enemies, and you and your sons will join me here in slumber."

Saul's body shook from sobs while Jonathan's own body rattled at the knees from fear.

"The wrath of the Lord is fierce." Samuel's voice drifted as his figure quickly faded away.

At last the fire that had blown out suddenly burst back into flames, and the room lit up as it was before.

"Go now," the old woman begged them. "You have tired me out, and I fear that I may not recover from this act." She leaned back in her chair and closed her eyes.

Jonathan's limbs quaked as he used her chair to pull himself back to his feet. He then leaned down and helped his father to also stand upright.

"Let us run from here," Jonathan beseeched Saul in terror. "We do not know if we were visited by Samuel or a malevolent spirit." He grabbed his father's arm and pulled him toward the door. "Either way, I fear we have participated in a great evil, and I have no intention of remaining here any longer."

Unwilling to abide any delays, he dragged the king back to their horses and helped him mount his before they rode away at a furious pace for the camp at Gilboa.

I will never again ask another to foresee my future, Jonathan told himself on the hectic ride back. The experience with the ghost, as well as the witch, had so completely shaken him to his core that Jonathan vowed to be a different person from this day forward.

"No man, or spirit of the dead, will ever foretell what my life will be again," he said under his breath between gallops. "Would that I should experience things as they come—for myself—and not have to live with this burden of prediction."

In an urgent need to break free from the shadows of the grave, Jonathan also promised himself that, after this battle, no matter what happened with the Philistines, he would loosen the blind loyalty that had chained him to his father's throne most of his life. *I will be at the side of my beloved,* he avowed to himself.

Whether or not he could force Saul to bury his one-sided hatred for David in the ground alongside Samuel's memory, he would no longer be separated from him. Yes, he promised himself that, while he would beg the king for David's complete restoration, nothing short of death itself would stop him from walking in love in the daylight of his life. Either Saul would at last restore David to their lives forever, or Jonathan would ride for Judah with great urgency.

As the camp came into view, he clung to his fresh hopes for the future. *Never again will I allow the years, or the delusions of a scared and feeble-minded ruler, to stand between us.*

Day was at last fully soaked in the sunlight of new beginnings.

Mount Gilboa

A jarring blast of the shofar split the air in two and announced the moment. At its call, Jonathan nocked his bow and marched forward into battle against the Philistines. As his feet moved, he turned his head to his left and found his brother Shua, a look of determination on his usually jovial face. To his right, Abinadab gripped his spear and steeled his jaw in strength and resolution.

These are my rocks, he thought to himself. *I trust them with my life.*

Step by step they moved forward, but his mind drifted back to their youth, and in his heart he laughed at how they used to annoy him so. *I would give anything to see the two of them wrestle on the ground again or hurl insults in my direction.*

There was an unease that circled the air like carrion birds when the words of the shadow of Samuel flew over his mind. He shook them loose and locked his gaze on his uncle, Abner. The general was riding on a donkey a few cubits up front, leading all of the Israelites out in one massive wave against the endless seawall of Philistines that stood ready to split them on the opposite side of the valley.

"Ready!" Abner commanded, and all weapons were raised into the air. "For the king of Israel," he shouted, and every Hebrew man ran out with great purpose in the direction of the gentile swarm.

"For your land . . . for your home . . . for your God," Abner continued to yell, but his voice became drowned out in the great roar of battle cries.

The distance between them and their enemy closed so quickly that within seconds Jonathan heard thwaps and groans as iron points from Philistine arrows broke through the armor of his fellow soldiers. With great fury, he lifted his own bow into the air and loosed a shaft, watching it arc above the heads of his father's men and descend quickly into the neck of a lowbrow commander.

As the unnamed Philistine leader fell dead off his horse, a torrent of curses heralded a heated advance from the enemy. Jonathan barely had time to inhale before the group surged into the Israelite army and the two forces met with a deafening clash of weapons.

A bow no longer befitting of this type of hand-to-hand battle, Jonathan tossed his to the ground and pulled a sword from his back, swinging it wildly into the air. Metal slammed into metal as he repelled an advance. He replied with a thrust of his weapon, which pierced flesh. But where one Philistine fell, three more seemed to take his place. Over the sound of an endless din of scrapes and snaps that filled his ears, the music of war became broken by three disheartening blasts of the horn.

Jonathan's spirit fell at the sound. The rarely heard tones undeniably meant that the Israelites were in danger. Whether they were outnumbered or simply outflanked, they had been called to retreat.

His first instinct was to protect his brothers, so he parried his way through the crowd until he found the two of them, shoulder to shoulder in battle.

"This way," he shouted above the thunderclaps of weaponry.

Shua's head, which was dripping with sweat and blood, turned in surprise to Abinadab, who grabbed his arm and pulled him toward Jonathan. Once his kin were at his side, Jonathan pushed and fought his way across the sea of mayhem as he looked for a spot where he could carry them out of the madness and lead them to his father and swiftly back to Gibeah.

"There will be other days for battles," he said decisively when Shua wanted to run back into the fray.

At last, Jonathan saw a break in the terrain, and he pulled his brothers out of the melee and onto a path that led up the side of the mountain they had camped on top of the night before. A small group of Philistine fighters burst out after them, and Jonathan ducked with his brothers behind some rocks and leaned down to whisper in their ears.

"Let us get to the top of Mount Gilboa," he said softly between breaths. "From there we will be able to see how best to respond to the Philistine advance or, if necessary, plot our best route home."

His brothers panted and nodded. Together they snuck away from the Philistines that were nearby and worked their way up the winding pathway until at last they could see its summit.

"There." Jonathan pointed. "We need only make it over those rocks and we'll be at the top, where we will also find our father."

Just then, two figures emerged in the very spot Jonathan had pointed to. *That's not the king*, he worried to himself. But as the men looked down over the edge of the mountain, Jonathan recognized it was Armoni and Mephibosheth, and he breathed a sigh of relief. These were not Philistines, and his father had not been captured.

"Help, brothers," Jonathan called out with a wave as he saw the group of Philistines that still searched for them down below come closer. "Grab your bows and arrows. We need cover so that we can make it up the mountain to you safely.

Mephibosheth looked past them, and then his face transformed into a smug smile. He leaned over and whispered something into his brother's ear. Armoni's eyes widened, and he also beamed a great smile, then they both nodded to Jonathan.

"We will help, alright," Armoni said sarcastically.

Jonathan's brief sigh of relief was replaced almost instantly with rage when Armoni began to jump up and down and wave and shout at the Philistines down at the base of the mountain. "Up here," he yelled.

"What are you doing?" Jonathan shrieked.

"Look over there and you will find the king's sons!" Armoni pointed to where Jonathan and his brothers stood behind a stone. "It is Saul's sons!"

Jonathan's head felt like it was going to explode. "Curse the day those maggots were born," he hissed to his brothers. "I will pull them apart with my bare hands when I make it up this mountain—"

His vow was disrupted by a volley of arrows that came at them from down below.

"Duck!" Abinadab yelled. But it was too late, as one of the arrows had already landed right in the neck of their younger brother.

"Shua," Jonathan cried as he rushed to his side. He placed Malchishua's head into his lap. His brother smiled crookedly before his eyes went dim.

"No!" Jonathan screamed out in pain as he lowered Shua's head to the ground. "No . . ."

He looked back up at his half-brothers and glared before he clutched the hilt of his sword tightly and turned to run down the hill, directly at the small group of Philistines who were on their way up to kill the two of them that remained.

"Wait," Abinadab shouted, but Jonathan was too enraged to hear him.

In less than five paces, he was amid the enemy. With a great roar of mourning, he raised his sword, which had already sliced the neck of one Philistine before he swung it around and buried the blade deep into the chest of another.

Abinadab caught up to him and also began to strike and block their foes with furious movements.

It seemed as if they would prevail and avenge their brother, until from his side, Jonathan heard Abinadab let out a small grunt that sounded as if he had swallowed a stone.

From the corner of his eye, he saw the figure of his other brother fall to the ground in a heap. With a savage roar, Jonathan swung his sword more violently than before, but it was too late. No amount of work could stave off the attacks of his enemies, who now surrounded him on all sides.

With Jonathan encircled completely, the small group of Philistines slowly surged toward him with the tips of their spears edging closer and closer to his body. He knew that there was no escape, so he dropped his blade and looked up at the mountain where his half-brothers stood. As the two watched from above, another figure emerged just behind them. The concubine Rizpah put a hand on each of her sons' shoulders and smiled.

Jonathan lowered his head to stare into the faces of his attackers. He had resigned himself to death, but was not prepared to find himself looking directly into the eyes of Doeg. The Edomite, like the others, had a spear in his hand, but he had a salty grin on his face that was unlike the rest.

"You should have chosen me," he said bluntly.

"I couldn't have." Jonathan shrugged as an image of David flashed through his mind. He lifted his gaze up toward the heavens, and the words of the stranger who had spoken to him outside of Samuel's tomb flooded his ears.

For did not the hand remain strong?

At this memory, he began to pray.

Epilogue

The tamarisk tree stood proudly alongside a desert wash. It was not directly in the streambed, or the bones of Jonathan and King Saul would never have been placed there underneath it for fear of their being washed away in the rains. Instead, this tree had been chosen because it stood vigil close enough to the water to carry the flood of tears the many mourners that visited would send down its nearby channel.

David sat down in the sandy soil and leaned his back against the gnarly gray bark of this salt cedar. He lifted his gaze up through the wispy branches that spread out in asymmetry in many directions. Though these limbs' advancement was chaotic, there was beauty in their lack of conformity. High at the top, where their arms reached out the farthest, David could see a cloud of pale pink blossoms that sprouted in gentle reverence.

"It has been a year already," he spoke into the air.

A great swooping sound closed in as a large white bittern landed loudly on a branch above him. A cascade of petals showered down on David's head as the bird erupted into a hollow call like the bellowing of a bull. Once it became silent again, its wings began to thrash against the branches as it lifted off and swooped farther along the stretch of dried-up ravines.

David shook the flowers off his head, and they fell onto his lap.

He chuckled. "Hey, I'm the one who does the dramatic entrances!"

Then he lifted a lyre and rested it against his chest.

"Sorry Saul," he said as he sat back. "I know you probably don't want to be forced to listen to this drivel, but it was not I who buried you with your son under this tree. I promise you both, though, once all is settled, I will take your bones and lay them myself in the land of Benjamin at Zela in Kish's tomb. No man should be placed here forever."

He sat in silence for a few minutes.

"Oh," David started again. "I need to catch you up, Jonathan, as much has happened. Some good, some bad. How am I to really know which is which, though?" He shrugged.

"Let's see . . . I wanted you to hear from me before anyone else that I married your mother, Ahinoam. I always did think she was beautiful, and after your father died, she was without a husband and without a home. How can a woman so elegant be homeless? Well, I couldn't allow it, so I took her in as an honor to you and your memory. It was either that or leave her in the hands of Rizpah, and we both know that concubine would have loved nothing better than to see your mother become her washer-woman." David laughed at his own words.

"Speaking of Rizpah," he continued, "she did not waste any time. At first she tried to become my wife as well, but I've seen all too well what her presence can do to a household. Instead, they say she has been making moves to seduce Abner again, but I hope to Sheol that your uncle is smarter than your father was when it comes to her. Oh . . . sorry, Saul."

He paused for a moment.

"I don't know why her two sons thought they would ever be king. They must have forgotten that you still had another brother, because Ish-Bosheth has been made the ruler of Israel." David clutched his side in laughter. "Can you believe that little snot-nosed thing is a king? Ha!"

He strained his ear as if he heard something.

"Me?" he replied to the lifeless earth. "Oh, I became a king too, but only of Judah. You probably know all of this already, wherever you are, but yes, I am a king, and the land is divided into two. I would treat with your brother, but tensions are high because of Saul's other blood relatives."

He grinned. "You always did know the truth. Yes, I have been prom-ised all of Israel. I mean, before, when you were alive, I couldn't just say it—though you knew it! What was I supposed to do? Smugly tell you that I would be king over everything and that you and your father and all of your brothers would die? I could never do that. Besides, I didn't know that part. If I had, I'm not sure it would have changed anything."

David lowered his head and fell silent once again.

"Your son, Sheth, lives with me now," he whispered eventually. "I will raise him as my own, as if he were yours and mine. Ours," he emphasized. "Though it saddens me to tell you that he is lame now."

"How?" David picked a pebble up and tossed it. "Well, when the great battle erupted, his nurse grabbed him by the arm and ran with all of her might downhill to escape them. They tumbled and fell into a ravine together. The Philistines never found him, but when the Israelites did, the nurse was dead and Sheth's legs were so shattered that he will never be able to walk again. Oh, but don't worry! He will live as if he had a thousand pairs of legs, because I will give him more servants and more love than anyone alive because he is a part of you. The only part of you I have left, really."

After a minute, he plucked the strings of his instrument and hummed for a while.

"I'll have to go soon." He paused his music. "There is much to do, and I know you will be with me whether I am by this tree or not. Remember, you promised to follow me in my heart everywhere."

Sweet music once again flowed from the lyre, this time more loudly than before. At last, David lifted his head and sang.

> *More wonderful,*
> *more wonderful than that of woman.*

> *Under stars we proclaimed,*
> *lips touched, we were changed.*
> *And forevermore you will be*
> *more wonderful than woman to me.*

> *You were loyal, you were sweet,*
> *me tempestuous, us complete.*
> *And forever more you will be*
> *more wonderful than that of woman.*

David stopped his singing and sniffled. Tears soaked his cheeks, and he closed his eyes. Finally, he put his lyre onto the ground and stood up.

"I will come back for you . . . one day," he said to the sandy dirt. "And then, after that, I will join you, wherever you are, and no one and nothing will ever separate us again."

He leaned down and picked up his instrument. Choking back what remained of his tears, he lifted up his head to the horizon. There in the distance stood a hundred men who had traveled with him to Jabesh, along with his wives, Abigail, Ahinoam, and Michal, who had been returned to him after Saul's death. He smiled at the sight of the baby in Abigail's arms. He looked back once more at the base of the tree before he turned and walked away.